Sexy Be

Sexy Beast VII

KATE DOUGLAS
ANITRA LYNN McLEOD
SHELLI STEVENS

APHRODISIA

KENSINGTON BOOKS

http://www.kensingtonbooks.com

CONTENTS

Chanku Challenge 1
Kate Douglas

Eye of the Beholder 103
Anitra Lynn McLeod

His to Reclaim 211
Shelli Stevens

Chanku Challenge

Kate Douglas

Forward

They live among us, often unaware of their true birthright as they try to exist in a world that, in many ways, forces them to abide by laws and customs contrary to their nature. Ruled by a powerful libido as well as an innate sense of honor and a loyalty to their own kind so deeply ingrained it cannot be denied, they often live lives of quiet desperation until their feral nature is finally, often explosively, unleashed.

Descendants of an ancient race born upon the Tibetan steppe, they are more than human—so much more than they appear to the world around them.

They are shapeshifters.

They are Chanku.

1

His thick paws made barely a sound as Nick Barden trotted along beside his mate. He and Beth followed three of their packmates along the service road running near the large wild wolf compounds at the sanctuary run by Chanku shapeshifters Ulrich Mason and Millie West.

At some level, Nick realized he should be loving every second of this chance to run free in the beautiful northern Colorado mountains—here he could take this form without fear of discovery or attack, without the stink of the city burning his sensitive nostrils.

Instead, he hardly noticed the myriad scents and sounds teasing his wolven senses—not the fresh mountain air or even the altogether unique freedom of running as a wolf through dark, pristine forest. No, he was much too aware of the female beside him to appreciate any of it.

Too aware of her displeasure and her silent disapproval to notice the scent of fresh game or even his own unique abilities in this powerful body.

Nothing he did seemed to please her. Not anymore.

His ass still hurt from Ulrich's screwing the other night, but when he looked back at the way he'd been acting for the past week, he figured he'd deserved what he got and then some. The power play Beth had talked him into had backfired—more literally than he'd expected.

Couldn't she see that Ulrich Mason wasn't the problem? He'd never done anything to Beth that wasn't perfectly kind and accepting. Beth's misplaced animosity was totally unfair, all part of her own convoluted baggage. Baggage she needed to deal with now if she and Nick wanted to remain part of this close-knit pack.

If he didn't love her so much, Nick never would have gone along with her stupid wishes.

There was no denying the fact he'd eventually enjoyed Ulrich's powerful response to his stupid challenge. Sex with a dominant male was worth the pain, worth the pure sense of humiliation Nick had suffered.

It had raised his level of arousal even higher.

He wished Beth would lay off. She'd focused her anger on him now, instead of on Ulrich, and it was so thick he could practically see it vibrating in the air between them. In fact, her anger was just about the only thing they had between them anymore. She'd shut him out ever since he'd blocked her constant bitching that night, even though Nick was the one who had ended up paying for the failure of Beth's stupid plan. When he chose to follow Ulrich's lead rather than hers, it meant getting his ass reamed out in a reactive display of dominance by the old guy.

Okay. So he got the message, along with some really great sex. Now why couldn't Beth figure it out? There was no point in challenging Ulrich. Nick didn't want to fight him. For one thing, he really liked and admired the man.

For another, he'd lose.

Ulrich was smart, he was cunning, and he was strong. He had age and experience on his side, and he was a born leader whether he was in his wolf form, snarling with teeth bared and hackles raised, or staring a man down from his impressive height on two legs. No matter, it was something Nick knew he'd never be able to pull off in any form.

Why couldn't Beth accept him for what he was? In this society, this world of Chanku, he was just a pup. Barely twenty-four years old, he'd been nothing but a loser on the streets of San Francisco. Why did Beth seem to think his ability to shift would make him anything different?

Was it the fact he'd killed that guy to protect Tala? Was that why Beth expected him to be more aggressive? If that was the case, she was dead wrong. He'd killed without thinking, shifting before he even knew he had the ability.

And he'd bonded with a woman he loved before either of them really thought about the permanence of their act.

He watched Daci, Deacon, and Matt trotting together up ahead. The three of them had slipped into an amazing union, and they weren't even mated. He and Beth were mates, yet they hardly spoke to each other. He missed the easygoing relationship he'd had with Matt and Deacon, missed the freedom and the fun they'd all had together, but he missed Beth most of all. Missed the beautiful, shy young woman he'd fallen in love with.

He glanced at Beth and realized she watched him. Was she reading his thoughts? He'd been blocking . . . or at least he thought he was.

She veered off the road and trotted down a narrow trail that led deeper into the woods. Nick hesitated then decided to follow her. She stopped after a short distance and turned to face him, standing in a brilliant ray of late afternoon sunlight, dead center in the middle of a small meadow.

He halted a few feet away, ears flat, tail down. It was easier this way, acting the submissive role with Beth. It seemed to make her happy, though at this point he hardly cared.

She shifted. He faced her for a moment, still the wolf. She stared at him, her dark brows crinkled in that way she had, her arms folded over her bare chest like a disapproving teacher. He held her gaze for a moment longer. She didn't move. Didn't say a word.

Oh, hell. If he wanted to see what she wanted . . . Nick shifted and stood on two feet, wary and uncertain.

Beth raised her chin and stared at him. Sunlight poured across her beautiful olive skin and raised red highlights in her long, dark hair. Her amber-eyed gaze, so much like his own, bored into him. He held her stare.

"It's not working," she said, clasping her hands over her smooth belly. In control, as always. Naked, beautiful, standing there with a sense of entitlement, of power, like an Egyptian goddess here in the midst of the Colorado forest.

"We never should have bonded. I want out."

Her words, a statement, not a request, came as a relief. At least he wasn't the only one who felt that way.

Unfortunately, it wasn't an option.

He actually smiled when he answered her. "Great. So do I, but it's a little late for that, Beth. You heard what Tala said. A pair bond is forever. You wanted me, you've got me."

She jerked back as if he'd slapped her. "You don't want me?"

Not at all surprised by her contrary question, Nick shook his head. "You're supposed to be the one who can tell when a guy's lying or telling the truth. You tell me."

She shook her head as if some of the fight had gone out of her. "I can't tell anymore, Nick. Not with you. It doesn't work with you."

"Does it matter? You just said you want out. You've shut me out for days. We don't have sex with each other, even after a run. It's pretty obvious you don't love me anymore." He was standing up straighter, feeling taller than he had since they'd first linked, even though every word he spoke chipped away more of their bond. "So, I guess my answer's no, Beth. I don't want you. Not anymore. Not the way you are now." He shook his head, no longer smiling.

"I loved a girl who was sweet and kind, who cared about me, about the future we planned together. All you care about now is power. You're twenty-one years old, Beth. You're a baby in this pack, just like me. You have no power. Not over me, not over yourself, and definitely not over any of the others. Get used to it."

He stared at her for a long moment, holding her gaze until she finally looked away. Obviously, this conversation was over.

He shifted. *I'm going back to the others. You can come if you want to. Or not.* Nick glanced over his shoulder and watched her face. She looked brittle, like she might shatter as easily as glass. He felt bad about that, about hurting her, but he didn't trust her. Not anymore.

He still loved her, though. Goddess help him, he loved her.

With one last look, Nick whirled around and raced back along the trail. Dry grass crackled beneath his feet. A gentle wind blew and leaves dropped all around, but he focused on the trail ahead. He didn't want to think of the young woman he'd left behind.

He left her standing in the meadow, looking stunned and alone. At least she wasn't angry at him now, but he didn't feel like he'd won a victory. No, he just felt empty.

Empty and very much alone.

It was the ear-splitting *rat-a-tat-tat* of a woodpecker working away on a thick branch overhead that finally jerked Beth out of the fog Nick had left her in. She sat down hard on the rough ground and dropped her forehead to her knees.

Well, what the hell did you expect? That he'd beg for forgiveness? That he'd say everything was just hunky-dory?

No, in all honesty, she had to admit he'd behaved much more admirably than she had. First sign of trouble, and all she'd wanted was out.

Of course, the trouble was all of her own making.

It wasn't easy to run away from yourself. Beth lay back in the dried grass and scratchy pine needles and stared at the tiny bits of blue sky visible between the canopy of leaves. The woodpecker stopped its pecking and flew away. She heard the sharp buzz of a bee searching for one last flower before winter and felt the cool brush of air across her naked thighs and belly.

Her nipples tightened from the chill, and she thought of that first time with Nick, when he'd drawn her nipple between his lips, pressed it with his tongue, and held it against the roof of his mouth.

She'd never felt anything so sweet, never known love like that in her life. When he'd filled her, when he'd stretched her with his length and width and pressed deep inside, she'd expected pain, a repeat of the violation that was all she'd ever known.

She'd felt only pleasure.

He'd chased away the memories. The nightmares, actually. Nightmares she'd lived with ever since she'd been a sixteen-year-old virgin and her stepfather had raped her. That one brutal, agonizing act on the eve of her mother's funeral had taken more from her than any girl should have to give.

No one man should have the power to defile a person's entire life, but her stepfather had managed. He'd taken what should have been hers to give, and he'd ruined it forever.

Then she'd met Nick. Gentle and kind, he'd offered her friendship, and then he'd offered love. They'd chosen together to cement their relationship with the mating bond. Beth hadn't had any doubts then. She'd thought Nick was the one who would keep her safe, the one to take the darkness that covered her soul and strip it away—and for a special but much too brief time, he had.

If only she hadn't joined Tala that night when they had sex with Ulrich. It wasn't Ulrich's fault he was older, that his age and even his general appearance reminded her of her stepfather. He hadn't hurt her. Anything but . . . in fact, Ulrich had given her pleasure.

Maybe that was the problem—the fact she'd had a wonderful sexual experience with a man similar enough in looks to her stepfather to totally reawaken the memories.

Without realizing it, Ulrich had brought back all her ghosts. His had become the face in her nightmares.

It wasn't fair to Ulrich, but it wasn't fair to her, either. She'd thought those nightmares were a thing of the past.

Now they were back, worse than ever. Nick could have been the answer. He could have fought her demons if he'd been man enough, but he wasn't willing to challenge someone he saw as a mentor. He'd chased away the nightmares once. For some convoluted reason, she was certain that if he challenged Ulrich and won, they'd be gone forever.

Or would they?

Now she'd never know. Nick had looked totally disgusted with her, and she really couldn't blame him. It wasn't fair to ask something of a guy that just wasn't part of his nature. Why couldn't Nick, the Nick she'd fallen in love with, have been enough? Why did she need to make him into something he wasn't?

It wasn't fair to him. Not to her, either. Like an absolute idiot, she'd managed to chase away the best thing that had ever happened to her.

The sun disappeared behind the hills while Beth lay there on the hard ground. Pebbles dug into her butt and pine needles poked her thighs and back, but she couldn't find the energy to move.

Where would she go? Nick wouldn't want her back. Not after what she'd said to him today. He'd barely tolerated her since that fiasco the other night when he'd ended up getting royally fucked in the ass.

She wasn't sure if he'd actually liked it or not. In some perverse way, Beth had. She must be totally sick to have gotten so turned on watching Ulrich slam into her mate the way he had. The sex had started out so brutal, so typically male, but Nick hadn't fought. He'd merely bowed his head and accepted Ulrich's pounding violation—accepted it and eventually climaxed from it.

In fact, all of them—Ulrich, Matt, Nick, Millie, and even Beth—had achieved something amazing with their simultaneous orgasm, but it hadn't really mattered. Nick had blocked her long before his climax, just as she'd blocked him. That night, aroused, angry, frustrated with each other, they'd essentially severed the special link that bound them together.

Neither of them had attempted to reconnect since. It was like cutting off part of her body, going through the motions each day without Nick's thoughts in her head.

He'd slept in Matt's old room that first night, and the next couple nights since, sharing the cabin but not her bed. She missed sleeping beside him. Hated running beside him and not connecting. She felt the pain in every part of her body, but the place it hurt most remained the hardest to touch.

Her heart actually ached. What had she expected? That he would promise to challenge Ulrich? Even if he won, what would that solve?

Beth opened her eyes. A narrow sliver of moon was rising. It was almost entirely dark, and still she lay shivering on the hard ground. She thought of shifting, of just staying the night in the woods as a wolf, but somehow that didn't seem right. Not with the convoluted thoughts swirling darkly in her mind.

Instead, she folded her hands over her waist and closed her eyes against the moonlight. Naked, vulnerable, her body cold and aching with the night's chill.

Alone, with nowhere to go.

2

———

Head down, tail dragging, Nick wandered aimlessly through unfamiliar forest. Finally, as a pale sliver of moon rose over the treetops, he turned back toward the cabins. He hadn't really wanted to join up with Matt, Deacon, and Daci. The last thing they needed was someone like him tagging along and bringing his shitty mood with him.

Shitty and horny. Beth hadn't come near him in days, not since the fiasco with Ulrich. He'd shifted a number of times since then, and his arousal had built, growing along with the certainty that there was no hope for him and Beth. He couldn't make her love him. Not the way he loved her.

Lights were on in Daci's little cabin. Now, she was something else, coming here in search of answers in spite of the fact her father had been the worst enemy the Chanku had ever known. The baggage in Daci's past didn't seem to get in the way of her relationship with Deacon, and it hadn't kept her from adding Matt to their union.

She'd kept the cabin Millie had cleaned up for her and Deacon when they first arrived. It was a tiny, one-room place with little more than a big bed in the main room. Matt had moved out of the room in the cabin he'd shared with Beth and Nick and into Daci and Deacon's cabin, and the three of them filled the small place to overflowing.

If it weren't for the fact Nick and Beth needed separate rooms, Daci and her men should be the ones in the larger space. Now her little cabin glowed with light and laughter, while Nick and Beth's larger one stood like a dark and foreboding sentinel against the edge of the forest.

Somehow, Nick ended up trotting toward Daci's cabin, drawn like a moth to the light. Daci opened the door before he'd even climbed the steps to the porch. She was dressed in a pale green sarong that did amazing things for her slim figure.

"I thought I sensed you out there," she said, looking past him, toward the dark forest. "You guys just disappeared on us. Where's Beth?" Frowning, she stared down at Nick.

Nick shifted, but he couldn't meet Daci's steady gaze. Finally, he mumbled, "She wanted time by herself." He looked down at his bare feet and blurted out, "She wants to end our bond."

He heard Daci's sudden intake of breath and raised his head. She glared at him. "I hope you told her tough shit. It's a lifetime thing, Nick. She can't just turn it off." She took a deep breath as if to calm herself and held the door wide, welcoming him. "C'mon in."

Matt and Deacon sprawled on the big bed that dominated the main room of the cabin. Matt had on a silly-looking pair of striped knit boxers that clung to his strong legs. Deacon was wearing soft sweatpants, but even relaxed, his lean chest rippled with muscle.

Both men were taller than Nick, physically more formidable, yet they'd chosen to share this one young woman, each to love her without jealousy or competition.

He and Beth couldn't even work out a simple relationship between the two of them.

Nick stepped inside, but he stood in the doorway, feeling oddly vulnerable. He wasn't as big or as well built as Matt or Deacon, and he'd failed as a mate to the woman he loved. Even worse, he was the only naked person in the room.

Naked and aroused. He couldn't will his boner down for the life of him, and it was obvious the three of them had showered, which meant they'd either just had sex or were planning to. He glanced at Daci standing quietly beside him. "I shouldn't have come here. I'm sorry, guys. I'll just go back to my place." He turned away and grabbed the door handle.

Daci's small hand covered his. "No, you won't."

Nick turned and caught her soft gaze. Pity was the worst thing of all. He straightened up. "I don't need your sympathy, Daci. We'll work it out. Beth'll be home later, and we'll . . ."

Daci shook her head. She grabbed his hand and tugged Nick toward the bed. "You're in no condition to be alone, Nick. Not when you've got friends here who care about you."

Deacon reached for him, wrapped his fingers around Nick's other hand, and gently pulled him closer. "C'mon, Nick. There's plenty of room."

Matt scooted over, and Daci gave Nick a push. Her small hands felt like licks of fire against his chest. He sat on the edge of the bed. Daci didn't say a word, but she knelt between his knees and ran her fingertips over his thighs. His cock jutted up between his legs, brick red and weeping, but Daci ignored it. She touched his legs, his belly, the line of his flanks, stroking him with her fingers.

Damn, it felt so good he almost cried. Her small hands drifted over his chilled flesh, leaving invisible trails of heat behind. She poured caring and love and a sense of belonging into every stroke of her fingers, every sweep of her hands. It wasn't merely the fact she touched him in all the right places, but the fact Daci touched because she cared.

Beth had cared, in the beginning.

Matt and Deacon pressed close behind him, chests hard, yet warm and comforting as they ran their hands over his back, his shoulders and arms. His arousal grew, but the emotional tension, the stress of the past few days, seemed to melt away beneath their caring touch.

When Daci leaned forward and took the slick head of his cock between her lips, it seemed like the most natural thing in the world. Nick sighed, clenching his muscles to keep from coming as Matt and Deacon gently forced him back until he lay across the bed with his legs hanging over the side.

They stroked his chest, gently pinched his nipples, and ran their fingers along his rib cage while Daci's tongue and lips worked the full length of his erection. The soft glide of wet lips and the searching tip of her tongue made him ache with the powerful pleasure she gave him. Matt and Deacon's loving attention added layers of emotion to the arousal he felt and a sense of belonging that had been missing the past few days.

Beth—the different ways she'd loved him and the callous manner in which she'd denied their love—slipped into Nick's mind. He tensed and his erection softened. Obviously sensing the direction his thoughts were taking his libido, Daci raised her head. Her tongue tickled the sensitive spot beneath the crown of his penis, and her pink lips stretched around his thick shaft, but she frowned at him.

Groaning, Nick concentrated once again on Daci's mouth, on Matt and Deacon's warm bodies and even warmer hands. Blood surged into his cock until his increased size stretched Daci's lips wide. Smiling around her mouthful, she carefully worked her lips down his length. He felt the soft tissues at the back of her throat, the ripple of muscles as she swallowed him.

Her lips kissed his groin, and she slowly backed away until he was almost free of her mouth. Then, once again, she took him deep. This time, she slipped her hands over the tops of his thighs and reached between his legs. Lifting the weight of his sac in her fingers, she gently fondled the hard nuts inside.

Nick closed his eyes and drifted in a sea of sensual, loving touch—the guys' warm hands on his body, Daci's warmer mouth around his cock. He opened to their thoughts and found a kaleidoscope of sensual images and longings, felt a powerful sense of love and commitment to the pack.

Commitment to him. To Nick Barden—packmate, lover.

Loving thoughts of helping him through the long night, of being one with their brother, their mate.

He floated in sensation, in a tide of love and longing. The curved edge of a hard cock brushed his chin, and he opened his mouth. He wasn't certain which of the guys was stretching his lips wide until his tongue traced the smooth crown and lapped over the edge to follow the silky length beyond. *Matt.* He was sucking Matt's cock. If it had been Deacon, his tongue would have slipped over the foreskin, but all he felt was Matt's smooth glans and the salty sweet taste of his pre-cum.

Hands roamed across Nick's torso, fingers cupped his balls, while soft lips surrounded his cock. He mimicked Daci's suckling and gave the same attention to Matt, reveling in the gentle loving all three of his friends lavished on his body.

In the back of his mind, he thought of Beth. She should be here now, sharing this experience, being part of the warmth and love, but he couldn't let the thoughts out. Instead, he kept his secrets—his failure—locked behind solid barriers in his mind.

Someone gently tugged him across the bed until his entire length was stretched out in the middle. He kept his eyes closed, lost in the fantasy of touch and taste, warmth and softness. So long as his eyes were closed, he could imagine that one of the warm mouths or stroking hands belonged to Beth; that one of the bodies pressed close to his belonged to the woman he loved.

The thick shaft slipped out of his mouth. He trapped the crown between his lips, suckled the smooth glans, and ran the tip of his tongue over the narrow slit. Slowly, Matt pulled away, but his thick erection with its salty drops of fluid was replaced by the sweet flavor of Daci's mouth. Her tongue traced the seam of Nick's lips, and her kiss lingered, warm and loving.

He barely knew her, but Daci seemed to understand exactly what he craved. Not sex so much as connection, the feeling that he was with others like him, others who understood what it was like to feel alone in the world.

His life had never been easy, but with Beth, it had suddenly taken on a sense of purpose. He'd felt that purpose slip away out there in the meadow today. Once again, he'd been that homeless kid, wondering where he'd sleep tonight, wondering if anyone would ever love him.

Now, though, he realized he wasn't nearly as alone as he'd been for so many years.

He was Chanku. A valued member of the pack. Part of a family that cared about him, no matter whether he was an alpha or not. No matter if he'd been a loser in his other life. This was a new life, this life of Chanku. Even when he stumbled, there were others to help him up, to care about him. To make him feel wanted and loved.

He tried to thank Daci, with feelings, not words. She didn't respond, but she didn't have to. Her touch told him more than words ever could.

Slowly, she ended the kiss, sucking gently on his lips before she moved away.

Before Nick had time to wonder what was coming next, someone stretched a condom over his straining cock. Large, strong hands smoothed the latex over his full length, cupped his balls, and softly massaged the smooth skin along his perineum. A fingertip circled the sensitive portal to his ass, and he clenched his buttocks in response. His cock seemed to swell even more within the latex sheath.

His legs were stretched out, his feet placed close together. He felt the glide of warm, muscular skin against the outside of his thighs, the roughness of hair-covered legs as one of the guys knelt over his groin. Someone slathered his latex-covered glans with what felt like warm cream. Big, strong hands encircled his length, stroking, making him harder, thicker.

With his eyes tightly closed, he pictured his cock growing, the length stretching. Unseen hands held him at a perfect angle to meet the warm, damp cleft between two male cheeks. There was no need to thrust, not when one of the guys—he wasn't sure if it was Matt or Deacon—pressed against Nick's hard cock and forced entry. Nick groaned, and his hips lifted involuntarily, but it was all he needed to breach the opening. The broad flare of his cock compressed and slipped through the taut ring of anal muscle, sliding deep into a slick channel that flexed convulsively around his length.

Someone—Daci, he thought from the smaller hands—tied a blindfold over his eyes. The warm fabric blocked all light and somehow made him feel more secure. She grasped his hands, raised them over his head, and gently tied them together at the wrists. He tugged, but it appeared he'd been carefully secured to the headboard.

No one made a sound. He was aware of soft restraints holding his ankles, anchoring his legs to the footboard of the big bed. The solid weight of a male body held his legs to the bed. His cock was tightly surrounded by heat and rippling muscle.

There was no reason to try and escape, not when he trusted them completely. The scent of clean bodies and hot sex seemed more powerful when he was so securely trussed and deprived of sight. The scrape of a finger, the brush of lips, the heat and warmth surrounding his cock—everything seemed to flow with the steady beat of his heart, the slow rise and fall of his chest.

Tied, blindfolded, surrounded by warmth and love, Nick arched against the one who covered his groin, who raised and lowered in a slow but steady rhythm over his sheathed cock.

Securely restrained, he had no choice but to go with his body's needs, with the needs of the silent yet caring friends who made love to him. Caressed by wet heat and rippling muscles contracting with each gentle slide, Nick felt the worries of his life melting away.

When he finally climaxed, it was little more than a gentle and loving finish to a horrible day. No scream of completion, no sense of jubilation. He groaned and raised his hips, muscles tensing, convulsing with the hot coil of orgasm. His sperm rushing to fill the condom left him with no more than the relief of days of pent-up arousal and a sense that he was loved and among friends. He drifted off to sleep, his hands still restrained, his legs still tied, while someone bathed his body with a warm cloth and another removed the spent condom.

There was no tension in him. He was loved. Protected. Ready to face whatever might come next. But even as his packmates had loved him, had eased his loneliness, he'd been left with a new sense of purpose. He would not quit Beth. Never. No matter that she wanted to give up on him . . . on the two of them.

That was not the way of Chanku. Not the way the pack survived. A bond was forever. Love was forever, and Beth was his bonded mate. If they hadn't loved enough, the bond wouldn't have happened.

If Beth hadn't truly loved Nick, she never could have taken him into her heart, her body . . . her mind. She had willingly given herself, and in return, she had taken Nick. She had taken his heart and soul, forever. No matter what she said, Beth could never give him back that part that was now irrevocably hers.

No matter what she might say or think, Beth was his mate. Forever. Somehow, he would help her see the truth. He couldn't change the man he was, but would Beth have loved him if he'd been anyone different? It didn't matter. In the short time they'd been together, both of them had grown.

Both of them had changed. Discovered new parts of themselves, new powers and needs.

Both he and Beth had faced an entirely new reality, one that would continue to change and continue to test them. They couldn't make choices based on a past that no longer had relevance.

It was time to look to the future, to the new life stretching out ahead of them. A life Nick couldn't imagine without his mate.

If he had to, Nick figured he'd just love enough for both of them.

Millie West hiked slowly up the trail to the small cabin she shared with her mate. Sometimes the director's job just sucked. She'd had one hell of a long day, with one crisis after another. She'd dealt with federal inspectors and ranchers complaining about stock losses. She'd had an injured, half-grown pup brought in, one that someone had tried to keep as a pet in a pen he could barely turn around in. The poor thing was traumatized by its life in a cage, its unhealthy diet, and its lack of companionship.

Didn't those idiots realize wolves were pack animals? They needed each other . . . just like she needed her mate.

Millie hoped it would survive and learn to adapt to the ways of the wild. Hoped it wasn't too late for the little guy. At least the rest of the sanctuary's wolves were fed, and her employees had all gone home for the day. For now, though, her body ached, her feet hurt, and she was tired and grumpy.

If only she could go home to a quiet cabin with no one there beside Ulrich, but with the addition of their guests, that wasn't going to happen.

As much as she loved the younger Chanku, they were wearing her out.

Too much energy, too many crises, and too many mouths to feed. None of them seemed to know how to cook, and damn it all, but she was ready for some alone time.

It wasn't to be. Ulrich sat on the front deck, deep in conversation with Matt, Deacon, and Daci. The threesome appeared much more somber than usual. Of course, Deacon always looked somber, hence his name, but Matt generally had a smile on his gorgeous face and a twinkle in his eyes. Daci was as full of sass and mischief as any beautiful young woman with two handsome men as her lovers should be.

To be that young, and so carefree. Aching all over, Millie slowly climbed the front stairs. Nick and Beth were nowhere to be seen, but they'd been keeping to themselves since Nick's little power play a few nights earlier.

Ah, the drama of the young . . . One more thing she did not want to worry about . . . the Drama Queen and her Lothario.

"Hello, m'love." Ulrich grabbed Millie's hand as she reached the deck and tugged gently.

She tumbled willingly into his lap and kissed him. "Hello to you, too. What's up?"

Ric nodded toward the younger Chanku. "They're worried about Nick and Beth. Seems they're not getting along at all."

"They want out of their pair bond," Daci said. "That's what Nick told us. Except he still loves Beth, but . . ."

Matt chimed in. "They're just not connecting. Nick's miserable."

"So's Beth." Daci glanced at the rest of them. "I mean, I think she's the one causing the trouble, but none of us can figure out why. It's like that scene the other night, before Deacon and I got here, when she wanted Nick to go after Ulrich."

"You've talked about it?" Millie glanced from one to the other and back at Ric. "I was oblivious to a lot of the undercurrents."

Ric leaned close and kissed her on the nose. "That's okay, sweetie. I love you anyway."

The kids laughed, but Millie waved Ric off. "Damn right you do, old man. I'm the only one who'll have you."

"There is that." Ric hugged her close, and Millie felt her body respond. It didn't take much with this man.

She hated to ask, but, "So where are Nick and Beth tonight?"

Deacon shook his head. "Nick's back at our cabin, sleeping. Beth didn't come home with him after we ran. They split off from us, but only Nick came back."

Frowning, Millie glanced at Ric. "Has anyone gone to look for her?"

The kids shook their heads.

"Can you sense her? Is she nearby?" She really didn't want to get involved, but . . .

Ric shook his head. "No. I could pick up only Nick's presence. He's miserable, but he's alone." He winked at Daci. "The kids took care of him tonight, made sure he'd sleep for a while."

Sighing, Millie disengaged herself from Ric's comforting embrace and stood up. There was no way she'd be able to relax now, not while she worried about Beth. The girl had way too many issues, but she was a good kid.

Just a bit too confused . . . and a tad on the dramatic side, something neither Millie nor Ric knew how to deal with. Neither of them had any idea what was behind Beth's strange moods—they didn't know what demons drove her. But no matter. Millie couldn't leave her out there in the woods . . . not after spending her own youth so terribly alone, with no one to turn to for anything.

"Daci, you interested in a run? I think we need to go find

Beth. I hate to think of her out there by herself, especially if she and Nick are having problems."

Daci nodded and stood up, slipping out of her sweatshirt as she rose. All three men turned appreciative eyes on both women as they disrobed before shifting.

Millie struck a pose and stuck out her tongue at the three guys. "I expect dinner when we get home, so get your eyeful of naked woman while you can, and then get your butts into the kitchen and get to work."

Daci laughed as she folded her jeans and handed them to Matt. "Millie, I like the way you think. Interested in giving lessons? I sure don't have your knack for giving orders. . . . We need to talk." Then she shifted and, with a swish of her tail, leapt cleanly over the deck railing.

Millie followed, smiling to herself over the men's laughter as the two of them trotted into the dark forest. Funny how she'd wanted nothing more than a quiet evening, and now she was actually looking forward to her run through the woods with Daci.

Their Chanku senses would lead them to Beth. If only she had some idea what to do once they found her.

3

Millie sensed a disturbance in the forest long before she realized it was Beth's misery she'd picked up. If she'd been human, she might have laughed. All she'd asked for was a quiet night home alone with Ric. Instead, she was running through thick shrubs, towering pines, and a dark and chilly night in search of the resident drama queen.

This way. She nodded to her companion and slipped off the main trail heading into the dark woods. Daci followed along the narrow track. As familiar with this forest as she was, Millie knew it led to a small, secluded meadow.

She wasn't sure what she'd find, but Beth, lying naked and human upon the cold ground, her arms crossed over her waist like a virgin sacrifice, certainly wasn't it.

She paused at the edge of the meadow with Daci alongside. *Beth? Are you okay?*

"Go away, Millie. Daci. Just leave me alone."

Millie trotted across the meadow. *Sorry,* she said. *It doesn't work that way. We're a pack. Whether you like it or not, we're all in this together.*

Beth shook her head. Slowly, she turned and sat up, but she didn't shift, and she didn't look at the two wolves. Silvery streaks across her face tracked tears she'd shed. The night was growing colder, and Beth shivered. Millie had the strong suspicion she was actually enjoying her misery.

"No, Millie. You're wrong. I'm not enjoying it."

Beth raised her head, and Millie was struck with the young woman's almost ethereal beauty. Her amber eyes were luminous, the thick lashes clumped together from her tears.

"I don't know what to do. I can't go back to Nick. He doesn't want me." Beth turned away, shivering, crying. "I don't blame him. There's not much here to want."

Millie shifted. She wrapped her arms around Beth and hugged her close. "Oh, Beth, honey. C'mon. Don't you think you're being just a bit melodramatic? Nick still loves you or he wouldn't be so miserable."

Daci waited in the background. Beth curled into Millie's embrace and cried even harder. Millie sighed. Obviously, her approach was getting her nowhere fast, and that quiet evening with Ric seemed farther away than ever.

"Open to me, Beth. Whatever's happened, it's easier to say it without words. Show me what's wrong so I can help."

"You can't help, Millie. No one can."

Millie would have rolled her eyes, but there was no one watching who could appreciate it. Damn, she really wanted to be home, sipping a glass of wine, cuddling with her mate . . .

"You're wrong. There's nothing broken that can't be fixed. Trust me. I'm a perfect example. So is Daci. Almost all of us have some sort of crap in our backgrounds, but with a little time and some hard work, we get past it. Give it up, Beth. Tell me what's wrong before I decide to just climb into your head and find the truth."

Beth jerked out of her embrace. "You'd do that? But that's . . ."

"Yes, I would." Millie touched Beth's shoulder. "I'd do it

because I care. I don't like seeing you like this. What's the problem? It's not just Nick. There's more to all this business than your troubles with your mate. Why are you trying to get him to challenge Ric? You know he won't do it. He loves Ric. I thought you did, too."

Beth bowed her head and trembled even harder.

Millie felt her patience begin to shred. "Beth, shift. You're freezing and so am I. Daci's the only smart one in the bunch." She turned and smiled at the wolf sitting silently behind her. "We can talk better without words, and I'm going to get to the bottom of this before we go back to the cabin."

Beth hiccupped and sniffed. "You sound like my mother. I miss her. I never thought I'd miss getting yelled at."

"I never knew my mother, and I'm not yelling. You're lucky you've got that memory. Now are you going to shift?"

Beth nodded, and just as easily, a large wolf sat beside Millie with her ears laid back against her broad skull. Millie shifted, but instead of asking Beth again, she slipped quickly into her unguarded thoughts.

It took only moments to find dark memories eating away at the young woman, but instead of sympathy, Millie's hackles rose and she growled. Before Beth had time to react, Millie sat back on her haunches and glared at the young wolf. *How dare you! How can you possibly confuse Ric with that bastard? They're nothing alike. They don't even look the same!*

Beth hung her head. *I know, but I can't make the memories go away. Being with Ulrich brought them back. I can't even let Nick touch me or I think of him. I can't bear to look at Ulrich. When I do, I feel my stepfather's hands on me, his cock tearing inside me, his . . .*

Disgusted, Millie stood up. She was tired and hungry and this little twit was wallowing in self-pity when Millie could have been home with her mate. Maybe she'd have more patience if it hadn't been such a long day, but it had, and she didn't.

Enough. Beth, you can't let nightmares and bad memories rule your life. Look to the future. Nick loves you. You love Nick. If the love weren't there, you would never have been able to bond. It flat out wouldn't have happened. The incident with your stepfather is part of your past, not your future. Get over it. Besides, you're part of a pack, now. It's not all about you.

Beth's head hung even lower.

Daci slipped between Beth and Millie. She flashed a fierce glare in Millie's direction. Then she turned to Beth. *Millie, I'll stay with Beth for a while. You've worked all day. Why don't you go back and let the guys know I'll be home later.*

Silence hung in the small glen. Cold chilled Millie to the bone. *Oh, Goddess.* She hung her head, shamed to her core. She'd just told a young girl to "get over" a brutal rape. She couldn't believe she'd done something so cruel. Mortified, Millie sighed. *Good idea, Daci. Beth, I am so sorry. It has been a long, difficult day. I wasn't thinking when I said those awful things. Will you forgive me?*

Beth looked directly into Millie's eyes and nodded. *There's nothing to forgive, Millie. You're absolutely right. I need to move on. It's just . . . I don't know how.*

That's okay. Daci turned a bright look on Millie. *I do. Everything will be fine.*

Ric was blessedly alone when Millie climbed the front steps to the cabin once again. She shifted when she reached the door and stepped inside. Ric looked up from his newspaper, set the paper aside, and opened his arms.

Millie collapsed into his lap, sobbing. She didn't try to tell him what had happened. Instead she merely opened her thoughts to the entire conversation with Beth and waited for Ric to tell her she'd been a cruel and heartless bitch.

"Ah, m'love. You pegged her perfectly. She is a drama queen."

"What?" Millie raised her head, sniffing loudly. Ric handed her a clean white handkerchief. "But I said horrible things, and . . ."

"That you did. Things she needs to hear. If Beth wears her past like a hair shirt, she'll never move on. A lot of us have issues with our past, but we deal with it. It's not always easy, but we don't wallow in our misery. We get on with things, unless there's a reason not to." He brushed Millie's tangled hair back from her eyes. "That night with Tala and Beth, the sex was great. Spontaneous and exciting, but Beth was no shrinking violet. She was the aggressor. The girl likes control, and I imagine that's why she's pushing Nick so hard."

Something seemed to click for Millie. She saw Beth, her dark eyes so sad and confused, and in those eyes she saw herself as a young girl living under the rule of her overbearing uncle, a man whose twisted sexuality had been a constant threat in Millie's young life.

"It's not that she likes control," she said, basically thinking aloud. "Beth *needs* control. When her stepfather raped her, he took away her chance to control her own life, her destiny. Somehow, she has to come to terms with what happened. I don't know how she's going to do that, but she'll have to do it on her terms."

"Daci can help her, then. That little gal has faced more demons than most of us, and she did it with honesty and determination. Don't worry, m'love. You can't solve everyone's problems for them, especially with someone who needs to work out control issues." Ric ran his hands along Millie's ribs, curled his fingers over her hip, and squeezed her left cheek. "I think I'm having control issues of my own." He leaned close and kissed her breast, circling the tip of his tongue around her nipple and then drawing the taut bead between his parted lips.

She felt the tiny nibbles, the wet heat of his mouth, the need that poured off of him with every touch, every breath. Stubble from his upper lip rasped her sensitive skin and raised chills across her chest.

Sighing, Millie leaned into his touch, pressing her breast against the searching warmth of his lips, running her fingers through his thick, white hair. She leaned closer and ran her tongue around the rim of his ear and nibbled with the sharp edges of her teeth. Pitching her voice low and sexy, Millie whispered into his ear, punctuating each word with little licks and nips. "That's good to hear. I love it when you lose control, when you're so hot and bothered you're nothing but a mindless sex machine." She kissed the top of his head and backed away. "So, what did you fix me for dinner?"

Ulrich leaned back and stared at her. "Dinner?" His cheeks were flushed and ruddy, his amber eyes dark with arousal.

"Yep. Dinner." Moving carefully over the full erection tenting his sweats, Millie slipped off his lap. Grinning broadly, she held out her hand and pulled him to his feet. "You promised you'd feed me when I got back. It's been a long day."

Grumbling, Ric carefully stood up. He adjusted his erection with a dramatic grimace, lightly swatted her on the butt, and followed her into the kitchen. "You don't know the half of it, m'dear. Not by a long shot."

Beth stared at Daci. *Do you really know how to help me?*

Nope. But we'll figure something out. Daci curled up beside Beth and rested her muzzle on the other wolf's shoulder. *Can you talk about it?*

Beth raised her head and stared straight ahead. *I never have. Not even to Nick. He knows only because he saw what happened the night we bonded. He saw my memories.*

Daci took a deep breath and then let it out. *I certainly won't try to force you if you're not ready to talk about it, but let's go back to your cabin so we can speak as women, not as wolves.*

Nick might be there.

I don't think so. We left him a bit tied up at my place.

Beth swung her head around and stared at Daci. Daci opened her thoughts and shared her vision of Nick, blindfolded and tied to the bed.

Then she showed Beth what the four of them had done earlier in the evening, how Matt had impaled himself on Nick's cock and taken a slow, sensual ride that took all of them over the edge. How Nick had thrust blindly with his arms and legs still bound, filling Matt with each powerful lunge.

Daci felt the hot stab of Beth's arousal, the sudden burst of sexual interest. *Haven't you guys ever done any bondage stuff? Never.*

Daci stood up. *Well, maybe it's time you did. I've got him all ready for you.*

Wide-eyed, Beth stared at her. *What if he's still angry with me?*

Daci snorted. It was the best laugh she could manage as a wolf. *I can assure you, Beth. If you go to a man, any man, with sex on your mind while he's naked, tied to a bed, and blindfolded, anger's going to be the last thing he's thinking about.*

Beth's silent laughter filled Daci's head as they turned and trotted back toward the cabin. Daci reached out for her men and managed to link with Matt. Nick was still asleep, still tied to the bed. Matt assured her that he and Deacon didn't mind a bit switching cabins tonight with Beth and Nick.

As they drew closer to the cabins, Beth linked with Daci. *I wish I had your confidence. Everyone thinks I'm so together, but I'm not. Not at all.*

Daci glanced over her shoulder. *That's funny. I didn't have any confidence at all. Not for a long time. I had so many issues about my childhood. Did you know I was a bastard? My father never acknowledged me, not in the legal sense, and I had all kinds of issues with him. Ulrich helped me find closure with my feelings for my father. That's an important step . . . closure. Maybe that's what you need with your stepfather.*

Beth glanced at Daci. *But how? I haven't seen him since the night he raped me—over five years ago.*

Maybe you need to see him. Maybe it's time to speak with him. Tell him that what he did to you was wrong.

I'd rather kill him. Beth trotted beside Daci. *I could do it, now that I'm the wolf.*

That you could. Daci paused and stared at Beth. *But it's something you need to do yourself. Nick can't do it for you. It's not fair to ask your mate to fight your battles.*

He's killed before. He shifted and killed a guy before any of us even knew who or what we were.

Daci stared at Beth. *I've heard the story, but Nick's not a killer by nature. What happened in San Francisco was a very unique circumstance. A creep was attacking a woman and Nick reacted. He didn't expect to shift. It just happened, and the wolf took control. Nick loves you, Beth, but you can't ask him to be someone he's not. You can't ask him to murder a man he doesn't even know. You can't put conditions on your love, either. You either love him or you don't.*

Daci stared into the amber eyes so like her own. Beth lowered her gaze and glanced away. After a long moment, Daci turned and started back to the cabin. She was aware of Beth following behind her, but the other wolf's thoughts were hidden behind powerful barriers.

She felt as if she was totally out of her league, but there were women Daci knew who would understand. Women who had suffered horrible assaults by men and found their own form of closure. One of them, Millie's daughter Manda, had been victimized by Daci's father, but she was still fragile, still finding her strength as Chanku.

Keisha Rialto and Tala Quinn, though, had come through their trauma as powerful, self-assured women. The act that linked them, the risks they'd taken, and the courage they'd found might be the key to Beth's issues.

Both women had been tortured and raped. Both women had shifted and killed their attackers. Each of them, Tala and Keisha, had emerged as powerful alpha bitches, sure of themselves and their place within the pack.

Maybe Beth was right. Maybe killing the man who had violated her soul as much as her body was the solution.

Keisha and Tala would know, and they were only a phone call away.

4

Alone now that Daci had gone to meet her guys, Beth hesitated at the door to the smaller cabin. Her fingers clasped the door handle, her mind touched the quiet, unguarded thoughts of her mate as he slept inside.

She shivered in the chill night air, but still she hesitated. Nick loved her. He wasn't blocking his feelings right now. He loved her, but he hated what she asked of him. Hated the way their relationship had become so twisted in the convoluted drama of Beth's past.

Hated the situation, but still loved her.

"Well, that's a start." She opened the door and slipped inside. The rush of warm air enveloped her like a comforting blanket as she quietly shut the door behind her.

Nick slept on, exhausted most likely by the trauma of the past few days as well as the powerful sex he'd shared with Daci and her guys just hours ago.

Thank goodness he'd had those packmates to turn to when his own mate had failed him so badly. Beth actually cringed when she thought of her behavior over the past few days. While

Nick had done everything in his power to be what she wanted, she'd shut him out, asked him to take actions that he found not only distasteful, but dishonorable.

Thank goodness for Millie and her unrestrained mouth. No one else had the courage to force Beth to face the bitch she'd become over the past few weeks. She'd been wrong. Dead wrong to expect Nick to go against his own personal code of honor. Asking him to fight Ulrich had reflected badly on her, not Nick.

Never again.

Now, with her thoughts swirling and her eyes stinging from unshed tears, she stood beside the bed, hands clasped over her flat belly, and watched him.

Merely looking at Nick made her hot. His beautiful eyes were still covered with the colorful bandana Daci had used to blindfold him, and his hands and feet were tightly restrained.

The blindfold didn't hide the dark slash of his cheekbones, his full lips, or the sharp curve of his jaw. Barely a shadow of beard shaded his cheeks.

She'd been attracted to his androgynous beauty from the first. A man whose features were so finely cut, so inherently beautiful he might have appeared feminine if not for his innate masculinity.

There was nothing feminine about his strength, his sense of honor, his lean but powerful physique. Broad, bony shoulders tapered to a narrow waist. His cock, huge even when flaccid, lay softly against his thigh. The sensitive glans was completely covered by his foreskin. Beth realized she was actually licking her lips, imagining the taste of him, picturing the blood engorging his cock, the way the loose skin now hiding the tip would stretch across his broad glans and finally slip behind the crown when he was fully aroused.

His dark hair had grown longer. A thick curl lay across the blindfold and long strands brushed his cheek. His caramel-colored skin glistened in the pale light, but the dark tufts of hair under his arms and the matching swirl of hair covering his groin drew her eye.

He was beyond beautiful, inside and out. And she'd hurt him with her pushy requests. She'd driven him away when he was willing to do almost anything she asked.

A tear slipped down her cheek. Then another.

And she remembered.

When she'd first met him almost a year ago, he'd been a typical street kid hanging out near Golden Gate Park in San Francisco. They'd called him Nicky, then. A kid's name, but he was little more than a boy, too pretty to be considered a man.

He'd been raised in foster homes and then turned loose on the streets at eighteen, where he'd found odd jobs and occasionally turned tricks. As beautiful as Nick was, he'd been more than popular, but whoring hadn't been his choice.

No, he preferred a quiet corner in the library where he could read until they kicked him out at night, or hanging out at the memorial garden in Golden Gate Park, nibbling on those sweet grasses—the grasses none of them realized were full of the nutrients that would enable those with the right DNA to achieve their Chanku birthright and the ability to shapeshift.

Covered in tattoos and piercings, with his dark amber eyes, dark hair, and dark skin, he could have passed for a young gangbanger, but he'd preferred the quiet of the park and a good book to the hangouts on Stanyan or the local coffee shops.

Beth had recognized a kindred soul, one not only damaged by life and circumstance, but as racially mixed as she was. Both of them with hearts and minds as confused as their DNA. Where Beth traced her ancestry to the Middle East, Nick's was mostly native American, but they each had the same tilted eyes, the same long, lean lines to their bodies, the same soft, caramel-colored skin.

Nick wasn't as big or as tall as many of the Chanku males,

but what he lacked in size he more than made up for in strength, in the scrappy street smarts that had helped him survive his convoluted childhood.

She knew his life hadn't been easy, but he never complained. He'd wanted so much to go on in school, but when the money wasn't there, he adjusted. He was a survivor, but he'd managed to live his life on his own terms, with his own code of honor.

Until Beth came along and tried to change the rules.

She knew everything there was to know about Nick, just as he knew her. They'd learned it all in their mating bond, but did they really understand each other?

Obviously not. If they did, she wouldn't have been pushing him, as Daci had accused her. Wouldn't have asked him to go up against a man he truly loved and admired, especially when it really wasn't the solution Beth needed.

Daci was right. This was Beth's battle and hers alone. She needed to face her stepfather, and she had to do it by herself, with her own courage, not Nick's. That meant she had to find the courage inside herself. And, in case she failed, if something went horribly wrong and she didn't make it back, she needed to leave Nick with something wonderful to remember her by.

Something only she could give him—herself. Her love. The assurance that she loved him for who and what he was, not for what she'd hoped he could do for her.

With that thought in mind, Beth scrubbed the tears from her face with both hands. Then she carefully placed one knee on the edge of the bed. The slight motion woke Nick.

"Daci?" He turned his head. "Is that you?"

"No. It's me."

She didn't say her name, only whispered the words, but Nick immediately smiled. "Beth? Are you okay? I've been worried about you. I didn't like leaving you out there, but . . ." He left unsaid what she knew he meant, that he hadn't known what to do.

Well, neither had she, but maybe, just maybe, she was beginning to figure it out.

Nick tugged at the restraints. "Turn me loose, okay? It looks like the guys decided to leave me tied up for the night. Are they here?"

Beth shook her head, realized he couldn't see her, and softly whispered, "No. Just you and me, Nick. And no . . . I'm not going to untie you. I've decided I like you like this."

Nick went very still. "How's that?"

"Restrained. Tied up. All for me, for my pleasure." Beth crawled up on the bed and straddled his long, lean body. She settled her warm pussy over the ridge of his suddenly not-so-flaccid cock and squeezed her thighs tightly against his flanks. Then she sighed.

"I have to admit, I also like you blindfolded. It's easier saying what I have to say when you can't see me." She took another deep breath and wished her racing heart would slow down a little bit. It might make it easier to get the words out. "I love you, Nick. I don't really want our mating bond ended. I've been so damned confused. I wasn't sure what I wanted, other than the fact I know I'll always love you. Always need you. From the first time I saw you, I knew you were the one. I'm so sorry for saying what I said, for asking you to do things I didn't have the right to ask. Things that wouldn't have made a difference in my screwed up life . . . at least not a difference for the better."

There was a long silence. She tested Nick's barriers, but they were high and tight, and she had no idea what he was thinking.

Maybe this wasn't such a good idea after all.

She felt Nick's chest rise and fall beneath her as he took one deep breath and then another.

"I love you, Beth. I'll admit it, I don't understand what's

going on in your head. Not when you close me out the way you have."

"Is that sort of an 'I'll show you mine if you'll show me yours' suggestion?" She laughed, but her laughter ended on a sob. "Okay."

Then she opened to Nick. Showed him her love for him, her fears, the black shadowed memories that pulsed over every thought she had.

At the same time, Nick's love for her blossomed in her own mind, his worries, his fears that he wasn't man enough for her, that his role as her mate was somehow lacking because he couldn't and wouldn't take on the pack's alpha.

Not because he didn't want to protect Beth, but because he couldn't see any reason to challenge a man he loved and admired. Knowing he would lose, not because he lacked strength, but because he lacked the desire to fight. Most of all, he realized challenging Ulrich wouldn't stop the demons haunting his mate.

Beth felt his thoughts with a deep ache in her chest. Nick had made his decisions for all the right reasons. She'd made hers for the wrong ones.

"You're right, you know." She leaned over and kissed him, tracing the soft swell of his lips with the tip of her tongue. Then she touched her nose to his, separated from warm skin by the bandana tied across his eyes. "Not about losing. I still think you could take Ulrich if you had to, but I'm glad you could see what a stupid idea it was. I'm sorry I asked, and I'm really sorry if Ulrich hurt you. He's so big."

The image of Ulrich Mason shoving his huge cock inside Nick's ass should have upset her. Instead she felt herself growing wetter, hotter.

And she felt Nick swelling beneath her, his cock stretching, thickening. He laughed. "That should let you know you don't have anything to be sorry about. Ulrich's amazing. No wonder Millie's always in such a great mood."

Beth kissed him once more and sat back, softly grinding her pussy against his cock. "She wasn't in such a great mood tonight. She and Daci came looking for me in the woods. When she found out I was upset with Ulrich just because he reminded me of my stepfather, she was really pissed."

Nick shrugged, about all he could do with his hands and feet tied. "Can you blame her? She loves him. You're going to have to get past that. And you're going to have to apologize to both Millie and Ulrich."

Beth sighed. "I know. I will. And I've got a few ideas about the other, but in the meantime . . ." She scooted down between his legs, stretched out on her belly, and took his thick cock in her mouth. His foreskin was entirely stretched back and the sensitive glans fully exposed. The dark tip glistened, a single milky drop balanced against his slit. She gently laved the slick surface with her tongue, wetting him even more with her saliva, and then sucked him deep inside her mouth. The bittersweet taste of his seed made her vaginal muscles clench in a desperate, needy rhythm. Nick moaned softly and writhed against his restraints.

She released him and blew soft little puffs of air against the sensitive glans. She ran her tongue along the sleek edge of his foreskin where it stretched over his shaft, and nuzzled against him with nose and lips, tasting, nipping, teasing.

Beth was already close to climax merely from her mate's taste, from inhaling his warm, musky scent. How could she have denied Nick, much less herself, these past few days?

Using just the tip of her tongue and sharp nips with her teeth, she teased him with tiny licks and bites. His body twisted and writhed beneath her as she sucked his cock deep. Her vaginal muscles clenched and rippled as her arousal grew, step by step, with Nick's, but when he was almost ready to come, she released him with a little puff of air across his glans.

She dipped her head lower. He shuddered when she ran her tongue over his wrinkled ball sac, drawing first one solid orb and then the other between her lips, rolling them over her tongue, sucking and licking until Nick was shivering with the need to come.

His muscles tightened against the restraints. The bed creaked as he struggled to free himself. His thoughts were open to her, a steaming cauldron of arousal, of pure, unadulterated lust growing deeper, darker as she took him closer to the edge.

Close, but not close enough. Reveling in the power, the sense of ultimate control, Beth continued her sensual assault on the man she'd chosen as her mate, on the one person who came closest to understanding the convoluted thoughts and memories that drove her.

She nuzzled close against his groin, tasting and touching, breathing him deep into her lungs. He was trembling harder now, but so was she, both of them skirting the edge of orgasm. Moaning softly, Nick gave up any semblance of fighting her, gave in to whatever course Beth chose for him.

Ulrich Mason had said she had the ability to see the truth in people, to know when they lied. If that was so, if she truly saw truth, then there was nothing but honesty in Nick's response. He loved her. Needed her. Hated her at this very moment for denying him completion, but at the same time, loved her for holding him here at the very edge.

Loved her for all her faults, all her fears.

Smiling, fighting her own raging desire, Beth crawled over his body, licking and sucking her way along his ribs, spending an inordinate amount of time on first one copper-colored nipple and then the other.

She bit down on the left. Nick jerked, but Beth felt the sensual bite like a shock of sensation between her legs. Nick tugged against the restraints, but he didn't say a word. She licked the bruised peak and turned her attentions to the nipple on his right, biting it even harder. Her pussy spasmed. Nick's cock twitched against her bottom, and he moaned, shoving his chest against her mouth.

She licked and bit and sucked, moving from one side to the other until Nick was twisting beneath her, his body sliding in her body's fluids as much as his own. Sweat covered his chest, and his lips parted as he dragged in deep breaths. Beth slowly moved higher, until she straddled his upper chest. Rising up on her knees, she gently pressed the wet folds of her sex to his mouth.

Growling with frustration, Nick stabbed her with his tongue, licked deep, and then wrapped his lips around her swollen clit and sucked, hard.

She climaxed, screaming his name, clasping her knees against the sides of his head as wave after wave of sensation rolled through her trembling body.

He licked her gently, taking her to another climax, and yet another. She heard a loud snap and felt his hands on her flanks—he'd broken free of the restraints Daci and the guys had used to hold him.

Nick's feet were still tied, but he lifted her. Wrapping his big hands around her slim flanks, he held her over him and then slowly lowered her shivering body down on his erect, engorged cock.

The broad flare of his glans met her swollen vaginal lips, parted them, slipped between their folds. He was huge, grown thick and hard with her teasing, and he stretched her wide and filled her deep as her buttocks finally rested on his upper thighs and her vaginal muscles clamped tightly around him.

Nick's hands clasped her flanks. She rocked forward, fitting him even deeper, until the broad crown of his cock pressed hard against the mouth of her womb. His fingers dug into her sides, and he tilted his hips, holding her against him, stretching her impossibly with his thick length. Then he lifted her, held her above him, and brought her down once more.

Sighing, perfectly willing now to relinquish control to the rhythm Nick set, Beth slowly raised her hips and began to move.

5

Nick left the blindfold tied around his eyes. He ignored the restraints holding his feet. He didn't have to see his mate to love her, but he needed her wet heat around him now, needed the clasp of her pussy rippling over his sensitive cock, the physical affirmation of her love for him.

He'd thought she was lost to him. No matter that she would always be his mate, always be the one he would love, he'd never imagined they would come together again, not like this. Tonight when she'd told him it was over, he'd felt his world slip away even as he'd accepted her decision. He couldn't hold her if she didn't love him, couldn't keep her if she wanted to leave—but she'd come back to him

Come back and apologized, though he knew she still didn't understand the demons haunting her, still needed to pursue some course of action to free herself from her memories.

Whatever she needed, he would give. Wherever she needed to go, he would follow, but if she had to pursue some course of action by herself, Nick realized he could give her that freedom as well.

He wouldn't like it, and he'd fear for her, but he'd have to allow her that freedom, no matter the cost to himself.

Whatever it took to bring her back to him, whole, complete, no longer haunted by a past he could never truly understand.

For now, though, he would love her. Love her and reassure her that he was hers, no matter what, forever. And remind her of something even more important than their fears, their drives, their individual needs.

It wasn't just him who was hurt by her actions. They were part of something larger, more complex. They were part of a pack. He needed to remind her who and what she was. What he was. That he was Nick Barden. He was her lover, her mate—and he was Chanku.

He chose that moment to shift, so that Beth straddled the wolf, not the man she'd teased to distraction. She cried out, filled to the point of pain by the thick knot of his wolven cock. Her fingers tightened in the dark fur covering his chest.

The restraints fell away, the blindfold hung about his neck like a collar. Nick rolled beneath her, twisting and turning in a tangle of human limbs and wolven legs until, bodies still connected, he covered Beth from behind. She could have shifted, but instead she lowered her cheek against her folded forearms and knelt, buttocks raised, open to him and submissive now, no longer the dominant partner.

Nick raked her shoulder with one heavy paw, leaving a trail of dark red scratches. Growling, he thrust hard and fast, loving his woman, at the same time reminding her who and what he was.

Her mate. Male. Wolf. Physically more powerful, willing to submit to the needs of his alpha bitch, yet strong enough to wrest control whenever he desired.

He desired that control now. Desired it and took it, driving into her like a battering ram, giving in to his hurt, his anger, his frustration with the woman who'd managed to tear him to pieces for most of the past week.

He opened his thoughts, absorbed hers. Experienced himself from Beth's point of view. Felt the sharp, stabbing thrust of his cock, the thick bulge of the knot that held them together. Felt her love as her body tipped once again over the edge.

Orgasm raged through him, a shock of pure sensation striking hard and fast. Nick jerked. His cock swelled even more. Beth raised her head and cried out, finding her climax precisely as Nick's swept over him, sharing the sweet, sharp current as it raced through her body.

His hips continued thrusting even as he collapsed, his full weight driving Beth to the rumpled blankets, his jaws wide and tongue hanging as he struggled to draw in enough breath to power his straining lungs.

Long minutes later, they remained atop the twisted bedding, still connected, bodies sated, hearts pounding, thoughts open.

I hope I didn't hurt you. That wasn't my intent. Her pussy tightened around his cock in answer. The swollen knot, such a bestial reminder of who and what they were, was finally shrinking.

"No. That was . . ." She paused, her thoughts in disarray. *That was unbelievable. More powerful than anything I . . .*

Her mind drifted off into an unintelligible sequence of remembered feelings and sensations. Nick grinned. He felt much the same.

He also felt a connection more powerful than he had the night they'd mated. With that thought in mind, he shifted and pulled Beth into his arms, tight against the swell of his chest. "I love you, Beth. You're mine, forever and always. Whatever it is that's haunting you, we'll find answers, but for now we both need to sleep. Together. I'm not letting go of you, okay?"

"Okay." She rolled within his embrace and kissed him. Then

she sighed and snuggled close. "I love you, Nick. I'm sorry for being such a bitch. I love you more than you can know."

"Are you sure this is what you want?" Whispering softly, Daci helped Beth load her few belongings into Daci's little Mini Cooper.

Beth kept her voice just as low. "I have to. Thank you so much for letting me borrow your car." She looked down at the keys in her hand and then smiled at Daci. "And thank you for calling Keisha and Tala. I'll let you know as soon as I get to San Francisco. I really hope Keisha can be there, though I know it's hard to get away with such a small baby."

Daci shook her head. "She was actually thrilled that you'd asked for her. She's dying to see the garden she designed, the one you guys used to hang out at." Daci grabbed both of Beth's shoulders and looked directly into her eyes. "I hate doing this behind Nick's back, but I do understand. We'll take good care of him. Just promise you'll be very careful. If anything happens to you, I'm the bitch in trouble."

Beth laughed and wrapped her arms around Daci. "I'll be careful. Tell Nick I'll be home in a week, maybe two, max, but please explain to him. You were so right. This is something I have to do on my own. I can't ask him to do it for me."

"I know. Drive carefully. I'll tell the others."

Beth quietly opened the car door and slipped inside. "I love you, Daci. I can never thank you enough."

Daci flashed her a grin. "Just bring my little car home safe or I'll haunt you forever." Then she quietly shut the door to her car.

Beth grinned at her, started the engine, and within seconds had disappeared into the gray early dawn. Daci stood alone in front of the cabin where Matt and Deacon slept. She glanced across the parking area at her little cabin where Nick stood, staring silently out the window.

She knew he'd watched the entire time Beth loaded the car and prepared to leave. Watched, but restrained himself from interfering. Beth had been so nervous, she hadn't even known he was there. Daci glanced once more at the dark cabin. Her men slept on, oblivious to her absence. Smiling, she turned away and went to Nick.

It was obvious he needed her now, more than Matt and Deacon did. Nick needed the reassurance that he'd made the right decision to let Beth fight her battles by herself.

Daci walked up the steps and the door swung wide. Nick leaned against the frame, but his gaze went beyond her. She turned to see what caught his eye—the morning sun glittering through the dust cloud that marked Beth's exit.

"Do you think she'll come back?" He blinked. His eyes sparkled from unshed tears.

"She'll be back. The question is, are you going to let her go by herself?"

He nodded. "For now, though it's not my place to *let* Beth do anything. . . . She'll do what she thinks is right, no matter what I want. It's her life. It should be her choice." He stepped back and Daci entered.

It was her cabin, after all, but she flashed him a grin. Unlike some guys, Nick obviously understood and respected Beth's right to decide her own life. "Agreed," she said. "Then what?"

Nick closed the door and leaned against it. "I'm not sure. Last night, when we made love, I realized there are parts of Beth I don't reach. Memories I don't think she's even aware of. Dark shadows in her mind that cling to what she's shared with me, but they're still dark. She needs to bring those memories into the light. I can't do it for her."

Daci touched his hand. The mating bond terrified her, for some reason. She'd still not agreed to a bond with Deacon and Matt, though both her men were ready. "Shouldn't you have found them when you bonded? I didn't think there were any secrets left after a mating bond."

Nick sighed. "I thought so, too, but obviously that's not always the case. At least not with Beth and me. Maybe we were too young. Maybe it wasn't a true mating bond."

"I don't know. The guys and I, we . . ." Sighing, she took Nick's hand and led him toward the bed. They sat down beside each other, lost in their own questions. Nick slung his arm around her shoulders, but she knew that sex wasn't what he wanted right now.

No, Nick probably wanted the same thing she did. Answers. If only they knew the questions.

It's barely five in the morning. They're just sleeping. This place is huge and they might not hear, or . . . Beth looked down at the small bag at her feet and stared at the door. She'd knocked a couple of times already. What if they weren't asleep? What if they were gone? Daci said Tala expected her, but if they'd gotten called out on an emergency, Tala might have forgotten, or . . . Beth glanced over her shoulder at the Mini Cooper parked at the curb, right under the NO PARKING sign.

She raised her fist to knock one more time.

Suddenly the front door swung open. Tala was barely visible in the big fluffy robe she'd wrapped around herself, and her hair was tangled and uncombed . . . like she'd been sound asleep.

"Beth! What the hell are you doing here so early? It's not even light out yet!"

Beth shrugged and stared down at her feet. "I'm sorry. I know it's too early. I was going to wait to knock until later, but I felt silly sitting out front in the car, and I couldn't find parking, and if I don't move it right away I'll . . ."

Laughing, Tala swung the door wide. "Don't worry! We've got room in the garage. Daci called and said you'd be coming, but I didn't expect you until at least tonight or tomorrow. Let's get your car moved before someone comes along and tows it, and then come on in and I'll put on a pot of coffee."

"You're sure?"

Tala just shook her head. "Well of course I'm sure, you idiot. What do you think?"

Not quite certain what to think, Beth shrugged and tossed her bag through the open door. Tala must have hit a button nearby. Cranking and squeaking, the garage door slowly opened. It felt like a sign.

She was welcome here. Suddenly the day didn't seem nearly as dark and her future didn't feel as bleak. Smiling for the first time in what felt like forever, Beth went to move the car off the street.

Tala stuck her head inside the refrigerator and wondered what to fix for breakfast. It was still early, but she figured Beth must be starved. She was sitting at the kitchen table, sipping coffee and chatting about her long drive to San Francisco, when AJ wandered in, grumbling about the early hour.

"Beth! It's practically the middle of the night. When did you get in?" He winked at Tala and flashed his million megawatt smile at Beth. The guy was always gorgeous, but when he decided to turn on the charm, Tala knew there wasn't a woman alive who could ignore him.

AJ leaned over and gave Beth a kiss. Startled, she almost choked on her coffee. She was still sputtering when Mik walked in right behind AJ. He picked Beth up, wrapped his arms around her in a big hug, kissed her soundly, and plopped her back down in her chair.

He didn't seem to notice that she froze, that her eyes went wide with fear. Tala sent her a calming thought. Beth blinked rapidly and then forced a laugh. She made a big show of wiping

Mik's kiss off her face. "Early," she said, with a grateful glance in Tala's direction. "I drove all day and all night with just a couple of stops to nap along the way." She settled back in her chair and held her cup out to AJ for a refill. "Thanks for letting me come here, guys."

AJ frowned as he filled her cup. "Where else would you go?"

Before Beth could answer, Mik said, "Nowhere. This is your home, Beth. You know that."

"Mik's right." Tala grabbed a carton of eggs and a package of bacon. She glanced up and grinned at Mik. Then she set the food on the counter next to the stove, folded her arms across her chest. "Beth, you'll always have a home here. You know you're always welcome."

Beth stared at her hands. Tala wondered what was going through her mind. Unlike Jazzy Blue, one of the other young Chanku who had stayed here for such a brief time, Beth had kept to herself when she hadn't practically been attached at the hip to Nick. She'd never relaxed at all around the guys—not even with Tala.

Maybe the fact she'd chosen to return to the place where it all started meant something important, well beyond her issues with her stepfather. Maybe it meant she'd finally, truly understood what being Chanku actually meant.

She'd been a shapeshifter for such a short time. Tala remembered those early days when she'd first realized she was Chanku—not only had it brought back a wealth of memories she'd blocked for years, it had given her an entirely new family, a new appreciation for her own self-worth.

No one really knew what demons Beth still had to fight.

Tala sat down at the table and squeezed Beth's hand. "Where else would you go? We're family, Beth. All of us. No matter what happens, we have to learn to count on each other. Face it, we're all we've got!"

Beth glanced at Mik and AJ and smiled at Tala. "Thanks. I didn't know where else to go ... what to do. It wasn't fair for either Nick or Ulrich to have me hanging around, not with my emotions so screwed up." She hung her head. "I can't believe the horrible things I said about Ulrich."

Mik laughed, turned a kitchen chair around, and straddled it. "Ulrich's tough, but from what Tala said, I imagine you really pissed off Millie."

This time Beth grinned. "You don't know the half of it. I really needed to get out of there, and quick. I think Millie was ready to bite me."

AJ leaned over Tala and kissed the top of her head before he sat down beside her. "Well, just as a warning, don't say anything bad about Mik or me, or Tala might go for your throat. You know how she is when anyone messes with her men."

Beth nodded sagely. "I'll remember that."

Tala snorted. "Oh, cut it out, AJ. You are so full of yourself."

AJ cocked one dark eyebrow. "As I recall, just a few hours ago you were the one full of myself...." He nodded toward Mik. "And himself."

"And the vibrator," Mik said, interrupting. "Don't forget that honkin' big vibrator she likes to ..."

Tala's face flamed. She never blushed! "Cut it out, now, or no breakfast."

AJ slowly shook his head. "She's fightin' dirty, man. We better cool it."

Mik nodded. Beth giggled and covered her mouth with her hand, but when she looked up at Tala, there were tears in her eyes.

I want this, she said. *I want this same kind of ease with men that you have.*

Keisha will be here later this afternoon, Tala said. *Once we put our heads together, we'll figure out exactly what we need to do next. First, you'd better eat. Then I want you to get some sleep. We'll deal with everything else when you're rested.*

6

Beth crawled into bed in the same room she'd shared with Nick just a few short weeks ago, when they'd first come to this place. She lay there in the crisp sheets, remembering that amazing day when they'd all been hanging out in the park with nothing more important to worry about than where each of them would sleep that night.

She shivered with the clarity of her memories. Tala had come walking toward the garden, a complete stranger to all of them at the time. They'd noticed her—she was tiny and really cute, but it was painfully obvious she didn't realize she was followed by two young guys, gangbangers from the looks of them. They'd started out hassling her, and then one of the guys had grabbed her.

That's when, for the six of them, life took an amazing turn. The assault had happened so fast, none of them had time to react. None except Nick. Suddenly, the quiet boy Beth had been shyly flirting with all summer was gone. In his place was a huge, snarling wolf, a terrifying creature out of her worst nightmares. He'd jumped right over Jazzy and gone straight for the throat of the one hurting Tala.

Only they hadn't known her name. Not then. Not until one of the kids was lying dead on the ground and the other had run off, screaming. Not until the wolf had turned into Nick once again and collapsed, unconscious, to lie naked next to the body of the one he'd just killed.

Tala hadn't hesitated. She'd recognized all six of them as Chanku, called Mik and AJ for help and loaded the stunned group of kids into their SUV. At that moment, everything Beth had ever believed about herself had disappeared.

Her life was forever changed.

Just as Nick and Deacon, Jazzy Blue, Logan, and Matt's lives would never be the same again. They weren't lost, homeless kids trying to survive in the City by the Bay anymore. No, they were Chanku, members of an ancient race, shapeshifters with amazing abilities each of them were still coming to terms with.

Only Beth wasn't making the transition as seamlessly as the others. Logan had discovered he was a doctor suffering from amnesia, Jazzy Blue had finally remembered how she'd ended up in the sex trade as a child, Matt and Deacon now understood why they'd never really fit in anywhere, why they'd viewed the world from such a strange perspective.

Nick had found peace, and Beth . . . well, she'd had memories she'd been trying to forget shoved right down her throat once again. Memories of a brutal rape when her stepfather took her virginity the night before her mother's funeral. A horrible enough act on its own, yet the memory was somehow incomplete, as if there was more she should know.

How could there possibly be more? Wasn't the truth bad enough? It wasn't right. How come the others were able to find peace with their Chanku heritage while all she got from this new reality was more pain?

Not entirely true. I found Nick.

But would she be able to keep him? If she couldn't get her life together, Beth knew damned well Nick wouldn't hang around. He had too much to offer to a mate to be saddled with someone like Beth. Someone so trapped in the past they couldn't live their own future.

Daci was right. She needed closure, and there was only one way that was going to happen, but was she strong enough? Could she face the man who'd taken so much from her? Was that the solution—to fight now for her honor, something she'd been unable to do five years ago? Would she have the nerve?

Daci had insisted Beth needed to do it on her own . . . so why was she waiting on Keisha? Why had she come running to Tala?

Was it fair to deny Nick, her bonded mate, the chance to help her, yet involve women who had lives of their own? Mates who loved them? Keisha had a child. Was she bringing Lily Milina with her? Packing up a child and flying to San Francisco, all because Beth had issues? Because she couldn't deal with her past?

Millie thought she was a drama queen. Was she really that shallow? That selfish? Mind spinning, her entire life slowly unraveling, Beth felt her thoughts slipping deeper and deeper into the quagmire of questions and confusion that had haunted her over the past weeks. Finally, the confusion slipped into despair and, still without answers, she drifted into restless slumber.

Nick awoke in a tangle of arms and legs, none of which belonged to his mate. Damn but he missed her. She'd been gone for less than twenty-four hours, and it felt like months since he'd held her.

At least his friends hadn't left him alone to stew in his misery. He'd fallen asleep between Daci's legs. His last memory was the taste of her release and the soft cries she'd made during climax. Matt snored softly with Daci's left nipple pressing into his cheek . . . he'd obviously nodded off while suckling her breast. Deacon lay across Nick's thighs with one arm wrapped around his waist and his long fingers still grasping Nick's cock.

So why did he awaken with thoughts of Beth making him hard? She'd chosen to leave him, and while Daci promised him his mate would be back, Beth hadn't wanted Nick with her.

She hadn't wanted her mate beside her when she faced her nightmares. Logically, Nick understood her reasoning, but his heart didn't follow logic. Neither did his libido. He'd had some amazing sex throughout the night, but none of his buddies came close to his mate.

They were all talented lovers with open hearts and sex drives that matched Nick's, but none of them touched his heart or his soul the way Beth could. What Daci, Matt, and Deacon offered made for great sex, but not perfect sex.

Not the way it was with Beth.

He tried to roll away from Daci without waking her, but Deacon's long fingers tightened around his cock, and Daci's thighs closed against the sides of his head. Her scent drew him. Nick ran his tongue between her puffy lips, tasting the first drops of her arousal. Daci moaned and arched her back, but her eyes stayed closed.

Her thoughts were open. Sleepy, relaxed, her body waking from a night of what should have been sexual excess but had merely primed her for more. *Beth's going to be fine,* she said. *But I could really use some more . . .* Her mental voice drifted away on a sigh.

Nick chuckled as he shifted his body to accommodate Deacon's fingers. Then he sighed when Deacon ran his tongue over the broad crown of his cock. Slowly, Deacon drew him deep inside his mouth. The warmth, the suction, the light flick of his tongue, even the weight of Deacon's powerful male body pressing against Nick brought him as much a sense of peace as arousal.

Matt awakened with a sleepy yawn. He closed his lips around the tip of Daci's breast, and his cheeks hollowed with the strength of his suckling. Daci's thoughts flowed over all of them. Her love for Matt and Deacon drew Nick close as well, so that he felt a part of them, a link in their love for one another.

Yet as seductive as their love, as welcome as their need for him even as he needed each of them, it wasn't enough. As he made love to Daci with his mouth, it was Beth he tasted, and it was Beth he needed.

The three of them understood. Opening hearts and minds, they tasted and touched, gave and accepted, each of them showing Nick exactly how good it could be, how wonderful it would be when Beth finally came to terms with her past, when she finally opened herself to her future.

A future that Nick had to believe would include him.

Beth dreamed of Nick. Felt his hands on her body, his lips pressing against hers, but she awoke to the sound of gurgling and cooing, and a wet, sloppy kiss on her cheek. "Wha . . . ?"

Her eyes flashed open, and she looked directly into the sweet caramel face of a drooling baby girl dressed all in pink. Blinking, Beth looked beyond and caught Tala standing beside the bed, grinning.

"Meet Lily," Tala said, reaching for the baby. "And her mom, Keisha Rialto."

"Sorry about that. Here, let me take her." A beautiful woman with dark chocolate skin reached for the baby. "It was Tala's idea, not mine, to let Lily wake you up." She laughed. "Probably not the most exciting wake-up you've ever had, but it does the trick, doesn't it? It's good to meet you, Beth."

"I'm definitely awake!" Blinking in the late afternoon sunlight streaming into her bedroom, Beth scooted up in the bed. "It's good to meet you, too. I can't believe you flew all the way down here to . . ."

Keisha shook her head. "Not a problem. I've been wanting to make the trip anyway. The point is, we're family. Families help each other." She sat on the side of the bed and held Lily in her lap.

"Tala said you came here without your mate. Didn't he want to come?"

Beth shrugged and stared at her clasped fingers. "I don't know. I think so, but I finally realized he can't fight my battles for me. We've been having some rough patches. They were my fault."

Keisha laughed, and Beth jerked her head up. "What?"

"Been there, done that." Keisha's broad smile spoke volumes. "I put so many barriers in front of poor Anton that I'm amazed the man hung around, but ya know what? Those barriers taught us that we can get through anything, so long as we do it together. If your mate loves you, he wants the best for you. If that means you deal with it on your own, that's what he's going to make happen. If you need him beside you, he'll work that out as well. The important thing is honesty and appreciating the power of the love two bonded mates can have. It goes beyond anything else you'll ever know."

"I hope so. I can't imagine life without Nick in it." Beth took a deep breath. "I try to do the right thing, but somehow, I feel as if I'm missing something important. It's creating a rift between us that's scaring me to death."

"I understand." Keisha glanced away for a moment, as if organizing her thoughts. When she turned back to Beth, she'd obviously come to a major decision. "From what Tala says, we share an experience that makes us even closer. I want to help. It's not going to be easy for any of us, but we're all strong women. We can do it, especially if we do it together."

"Thank you." What else could she say? That she still wasn't sure? That she was terrified of facing her memories, much less the man himself? What if this was all a horrible mistake?

Keisha smiled and covered Beth's hand with hers. "I'm not intruding on your thoughts, but I imagine you're wondering if you're doing the right thing. That's why I'm here. To find out."

Before Beth could reply, there was a soft tap on the partially open door. Mik stuck his head in the room. "Hey, Keisha. I hear AJ and I get Lily for the afternoon. You're sure?"

"Only if you are." Keisha stood Lily up on her lap so the little girl could look at Mik. "Are you absolutely certain you two are up to a six-month-old?"

AJ stepped around Mik and reached for the baby. She grinned and giggled. AJ parked her on his hip. "You're kidding, right? Grown men run in terror from the two of us. What's a baby going to do that we can't handle?"

Keisha glanced at Tala and Beth, and the three of them burst into giggles.

"I'm not saying a thing," Keisha said, glancing toward Tala and Beth. "I don't want to lose my babysitters."

The tension ebbed away from Beth. Mik and AJ were so easy to be around, almost like big brothers. She'd heard so many wonderful things about Keisha, it was as if she'd known her for years. She already knew she loved Tala. Trusted her.

She could do this. Maybe.

Keisha stood up and ran her fingers through her daughter's dark hair. "I left all of her stuff in the room with the crib. There are bottles of breast milk in the refrigerator, and a few jars of strained carrots and bananas on the counter. I won't be far, if you need me for anything."

AJ shifted Lily on his hip and turned to Mik. "I'll take care of the bottles and, yuck, carrots and bananas. You get diaper duty."

Mik reached for Lily and deftly removed her from AJ's

grasp. He settled her in the crook of his massive arm and she looked like a tiny doll surrounded by all that rippling muscle. "Doesn't work that way, big guy. We share all of it. Remember, we're in training."

Keisha jerked her head around and stared at Tala. "Are you expecting?"

Laughing, Tala shook her head. "No, not yet, but these two have delusions of fatherhood. I want to be a little more sure I'm ready before we try and pop one out."

"Good idea. They don't pop all that easy. Believe me, life is not the same once you have one of these. A hundred percent better in most ways, but in others . . ." Keisha took the baby from Mik, held her up, and rubbed noses with her daughter. "You, my dear, are a lot of work."

Lily grinned and drooled, perfectly comfortable as she was handed from one grown-up to another. Keisha held Lily against her shoulder and reached for the diaper bag. Mik beat her to it and slung the big thing over his shoulder.

"Thanks, Mik." Keisha shifted the baby when she fussed. "I'm going to show the guys where everything is and see if we can get the princess fed before we get started. Beth, why don't you get a shower, find something comfortable to wear, and meet Tala and me in the sunroom on the top floor in half an hour."

Beth nodded and crawled out of bed as Keisha and Lily, Mik, and AJ left her room. Tala slipped an arm around her waist and gave her a hug.

"You've slept most of the day away. It's almost five. Keisha got here around noon, and she and Lily took a nap, too, so we're good to go, but first Keisha wants to do some serious linking. Are you up to that? To going back to the night it happened?"

"Do we have to?"

Tala nodded. "We have to. We also have to revisit our own

experiences. Keisha doesn't want any secrets. She wants you to know what happened to each of us, just as we need to understand exactly what happened to you. Once everything is out on the table, then we'll work on a solution." Gently, she stroked her hand over Beth's shoulder. "You can do it, you know. You can face your fears. It's not easy, but it makes you stronger."

Wasn't that why she'd driven all night? Why she'd left her mate? Beth nodded. Whatever it took, she was ready.

She'd have to be. If she wanted a future with Nick, she had no other choice.

7

Beth met Tala at the bottom of the stairs. Both of them wore soft, silken caftans belted at the waist. Tala's was a pale green while Beth had chosen a darker saffron shade of yellow.

She realized she was counting steps as they climbed the stairs to the third floor. She'd done that when she was little, before Frank, before her life changed.

Tension roiled through her body, and she almost turned around before they stepped into the sunroom on the top story of the converted mansion. Beth hadn't been up there before.

She'd had no idea what she was missing. "This is gorgeous . . . unbelievable!" She stood in the doorway, staring at the unobstructed view of the Pacific through huge windows that made up the entire western wall. Sunlight spilled in through glass skylights, where it all seemed to gather in shimmering waves over the brilliant turquoise sarong Keisha wore.

Beth thought she looked absolutely regal, like a queen awaiting her subjects, sitting there on a long white leather couch near the big picture window, sipping her glass of wine, with her dark hair flowing in curling waves past her shoulders.

"I'm surprised you never made it up here, but those few days you guys were all here were definitely hectic." Tala led Beth across the big room and sat down on Keisha's right with her toes curled under her butt.

Beth sat to Keisha's left, but for some strange reason, she felt stiff and awkward beside the other two. It was never easy, being the new kid on the block. She'd hated it when she and her mom moved when she was about twelve, when her mom bought a little house in Oakland for just the two of them. Adjusting wasn't easy for a shy child, but then her mother married Frank Michaels, and it got worse when he'd moved in with them.

She'd hated it then.

Hated Frank.

Beth shoved his leering image out of her mind. She took a deep breath and tried to relax, but her heart pounded in her chest, and she felt sweat beading on her forehead.

Keisha smiled and poured each of them a glass of wine. The chilled chardonnay left a tart but fruity taste on Beth's tongue. "Thank you. It's really good." She took another sip and tried to look relaxed, but her hands trembled.

"Of course it's good." Tala laughed. "You don't think I'd let my friends drink bad wine, do you?"

Keisha laughed, but Beth just stared at the wine. Thought about anything but why she was here with two women she admired but really didn't know very well. She sipped the wine again and realized she'd never tasted really good wine before meeting Tala and her men.

Of course, she'd never had or done a lot of things before that day.

Keisha smiled and held her glass up for a toast. "Thank you for making me feel so welcome, Tala," she said. "I have really missed this city. It's good to be back."

Tala clinked her glass against Keisha's and then Beth's. "You're always welcome. Look how many nights I've been in your home? Funny, isn't it? You miss the city and I miss those gorgeous mountains of yours. What's wrong with this picture?" She took a sip of wine.

Keisha sighed. "I know, but as much as I love it here, my heart's in the mountains."

Laughing, Tala grinned at Beth. "Don't let her fool you. Her heart's with Anton Cheval. I don't think it really matters where he is."

"There is that." Keisha turned to Beth. "Which reminds me, Beth. I want to know more about why you chose to come out here alone."

Beth took another swallow of wine and prayed for a little liquid courage. She looked down at the glass in her hands. It was almost empty, which surprised her. She didn't realize how fast she'd been drinking it. "Like I told you, I've been pretty awful to Nick," she said, staring at the amber liquid. "I asked him to do things he found dishonorable, thinking he could help me get past all my issues. We argued, but when we made up, I realized how wrong I'd been, asking him to solve my problems. He can't do it for me. I have to do it for myself."

Keisha nodded. "I understand. It's good you've come to the right decision, then."

They talked, about Keisha's memorial garden and her family, how she'd grown up without knowing her Chanku heritage even though she later learned her mother had been able to shift—had in fact been killed because of her birthright. No mention was made of Keisha's assault.

Tala talked about her dysfunctional family and the love she had for her brother Baylor and sister Lisa, but nothing was said of her assault, either.

Beth found herself relaxing, talking about growing up in the East Bay, how she'd always been afraid of her stepfather, even though she couldn't recall that he'd ever actually been abusive.

At least not in the beginning. It was harder to talk about her mother. They'd been so close, and she still missed her.

"I was never really certain what kind of cancer she had."

Keisha poured more wine in her glass without asking. Beth nodded her thanks, took a sip, and then another. As good as it was, it tasted even better the more she drank. Her tension seemed to ease with each swallow. "Mom wouldn't talk about her illness, and I don't remember her having surgery, but we all knew she was dying. She kept getting weaker and thinner, and then one day she was just gone."

Keisha covered Beth's hand with hers. "You're sure it was cancer?"

"That's what Frank said. He's my stepfather. Was my stepfather. He's nothing to me now. Why do you ask?"

Keisha frowned as if something didn't quite click. "You weren't adopted, were you?"

"No, and despite my darker skin, I look just like my mom."

Keisha stared into her wine. "Your mother was Chanku, even if she never had the nutrients that would enable her to shift, that she never embraced her birthright. It's not common for Chanku to get cancer, though it does happen. We're generally immune to most of the diseases that affect humans, whether or not we've had the nutrients."

Beth tried to remember, but so much of the last few months of her mother's life were a blur. One day she'd been healthy, and then she wasn't. There'd been little money for medical care, and Beth kept thinking she'd get better, but she didn't.

Instead, Beth remembered her mom growing weaker, her body failing and her mind slipping away until she was little more than a shell of the vibrant woman she'd been.

One morning when Beth awoke, her mother was gone. Frank said they'd taken her away in the night when she died.

He hadn't wanted to awaken Beth. Didn't think it would make any difference to her, once her mother was dead.

At least that was what he'd said.

Tala glanced at Keisha, but she asked Beth, "Was there an autopsy?"

Beth shook her head. "I don't know. I never asked. By then I was afraid of Frank. I tried to avoid him, but I didn't know where to go. It had always been just me and Mom until he moved in. We didn't have any other family, and she never told me who my real father was. Mom was blond, but she had amber eyes like mine. We looked alike, except I'm so dark, I always figured my father must have been Middle Eastern or Indian. I know for sure that Frank isn't my father. She didn't marry him until I was fourteen."

"Did he touch you before the attack? Had he ever physically or sexually abused you?" Keisha's soft voice soothed Beth even as the questions made her heart race in fear.

Beth shook her head. "He never actually did anything while my mom was alive. Not really, but I know he wanted to. It was the way he watched me. The way he'd manage to be outside the bathroom when I showered so that he'd 'accidentally' catch me wrapped in nothing but a towel. When he knocked on my bedroom door, he'd push first, to see if the door would open. I got a lock for my bedroom door and started taking a big, heavy robe with me to bathe. I covered up completely, but he still watched. It made my skin crawl. It still does when I think about it."

The sun went down while they talked. Beth felt the relaxing effects of the wine in spite of the deceptively gentle conversation that had drawn out more of her past than she'd wanted to share.

She stared as the huge, orange disk slipped beneath the horizon and thought of the way her mother had slipped away. Not with a burst of flame and glory like the setting sun. No, she'd been nothing more than a wisp of fog that merely dissipated into the air. One day she'd been alive, and then the woman who had given Beth life no longer had a life of her own.

She took another sip of wine.

A sound caught her attention, and Beth glanced up just in time to see Keisha share a knowing glance with Tala. Both women stood up and began to disrobe. Tala slipped her caftan over her head. Keisha untied her sarong and let the blue silk flutter lightly to the floor.

Without a word, they reached for Beth. Each took one of her hands and they led her to a small daybed in one corner of the large room. Tala released Beth's hand and began lighting candles set about the room. Flickering lights danced on the walls and were reflected in the big windows.

Keisha helped Beth slip her caftan over her head. "I want you to trust us," she said, smoothing the soft, cotton coverlet on the bed. "Lie down on your back. Open your thoughts. Find the one thought that brings you peace. Concentrate. Hold that thought in your heart."

Frowning, Beth did as she was told. As Nick's smile filled her mind, Keisha gently stretched Beth's hands over her head and secured them to the iron rungs of the headboard. Thoughts of Nick flashed out of existence, and Beth knew her eyes must be as big as saucers. She'd never been into bondage. Couldn't handle the thought of being tied up, out of control.

Before she could speak, Keisha pulled a dark scarf out from under the pillow and tied it around Beth's eyes. She felt her chest tighten and wondered why having her eyes covered made it hard to breathe.

"Relax. Trust us. We're not going to hurt you." Keisha's soft words did little to comfort her, especially when she felt her legs being pulled apart, felt padded cuffs securing her ankles.

She'd trusted Keisha and Tala, but they'd trussed her up like a damned turkey. "Why?" she asked, tugging at the headboard.

"Why are you tying me up?" She felt the panic begin to well up inside. Her heart raced. Her throat felt tight.

A soft hand pressed between breasts. Beth recognized Keisha's mental touch and forced herself to stop struggling. *We have to do this, Beth. Try to relax.*

The bed dipped beside her. "It's okay, Beth. We learned this from the master. Seriously. You've never met Anton, Keisha's mate, but he's discovered that sexual energy seems to empower Chanku." Tala chuckled. "And yes, the guys really hate it when I cut them off to build their frustration, but it works. When we reach a point where the body is crying for release, the mind seems to slip into another, more powerful gear. Barriers come down, power goes up. That's what Keisha and I want to do with you tonight. We're going to take you to the very pinnacle of arousal, but not let you slip over the edge. Once there, we're going into your thoughts, and you're going to enter ours."

Keisha's soft voice interrupted. "It's not going to be easy for you. Not only will we take you back to that horrible night with your stepfather, but we're going to take you through what Tala and I experienced as well. The memories are ugly, but what we are able to do with the knowledge we gain is empowering. It's hard to explain, but by restraining you, we've taken away your choice. When you know you can't get away, it makes it easier for your mind to accept what your body would love to forget. We won't hurt you." She laughed softly. "You may want to hurt us for what we make you see, but . . ."

Tala laughed. "Don't believe a word she says. That's the main reason you're tied up."

For some odd reason, Tala's gentle laughter calmed her. Beth took a deep breath. "Okay. What do I have to do?"

"Just lie there and enjoy it, sweetie. Tala and I will take care of everything."

Beth forced herself to relax. She hated the lack of control, the fact she couldn't see, couldn't get loose. She'd been the one free when Nick was tied up. That was different. She tugged once again at the restraints. The headboard creaked, but she was held fast.

Beth felt warm hands on her waist. Tala was right. She had no choice. No control. Forcing her fears into the background, she took a deep breath and tried to go with the flow. The wine had left her drowsy. She was relaxed, as long as she quit thinking about the restraints.

Quit thinking, stopped worrying, and let herself enjoy. Soft hands stroked her breasts and teased her nipples. Full lips coasted over her hip and grazed her pubic mound. Shivers raced across her legs, raised gooseflesh on her arms.

She reached out with her mind but sensed nothing. Both Keisha and Tala must have been blocking, leaving her mentally isolated amidst so many sensory impressions. The bed shuddered, and she felt an altered distribution of weight, the brush of coarse fur against her legs.

Which of the women had shifted?

She tried to picture the wolf as it nestled between her thighs— waiting patiently with amber eyes glowing, pink tongue and razor-sharp canines framed with dark, bristling whiskers. What was the wolf's intent? When would it reach forward with that long, mobile tongue?

Then the lips suckling her breast became more insistent, the hands stroking her belly and flanks grew more intimate, and the image if not the physical presence of the wolf faded.

A single finger parted her labia, dipped inside her moist center, trailed upward, and gently rubbed her clitoris. She raised her hips, powerfully aware of the wolf waiting patiently, lying between her thighs, all coarse hair and hot breath.

The wine left a fruity taste in her mouth, but her lips felt dry. She licked them, startled by the increased sensitivity as her tongue traced the contours of her own mouth. She ran her tongue over her upper lip, across the edges of her teeth.

She tugged lightly at the restraints holding her hands, aware of a powerful difference now. No longer fearing her restraints, she wanted the reassurance that all was still tight, that she couldn't move. Couldn't pull away.

She couldn't leave. Couldn't see. The blindfold heightened her other senses—taste and touch. Smell.

The musky scent of arousal filled her nostrils

A cold nose brushed her inner thigh and she moaned, arching her pelvis, reaching for more contact. Coarse whiskers scratched her sensitive skin. A long, wet tongue licked her once from ass to belly. Whimpering, she twisted beneath the hot stroke. Heavy paws across her thighs held her down. A long, hot tongue dipped inside her sex, stroked the inner walls, and penetrated deep and then deeper still.

Beth's breath hitched in her throat. Her muscles tensed, and she held her body immobile. The very tip of that hot tongue curled against her vaginal walls, stroking slow and deep before retreating to lap and lick her clit.

She quivered and her legs jerked against the restraints when it thrust inside once more. A cold nose brushed her clit, stiff whiskers abraded her inner thighs.

Licking, swirling deep inside, lapping at her cream, licking away the evidence of her growing arousal.

Fingers plucked at her left nipple, lips and teeth tugged at her right. Sensations seemed to explode, one upon the other. A deep coil of heat settled in her middle, and the muscles between her legs clenched, tightening then releasing in a slow, steady rhythm.

Each time she came close to orgasm, touch was withdrawn, and Beth would feel the tension begin to ease. The moment that happened, the sensual assault would begin anew. Over and over, Beth's body responded to the hot sweep of tongue, the sharp nibbles of teeth taking her closer and closer to the edge of orgasm.

Close, but not close enough. Frustration blossomed. How could they? Both Keisha and Tala denied her, kept her from taking that coveted leap off the precipice! Dear Goddess, she needed that final release, needed it now . . . anything to break the tension, end the sense of her body growing taut, stretching longer, tighter . . .

Beth writhed against the restraints, whimpering with need, unable to make the leap from extreme arousal to completion. Sound exploded in her mind—the thundering of her heart, the rush of air into her lungs. The rasp of tongue against her sex as the wolf slowly licked and teased her.

Close! So very close that she reached out with her mind, begging for completion, begging for more, the perfect touch that would finally take her over the edge.

Sobbing, her body writhing, fingers clutching at the soft restraints, Beth whimpered unintelligible gibberish, words without meaning, pleas that brought no response.

Then suddenly, without warning, Keisha was there, waiting as if she'd always waited, her mind open and searching. *Show us, Beth. Show us what happened that night five years ago. Take us there.*

I can't! Beth arched her back, silently begging for just enough, for more.

Why, Beth?

You'll hate me.

Never. Tala's soft denial seemed to float between them.

I thought the same thing, Keisha said. Her voice echoed in Beth's mind—strong, powerful. The sound of a woman in complete control.

My fears kept me apart from the man I loved, kept me prisoner, all because I couldn't bring myself to face the truth. Look into my thoughts, Beth. What I did was horrible. What happened to me an abomination. It no longer has power over me, not since I faced my deepest fears. Not since I took those fears and made them my strength. The memories can't hurt me. Not anymore.

Beth's body trembled as if she convulsed. Did she really want to know? Could she face Keisha's nightmares when she couldn't even face her own?

What choice did she have? Blindfolded, restrained, her body shivering on the precipice, she opened her thoughts. Opened to Keisha, and met her demons—demons that no longer held any power to hurt.

It was all Beth could do not to scream. Keisha shared her rape and its bloody aftermath, linking completely. Beth became Keisha, naked and bleeding, straddling one of her attackers, her insides torn and bloodied from repeated penetrations as the man brutally shoved into her from below. Another man held her head while he drove his cock down her throat. The pain was excruciating, the gag reflex overwhelming, but there was nothing she could do. No way to fight back—not with her hands tied behind her with wide strips of tape, her hips roughly held by the man beneath her.

Fear—blinding, overwhelming fear—and pain, so much pain Keisha's body began to shut down, to find another level of being, another existence. Then the sensation of someone else, the third man, behind her. Groping her, grabbing her hips, spreading her buttocks. Agony—blinding agony as he forced entrance, shoving himself deep inside her anus, ripping and tearing her flesh.

She wanted to scream but the cock in her mouth choked her. She wanted to die, but her life force was too strong.

She wanted to kill.

Wanted the taste of their blood, the sounds of their death screams—she wanted to live. Beth felt it then, the shift that had saved Keisha's life, the crackling of bones and straining of sinews unprepared for such an act, the shift that happened so quickly, Keisha's attackers were suddenly screwing a full-size she-wolf, a wolf that did exactly what any wild animal will do when it's frightened or in pain.

She attacked. The cock in her mouth went first. She simply snapped her jaws and jerked her head, tearing the man's genitals from his body. Turning with lightning speed, she ripped out the throat of the man who sodomized her, at the same time disemboweling the one beneath her with her hind feet. Sharp claws tore into his gut, shredding skin and tendon as if it were paper.

Her attack was fast and efficient, though only the man who'd had his throat torn died instantly. The others screamed for what seemed a long, long time.

Confused, exhausted, still in wolf form, Keisha stood alone in the middle of the blood-soaked room, her head hanging almost to the floor. Blood poured from her body, but she finally staggered to the door, only to discover paws were not made for dead bolts and doorknobs.

Finally, weak from loss of blood, she collapsed against a wall as far from the three men as she could get. Her mind shut down completely, blotting out the moans and screams, retreating from a world she couldn't endure. The images faded to black.

The wolf between Beth's legs laid its head on her thigh and sighed, as if exhausted from a long battle. The blindfold over Beth's eyes was wet with tears, and Tala's face, resting on her stomach, was just as damp.

The images, so stark in Keisha's memory, filled Beth's thoughts. The arousal that had simmered so powerfully only moments ago was gone, leaving behind nothing more than the ache of remembered desire. Before she had time to form any cohesive thoughts of her own, to try and understand the horrific experience Keisha had just shared with her, Beth felt the subtle intrusion of Tala's thoughts, the silent assault of yet another horrendous set of memories.

Her name was Mary Ellen Quinn, and she was a prostitute

in a small Southwestern town, but her pimp had set her up. The men weren't her typical johns. They were into bondage and sadism, and they'd essentially purchased the tiny dark-haired whore for a night of torture and deviant sex.

She'd proved to be a lot tougher than she looked. When Mary Ellen realized she wasn't meant to survive the night, when the pain had gone beyond suffering, she'd lost control. Somehow, what had been a tiny, dark-haired woman barely five feet tall, turned into a ferocious wolf—a wolf powerful enough, vicious enough, to attack and kill the two men who abused her.

They died screaming, but their deaths had a price.

She'd spent the next three years as a woman without a past. Mary Ellen had awakened as Tala, so traumatized by the events of that night she'd completely forgotten who she was, what had happened. It wasn't until a gang rape three years later that she'd found the courage to escape.

She would always wonder what might have become of her if she hadn't risked everything to hide in a big SUV that belonged to two of the most gorgeous men she'd ever seen. Miguel Fuentes and Andrew Jackson Temple—Mik and AJ—had been her saviors that night. Saviors who became beloved mates to their tiny Chanku bitch.

Beth shuddered, caught in the memories of the night when Tala made her first shift. Bloodied and beaten, she'd been so close to death she'd barely survived, yet the shift had given her the strength to protect herself.

Why hadn't that happened to Beth? She'd been brutally raped, but her attacker had walked away and left her torn and bleeding, her body bruised, her innocence lost. Why hadn't she fought back?

We need to know what happened that night. Beth, open completely. Show us your life when your mother was still alive. Show us who you were before this terrible thing happened.

Could she do that? Revisit a past she'd tried so hard to forget? She thought of Tala, of her amazing self-confidence, of the two men who loved her beyond anything else. Of Keisha, mate to the most powerful of all the Chanku, yet she held even more power than Anton Cheval—she held him in the palm of her hand.

Beth took a deep breath. *If I open my thoughts, if I remove all the barriers, can you find those memories for me? I don't know how to find them—I've spent the last five years trying to forget.*

The wolf whimpered. Lips brushed her mouth. Tala's lips. "We can, Beth. All of us together. We're going to take you to that peak once again, but this time, we're going over together. We'll find your past on the other side. Together."

8

This time, there was nothing remotely subtle about their fore-play. She sensed when Keisha shifted back to her human form. Heard the rustle of bedding as the women moved around her on the daybed. Beth heard a familiar buzzing noise and knew either Keisha or Tala had turned on a vibrator. Someone put a pillow under her butt, raising her hips. Fingers stroked her per-ineum, and she felt the slick glide of lubricated fingers between her cheeks.

The smooth tip of a finger pressed against her anus. The taut muscle fluttered in response, and the finger pressed harder. Beth lifted her hips, shocked when she felt three fingers stretch the tight anal ring and slip inside.

At the same time, the pulsing tip of the vibrator brushed her nipples, moving from one to the other. The peaks stiffened.

"This will hurt only at first."

Still dealing with the unexpected penetration, and before she could process Tala's soft warning, clips tightened on both nip-ples. Sharp and biting, the pain shot directly to her clit. Beth arched in reaction. The fingers stretching her anus slipped free, and the vibrator plunged deep.

The vibrations reverberated through her entire pelvic region. The clips on her nipples dug into the sensitive peaks, and a warm mouth covered her clit. Twisting against the tight restraints, Beth felt her grasp on reality slipping away.

She opened her thoughts and called to Tala and Keisha as her arousal increased. Her body hummed and her muscles rippled and fluttered in preparation for release. Sensation built upon sensation, and all the energy from the climax denied earlier added to the power growing inside.

Tala knelt over Beth's chest. Her thighs brushed the nipple clamps. The renewed bite sent another shock of sensation directly between Beth's legs. The rich scent of Tala's arousal added to Beth's. She raised her head and found Tala's sex with her tongue. Licking almost frantically between warm, womanly folds, searching with the tip of her tongue, Beth found Tala's clit. She wrapped her lips around the sensitive bud and sucked.

Tala moaned and her hips jerked forward with Beth's touch. Brushing the clamps once again, she tugged them against Beth's nipples with every rock and sway of her body.

Keisha straddled Beth's hips and opened her thoughts. She shared the visual of three women moving together, their bodies intimately linked. Beth hadn't realized that the vibrator filling her rectum was also buried deep in Keisha's pussy. Hadn't known that Tala and Keisha kissed deeply, nipples brushing against one another, their bodies swaying to a rhythm shared.

Rhythm and arousal, all three women joined now through an amazing link. Beth had never known this kind of arousal, nor had she experienced such amazing sex while totally under another's control. Tied and blindfolded, her body held down by both Tala and Keisha, it finally made sense.

The restraints gave her an amazing freedom, an ability to focus on pleasure, on sensations, on whatever the others chose to do to her, knowing that whatever they did was for her pleasure, not to inflict pain.

She trusted them never to hurt her. Trusted their love. Reveled in the awareness that everything Keisha and Tala did was *for* her, not *to* her.

Sensation grew. Arousal became a palpable mass of energy, a live and pulsing thing of power. Beth felt herself slipping away until she seemed to float. Tethered to yet separate from the group, her mind free of the fear that had been so much a part of her reality for so long. The strange feeling grew even as her arousal blossomed, the sense that she was no longer trapped within the body tied to the bed, the knowledge that she was more than Beth, more than Tala or Keisha, yet still very much connected.

Dear Goddess. I thought only Adam knew how to do this. Tala's mental voice echoed in Beth's head.

Do what?

This! This out of body thing. You've done this, Beth, not Keisha. Not me. Look down.

Beth looked. *Wow. What'd I do?*

She saw three women, their bodies swaying in a seductive rhythm as each of them found pleasure. Keisha's head was thrown back, her lips parted as she slowly thrust her hips against the vibrating dildo buried in Beth as well as herself. Tala'd caught her lips between her teeth. Passion etched her features in harsh relief. Her fingers twisted the nipple clamps pinching Beth's breasts. Beth's body swayed with Keisha's thrusts and her face was buried between Tala's legs as she feasted intimately on her friend.

It was an amazing, sensual tableau, more profound from this perspective, floating as a nebulous ball of sexual energy against the skylights. Fascinated, Beth lost herself in the beauty of three women moving as one, loving as one.

I think we should go back now, Beth. It's time. Keisha's soft voice of reason broke into Beth's dreamlike state.

Before she had a chance to wonder how she would actually return, Beth felt herself falling back into her body, falling even further as orgasm multiplied times three threw her screaming over the edge.

Keisha and Tala joined her, their bodies locked convulsively into a climax that went on forever, their minds locked into a link beyond anything Beth had ever known. A link that broke through the barriers, knocked down the walls.

A link that laid open a past she'd buried for so many years.

Nick held out his hand to shake Ulrich's. "You didn't really have to drive into Cheyenne on business, did you?"

Ric grinned. "Actually, son, I did. Had important business . . . I had to get you on an airplane."

Nick looked away and sighed. "I was afraid of that. I'm really sorry to be so much trouble, but I have to go to her. She's . . ." He took a deep breath. What was the point of explaining?

The older man just shook his head and placed one heavy hand on Nick's shoulder. "She's your mate, Nicholas. She's going through a tough time, and you should be with her. Don't ever apologize for doing the right thing." He grabbed Nick's hand and then pulled him into a tight hug. "It'll be okay. She's with Tala and Keisha. They're tough and smart, and they'll help her do what she has to do."

"I hope so."

A tinny voice over the loudspeaker called Nick's flight. "I need to go. I still have to get through security. Thank you. I didn't tell the others I was leaving. Will you explain what's—"

"No need. They know and understand. The rental car will

be waiting. It's under your name. You've got money for the trip, and I imagine you and Beth will be driving back together in Daci's car." He laughed. "I know for a fact that if you don't bring it back, we're going to have trouble. Daci loves that stupid little thing. Now go. The sooner this is taken care of, the sooner we get you home. We're all going to miss you. Both of you. Be safe."

Nick fought the sting of threatening tears. He couldn't speak, so he merely nodded, grabbed his bag, and walked quickly toward his gate. Ulrich would never know how much his simple words meant.

To have someone wish him well. Even more, to have someone he respected and admired actually want him to hurry and come back . . . *the sooner we get you home.*

He'd never had a home before. Not a real one. Not ever.

Now he did. It made this trip to find Beth more important than anything he'd ever done.

She was fourteen, and Mom's new husband was moving in. He'd been around, off and on, for a few months. At first, Beth thought he was pretty cool. He was really handsome, and he brought her presents and teased her. He made her feel special, and her mom smiled a lot more when he came to call.

After a while, though, about the time Frank married her mom, Beth realized he wasn't quite as great as he originally seemed.

She figured if she ignored him, maybe he'd go away.

Not that he was mean or rude or anything. Just the opposite. He was very good-looking and smiled a lot, but she realized there was no warmth behind the smile. He watched her mother with a look that seemed almost bored, but when he watched Beth, it was different. She couldn't quite put a name to it, but it made her uncomfortable.

He was a toucher. He liked to hug Beth before he left the

house to go to work in the morning, and he expected her to kiss him good night before she went to bed. Her mother encouraged it, and because she loved her mom, Beth learned to kiss Frank whenever he wanted and hug him when he wanted a hug.

She didn't have to like it, though. A couple of times he'd pulled her into his lap and hugged her. She hadn't made a scene, but she'd gotten free as quickly as she could. Her mom thought it was wonderful that her new husband loved Beth so much.

Mom didn't know what happened when she worked nights. She had no idea that by the time Beth was fifteen, her life with her stepfather was a nightmare. He'd progressed beyond simple hugs, and he'd started touching. First it was her hair, then the sides of her growing breasts.

The worst of it was, even though she knew it was wrong, even though she hated it, sometimes what he did felt really good.

She remembered falling asleep on the couch one night while watching a movie. When she awakened, Frank was sitting on the floor next to her with his fingers between her legs. Still groggy, she'd lain there a moment and drifted with the amazing response he was dragging out of her body. Her climax shocked her so much she pretended to sleep through it, but he knew what had happened.

It made him try more, touch more. When he grabbed her bottom, Beth finally told him to cut it out. He'd merely smiled and said he knew she really loved it when he did those things. Then he warned her. Said she'd better watch it, if she wanted to keep her mother safe.

It got worse over the next year. His touching was something she'd avoid when she could, but she couldn't stay away all the time. Her mom seemed to be changing, too. She got angry because Beth wasn't doing her homework, wasn't being a good daughter.

They fought when Beth was rude to Frank, but Beth couldn't

tell her mom the truth. She was afraid of what might happen if she did.

Then her mom got sick. She'd always been healthy. She'd been there for Beth, at least until Frank came into their lives.

The weaker Mom got, the more Frank groped.

The more he touched her, the more frightened Beth became. There was no money for doctors, but her mom said she'd get better. All she needed was rest and she'd be fine, but Beth heard her crying at night. Most nights, she heard Frank with her mother. He'd take Mom her favorite sweet tea and hold her in his arms and tell her lies.

And after her mother fell asleep, he'd come to Beth. How could she have forgotten? Memories slammed into her mind, things long forgotten. Horrible nightmare images of Frank holding her down, touching her body, threatening to hurt Mom if she told.

Making her touch him *there*. Beth knew it was wrong, but she couldn't tell her mom, not when Mom was so sick. Frank made her rub and squeeze his penis until he'd cry out and shoot stuff all over her. Then he'd sigh and smile and pat her on the head. Tell her what a good girl she was.

Even worse were the times he'd touch her. He knew where to touch Beth to make her body respond. She hated it, but she couldn't get away from him. Hated the guilt, hated the man.

Hated herself.

Her mom got worse. Beth begged her to see a doctor, but she said no, that there was nothing anyone could do to help her.

She patted me on the arm, Beth said. Crying so hard she couldn't verbalize the memories, she used her mind to share that horrible time with Tala and Keisha.

She kissed me and said she wasn't afraid of dying, now that she knew Frank was there to take care of me. I couldn't tell her the truth, not when she was so horribly ill. I couldn't tell her that he'd forced me to suck him off the night before, that he'd made me swallow when he came. I was barely sixteen, and I was so terrified.

Tala quietly released the restraints holding Beth and removed the blindfold. The nipple clamps and vibrator were gone, but she didn't know when they'd been removed. Keisha brushed her sweaty hair back from her eyes and hugged her. "It's okay now, sweetie. You're doing great. We're here for you, but you have to remember. What happened next?"

Beth took a deep breath and then another. Somehow she managed to get her tears under control, but she held tightly to both Tala and Keisha. "She died. I'd forgotten I was there when she died! How could I forget that? I was holding her hand, and she smiled at me. She said she loved me, and then she was gone. Frank had her cremated right away."

Shuddering, she forced herself to remember. There was more. How could she have forgotten what he'd said? Beth swallowed back the bile that filled her throat. *Oh, Goddess . . .* how could she have forgotten?

Her mouth felt dry, her tongue too thick. It was so hard to force the words out, to say them out loud, but they had to be said. She couldn't hide them anymore. "The next night, the night before Mom's memorial service, Frank came to my room. I can't believe I'd forgotten what he said. How could I forget?" She frowned, vaguely aware of Keisha's hand softly stroking her hair, of Tala's fingers tangled with hers.

Beth looked into Tala's amber eyes and saw pure, unconditional love. Understanding such as she'd never known in her life. It gave her the courage she needed. The courage she'd always lacked. "Frank told me he loved me. He got down on his knees beside the bed and held my hands, almost like he was proposing. Then he said that now that Mom was *out of the way*, he'd take care of me, that I belonged to him."

She shook her head and closed her eyes against the awful truth. "How could I have forgotten that? He acted as if I

should welcome him to my bed. As if he thought I loved him."
She shuddered. Keisha's arms tightened around her, and Beth
felt a new sense of anger that gave her strength. "He said he
loved me, and then he raped me. I ran away as soon as he left
my room. I haven't seen him since."

Beth took a deep breath and leaned against Keisha. She felt
oddly lethargic, as if the mere act of breathing was an effort, but
at the same time, there was a sense of lightness about her. The
feeling that a burden long held had been lifted.

"He poisoned her, didn't he?" She stared into Tala's eyes and
read the truth. "Something was in the tea he took to her every
night. Why didn't I know that? I could have saved her."

Keisha shook her head. "You couldn't have known. You still
don't know for sure, but it sounds plausible. He was grooming
you, sweetheart. That's what pedophiles do. They touch and
smile and build trust, but you saw through him. It was worse
for you, though, because your body betrayed you. The touches
that made you climax? You're Chanku. Even without the nutrients, your body would have responded to a practiced touch, no
matter what you felt for the man."

Tala squeezed Beth's hand. "The perverts who prey on children often live in a world of delusion. They create fantasy lives
that fit their sick desires. If they can't convince the children,
they still convince themselves what they're doing is perfectly
okay, even when they know it's dead wrong."

Keisha sighed. "I imagine you were his ultimate goal. He
probably married your mother to get at you."

"What if he's still doing the same thing? What if there's another child somewhere going through the hell he put me
through?"

Tala shook her head. "Don't worry. We'll find him. I've got
AJ searching the Internet right now."

Keisha chuckled and gave Beth a squeeze. "He's supposed to

be helping Mik watch Lily. Do you think the guys need a break?"

Tala stood up and grabbed her caftan. "Personally, I think we all need a break. I want a long, hot shower. No one's called for help yet. A few more minutes won't hurt them."

Beth slipped out of Keisha's comforting grasp. She felt out of sync, as if she'd slipped the bonds of reality. Suddenly she remembered. "Wow. What happened to us? That thing . . . you were there, weren't you? Above our bodies, looking down?"

Tala laughed. "Oh, yeah. I've done that before, with Adam."

Keisha blinked back tears. "So has Anton. It's what saved his life when they were attacked a couple months ago. It allowed him to save Lily's, too, but I don't know what it is. I don't think any of us do."

"I felt as if my soul separated from my body. I'd probably still be there, floating, if you hadn't told me to get back to my body, Keisha. Who made it happen?"

Tala slapped her on the back. "I told you. You did, m'dear. It was all about you."

"Oh, crap." Feeling lighter than she had in longer than she could remember, Beth giggled. "Millie's already convinced I'm a drama queen. This isn't going to help matters, is it?"

"Probably not. It definitely keeps things interesting, though." Tala tugged on Beth's hand. "Shower, then food. And then we're going to find your stepfather and deal with him."

Smiling as if she didn't have a care in the world, Keisha grabbed Beth's other hand. "And after he's dealt with, we're coming home to the guys for a lot of good, healthy sex."

If only Nick were there, and not only for the sex. There was so much she needed to share with him. That out of body thing was only part of it. The memories, too. How come he hadn't discovered all of her past when they bonded? How had she managed to hide her secrets from him?

So many things to apologize for.

Later. After they dealt with her stepfather. Smiling, Beth followed the women. She liked the sound of that. *Dealing with Frank.* As if he were merely a blip along the way and nothing more.

The way he should be.

9

Beth was glad Keisha had decided to stay with Lily and the guys. It was hard enough that Tala insisted on coming, like it wasn't a problem at all to drive across the Bay and all the way to Orinda at two in the morning.

Tala parked the SUV on a narrow street in the really expensive rural neighborhood where Frank Michaels now lived. She found a spot in dark shadows beside a large patch of oleander shrubs where they were completely hidden from his late wife's sprawling ranch style house. There were no other homes in view, and only a few pale lights marked the long walkway to the front door.

Beth couldn't believe Frank had ended up living here. Scum like him didn't deserve a beautiful home with trees all around and a swimming pool in the back.

Of course, she didn't deserve such loyal friends as Keisha and Tala, or a wonderful, loving mate like Nick. Not when she'd let her mother die.

She should have known what Frank was up to.

Should have been able to stop him before it was too late for her mom.

She glanced at Tala, sitting so patiently in the driver's seat. She looked like a little kid behind the wheel, but without her strength, Beth doubted she would have had the courage to face her worst nightmare.

"I'm going to knock on his door. I figure the shock value alone should help. You're sure he's alone?"

Tala nodded. "His wife just died a couple weeks ago. This is the third wife he's lost. Your mom was the second. I think Mik nailed it—if they'd done an autopsy, the coroner would have discovered ethylene glycol poisoning from drinking antifreeze. What do you want to bet the wives were all cremated? And that he liked to take each of them a cup of sweet tea before bed?"

Anger blossomed in Beth's heart. If Mik was right, that tea had contained just enough antifreeze to slowly kill her mom. Cremation would have destroyed the calcium oxalate crystals that formed in her body after drinking the poisoned tea, and she never would have guessed because antifreeze tasted sweet, the way the tea was supposed to taste.

"You're sure there are no children?"

Tala shook her head. "None. There were a couple of nieces, but her sister took the girls and moved to Oregon a few months ago."

"Probably to get away from Frank." Beth stared at the beautiful home hiding a monster, and shuddered.

"Quite possibly." Tala squeezed her hand. "The sisters were estranged, according to a neighbor Mik spoke to. Whatever it was happened suddenly. The little girls used to be here a lot."

"But not anymore." Beth took a deep breath and grabbed the door handle. "Thank goodness their mother got them away from him. I'm going in. Do you have the camera?"

"I do. Be careful."

"I will." Beth got out of the SUV and quietly closed the

door behind her. She heard Tala slip out on the other side, but there was no need to worry about her. Tala knew exactly what to do. She'd been working for Pack Dynamics, the pack's detective agency, long enough to have learned a lot more about catching the bad guys than Beth knew.

Beth walked quickly to the front door and rang the bell. After a moment, she pressed the button again. She heard cursing, saw the lights go on inside, and waited.

The porch light blinked on and the door flew open.

"Beth? What the hell are you . . . ?"

"Hello, Frank." She was glad her voice sounded so steady. Amazed, in fact, that now she finally faced him, she felt absolutely calm. He still looked much the same, and Goddess help her, he still reminded her of Ulrich. Tall and handsome, his hair was silver like Ulrich's, though his eyes were blue, not amber.

At least it explained why being with Ulrich had reawakened so many old fears.

"It's been so long, Beth. It's the middle of the night. . . . What brings you here?"

She shrugged. Smiled at him. "May I come in?"

Obviously confused, he stepped back and opened the door. He'd thrown on a bathrobe, but his hair was mussed and his feet were bare. Beth brushed by him and walked through the entryway, into a large, well-decorated living room.

She hoped he'd forget to lock the door, but even if he did lock it, Tala shouldn't have any trouble getting inside. The house was huge. There were doors and windows everywhere, and Tala was good at her job.

Beth paused in the middle of the room. Frank stopped a few feet away.

"Why are you here, Beth? I haven't seen you since . . . you never even went to your mother's funeral. You left so suddenly, I always wondered . . ."

She laughed. "What? You mean you didn't know why I left in the middle of the night? You raped me, Frank. The night before my mother's funeral. You came to my room and you raped me."

His eyes went wide. "I didn't rape you! You wanted me to make love to you. Don't you remember? You were hurting, Beth. You were so sad." He took a step forward, his hand outstretched. "You asked me to come to you. You were thrilled we could finally be together, once your mother was gone. You wanted me."

Tala and Keisha had been absolutely right. Beth stood a little straighter. So many things finally made sense. "You are sick, aren't you? You didn't love my mother. You wanted me. I was a child, Frank. A fourteen-year-old child when you showed up. The things you made me do . . ."

"Were things you wanted." He was suddenly much closer, invading her space, towering over her.

Tala's voice invaded her mind. *I'm here if you need me.*

Empowered, Beth tilted her chin and looked up at him. "I doubt there's a little girl alive who wants to suck on a man's cock. I doubt there's any child who likes being groped and fondled. I know that I, as a sixteen-year-old virgin, did not enjoy having my innocence ripped away by a grown man."

He grabbed her arm. Beth held still, but she glared at him. "Take your hands off of me."

Instead, he grabbed her other arm and held her in a viselike grip. His tone was placating, as if he indulged a child. "Ah, Beth . . . you wanted me. I gave you pleasure. How can you forget all those wonderful feelings I made you have? You want me now. That's why you're here, isn't it? You've always loved me. I knew it. That's why I married your mother. It was all for you."

"Is that why you killed her?"

His eyes went wide. Beth pushed into his thoughts, moving faster than lightning, past the sickening layer of filth and the memories her face had brought back to him. Past the images of two little girls swimming in the backyard pool, their prepubescent bodies calling to him like an addictive drug. He'd touched them, and they were perfect, but they'd known enough to tell their mom. She'd taken those beautiful little girls away.

At least he had pictures. Lots of pictures.

Disgusted, Beth learned where he kept the photos but skirted over the prurient details of what they contained. She moved on, deeper, until she saw the juice bottle of green liquid in the back of her mother's refrigerator and knew that was the poison he'd added to her tea at night.

Not a lot . . . just enough to slowly destroy her internal organs, to change the rhythm of her heart, to cloud her mind. Enough to kill her.

The same way he'd killed his first wife. The same way he'd killed the third. There was a similar bottle still in the kitchen in this house. He hadn't even tried to hide the evidence, he was that confident.

"What makes you think I killed anyone?" His fingers tightened around her arms, but she refused to back down. For the first time, Beth realized she was standing up to him, and she was doing it without fear.

"You kept the antifreeze in a bottle in the back of the refrigerator, and every night when you made Mom's tea, you poured just enough into the cup. Just enough, Frank. It didn't take all that long for her to start feeling sick, for her body to fail, but it was subtle enough that she never guessed. Never realized you were slowly killing her. Is that how you did it to your other wives? Antifreeze in their tea?"

He pushed her away and stepped back. "Where do you get your stupid ideas? Reading too many cheap detective stories?"

You go, girl.

Tala made a terrific cheering section. Beth stared directly into her stepfather's guileless blue eyes. "I know you molested your wife's nieces. They're awfully cute little girls, Frank. Cute enough that you took hundreds of pictures. They thought it was a game at first, didn't they? How come you never bribed me with toys and candy, Frank? You just did what you wanted to me." She pouted and looked sadly at him. "You gave them new bikes. Frank . . . that isn't fair."

His eyes went wide. "How'd you know about the bikes?"

"I know a lot of things, Frank. I know you have a mole on your dick. Not something most little girls know about their stepfathers, is it? I know you have tons of files of illegal pictures of little kids, including some pretty graphic shots of your nieces. I know you've killed at least three women."

If she hadn't been Chanku, if she didn't have such amazing senses, she might not have known when he decided to attack.

She read his intention a split second before he lunged.

Knowing it was coming gave her strength not to fight back. Tala's encouraging voice in her mind gave her a power she'd never expected. Beth let him tear her sweater over her head, and she screamed because he expected it. When he shoved her to the carpet and pulled her pants down, she struggled just enough to make him work, but she didn't break away.

When she was naked, he held her down with his knee against her chest and she fought him, but she knew it was what he wanted. When he shoved his bathrobe behind his back and spread her legs, she felt her strength coiling deep in her gut.

Until that moment, Beth wasn't certain whether or not she could kill. She'd given him a choice—admit his guilt or prove he was the monster of her memories. Now, as he pressed her body against the floor and fumbled with his pajama bottoms, Beth had no doubt—he was evil

But if she killed him, didn't that make her as evil as Frank? He grabbed his cock and shoved it between her legs.

Beth shifted.

Frank screamed and jerked away from her. She went for his

throat, but she didn't break the skin. Her weight and the speed of her attack rolled him to the ground. Then Beth spun around and clamped her jaws over his cock and balls and glared at him through wolven eyes.

He screamed again.

She visualized what she intended, how she'd bite down slowly but with enough force to tear his genitals from his body. Adrenaline pumping through her veins gave her the power to show him exactly how it would look—the blood and the disgusting mass of body parts hanging from her jaws, the gaping hole at his groin with his life's blood spilling forth.

Beth slowly clenched her jaws.

Frank's eyes rolled back in his head. His body went limp.

She hadn't left a mark on him, but she spit him out and backed away, sat on her haunches, and whined. Tala walked into the room, swinging her camera and smiling. She leaned over, touched the pulse point at Frank's neck. She held her fingers there for what seemed a terribly long time. Then she turned and frowned at Beth.

"He's dead. I thought he'd just passed out." She looked closely at his throat and then at his groin. "You didn't even break the skin. I don't get it."

I was in his head. I let him see me ripping his cock and balls off his body.

"Wow. Were you really going to do that?" Tala cocked an eyebrow and stared at Beth.

She shifted and began picking up her ripped clothes. "No, but he didn't know that." She slipped on her panties and jeans, pulled her sweater over her head. "I'm glad he's dead, but I didn't plan to kill him. I just wanted to scare him."

"You certainly did that. Scared him to death." Tala checked the room for any evidence of their visit. "Ripping his balls off would have left a huge mess. It would have been hard to explain to the police."

Beth laughed and gave Tala a big hug. "That's not what I was thinking at all. I didn't want the taste of his cock in my mouth. Blech."

Tala was still chuckling when they went in search of Frank's computer. By the time they'd looked through his pornographic files, neither woman was laughing. Tala downloaded them to a thumb drive and wiped away her fingerprints.

Then she called the police.

It was easy enough to explain, considering. Beth answered their questions. Yes, he'd been her stepfather, and yes, she'd suspected him of murdering her mother, especially after learning another wife had died under similar circumstances. And yes, he had raped her, but she'd never reported it.

She'd been too afraid, but she wasn't afraid now. She told them he'd tried to rape her tonight when she confronted him, but then he'd collapsed and died. She had no idea what caused his death. Beth held Tala's hand. Having a friend who believed had given her the courage to finally confront the bastard.

Once they showed the computer to the police, once the officers had seen the evidence of Frank's pedophilia and his collection of child pornography, there'd been very few questions left for Beth to answer.

A detective took information so he could contact her, thanked both women for their cooperation, and went to work gathering up the evidence of Frank Michaels's prurient life and convenient death.

No one seemed inclined to question Beth's story that he'd attacked her when she confronted him and then dropped dead. Stroke or heart attack . . . whatever the cause, it hadn't been anything she'd done to him. In fact, given the story, Beth thought the police were surprised she hadn't confronted him with a gun instead of a camera-toting friend.

The coroner showed up and removed the body. The police ran out of questions. It was a little after four thirty in the morning when Beth and Tala crossed the Bay Bridge into San Francisco, and almost five when they pulled into the garage.

Tala turned to Beth and touched her shoulder. "Are you okay?"

Beth nodded. She wasn't a hundred percent, but . . . "I've always thought I'd want to celebrate when he died. Last night I had the chance to kill him, but I realized I'm not a killer. I wanted him to suffer, to know the kind of fear I felt, the same fear those other little kids felt." She turned and looked at Tala, knowing her packmate would understand. "I'm glad he's dead. I'm relieved it's not entirely by my hand, but I don't regret my part in his death. Does that make sense?"

Tala nodded. "Entirely. He was evil and he didn't deserve to live, but you're right. We're not killers. We kill to defend ourselves, but what happened tonight . . . it was just. He needed to die. His death probably saved more children, more women."

"What will you do with the files you copied and downloaded?"

"I'll give them to Lucien Stone for Pack Dynamics. We do a lot of rescue work, lost children, kidnappings. There might be evidence in the pictures that will help us find missing kids."

Beth nodded. "That's good. Something good might actually come of this night."

Tala shot her a bright look. "Something good did happen, Beth. You faced your worst enemy, a man who was truly evil. You stood up to him, and you didn't back down. Not one inch. I was so damned proud of you back there."

Beth blinked, surprised at Tala's assessment. She was even more surprised to realize she agreed with her. She had faced him, and she'd held it together. She hadn't even been afraid. No, she'd been totally pissed off, but never afraid.

Smiling, she opened the door and crawled out of the SUV. "I'm exhausted. I think I could sleep for a week."

Tala came around the back of the car. "Nothing to stop you. I'm headed to bed, too."

"Actually, I need to call Nick first. I miss him so much! I want to apologize. I owe him more than he'll ever know."

Nick stepped out of the shadows. "I'm here, Beth. You don't have to call." He held his arms wide.

"Nick? You're here?" Beth couldn't move. She stared at him, felt his love and the strength of their bond. He'd come for her. In spite of everything, he'd come after her.

She took one step, and then another. He waited, arms wide, lips parted in a smile. Tears streamed down his face.

Tears like hers. With a laugh that broke on a cry, she threw herself into his embrace, and his arms tightened around her. Solid. Strong. Protective.

He covered her mouth with his, kissing Beth as if they'd been apart for months, not days. When they finally ended the kiss, Beth reached up and touched the tears on his face. "Don't cry," she whispered. "Not for me."

He pressed his forehead against hers. "For us, Beth. Tears of joy. I'm so glad it's over. I love you. Tala told the guys what happened. He's gone, and I am so proud of you. The most important thing? There's no more darkness."

Frowning, Beth pulled away and stared at him. "Darkness? What do you mean?"

He touched her forehead with his fingertip. "There. Inside you. Shadows on your memories. They've always been there, but not anymore. The shadows are gone." He wrapped an arm around her waist, and they followed Tala into the house.

Nick had known. He'd seen the shadows, but he'd loved her anyway. She had so many apologies to make. To Ulrich, for her bitchy behavior. To Millie, but most of all, to Nick. She owed him more than anything. She'd treated him horribly, but for some ungodly reason, he still loved her.

"Yeah," he said, leaning close to whisper in her ear. "Pretty stupid of me to love someone as wonderful as you. But just think how much fun we'll have with you making up to me."

Laughing, she punched him lightly on the shoulder. "You aren't supposed to eavesdrop," she said. "Those were private self-recriminations."

"You were broadcasting, sweetie." He stopped just inside the kitchen and turned Beth around in his arms. Mik, AJ, Keisha, and Tala waited with big smiles on their faces.

"Yep," AJ said. "We all heard you." He glanced at Mik. "Has she got anything to apologize to us for?"

Mik shrugged. "I'm sure we can think of something. I love the idea of a beautiful woman wanting to make up to me."

Tala stood up on her tiptoes, but Mik still had to lean over so she could kiss him. "Don't hold your breath, big guy. I'm all the woman you can handle."

But she wasn't. Not exactly. Much later, while Lily slept in her crib in the next room, Beth lay warm and relaxed in a pile of warm bodies, replete and completely at peace. Mik, Tala, Keisha, AJ, and Nick, all of them sprawled together in the huge bed in Tala's room.

Not once had she felt the need for control. There hadn't been a single moment where she'd been afraid, where her memories had intruded on their joined pleasure.

She'd been part of the pack. Loved, desired, a woman finally comfortable in her own skin.

Comfortable with her mate.

Nick pulled her into his arms and she went, gladly. It was exactly where she belonged.

10

―――――――

"Oh, look!" Keisha pushed Lily's stroller along the walkway leading to the memorial garden in Golden Gate Park. She paused in front of the beautifully landscaped area, the one she'd designed not all that long ago. "The plants have grown exactly as I imagined," she said. "I need to take pictures so I can show Anton."

Beth hadn't been back here since that day, just a few short weeks before, when her life had changed forever. She glanced at Nick when he squeezed her hand. Their thoughts collided, so closely aligned it was as if they were one person.

A single person with one shared thought. *I remember,* he said.

I remember. Beth held his hand and smiled up at him, and the memories spilled into her mind. *I was so frightened,* she said. *So confused. But you never hesitated. You saved Tala. You were amazing.*

I was frightened. Confused. The wolf took control. I hardly recall the attack.

I already loved you, she said.

I already loved you, too.

Keisha took pictures. She made them all stand together in front of the granite stone with the list of names carved on its face—names of Sherpas who had died while leading an expedition of local climbers in the Himalayas. Tall grasses native to their land waved softly in the light breeze.

The same grasses that ensured the birthright of the Chanku.

It was Keisha's turn, and she held Lily while Nick took pictures. Mik rounded up a gardener to get a shot of all of them together, laughing, with Lily squealing in delight.

Beth clung to Nick's arm and realized she couldn't have stopped smiling if her life depended on it. This all felt so amazingly normal. The sort of thing good friends would share. Something a family would celebrate with jokes and laughter and hugs all around.

Tourists walked by and smiled at the group of them. No one could possibly guess the truth, that they watched a pack of shapeshifters celebrating so much more than a beautiful day in the park.

Celebrating life. Even more, they celebrated survival. Each of them had survived a nightmare of one kind or another on their life's journey. Survived, and emerged stronger than before. Keisha and Tala, Mik, AJ, and Nick. All of them had stories that shouldn't have ended happily, yet they shared this sunny day with love and laughter and hope for the future.

Beth was thinking of her own journey as the little Mini Cooper headed east the next day. A journey she'd never expected to put behind her. She glanced to her left and grinned at the relaxed, confident look on her mate's face. He was still too pretty for words, but his confidence seemed to have grown and expanded over the past few days, as well.

"We're both different, you know."

Nick turned a lazy smile in her direction. "How so?"

"I like myself a lot more." Beth glanced down at her hands. "I always loved you, but I couldn't understand how you could love me. I didn't think there was anyone here"—she tapped her chest—"worth loving." She took a deep breath. "I guess it's finally dawned on me that I'm not as awful as I thought I was."

Nick threw his head back and laughed. "Shows you how much you know. I never once thought you were awful, but I felt the same way about myself. Figured someone like you could never really love a loser like me."

Beth leaned over and kissed his cheek. "We were both pretty stupid, weren't we?"

"Yeah, but not anymore." He winked at Beth. "Now I just hope we don't get lost. I've only flown between California and Colorado. I've never even driven out of San Francisco before, and we're almost to Nevada. Are you sure this is the right highway?"

Beth grinned at him and shrugged. Did it really matter? She knew they'd get home eventually. No matter where they were, so long as she was with Nick, she wasn't lost at all.

Not anymore.

Eye of the Beholder

Anitra Lynn McLeod

This one is for my mother,
who read me my first fairy tale,
and without knowing,
started me on the path to writing.
I miss you deeply.

1

Everything about Dauer of Hargarren reeked of evil.

Dragging her steps, Larra trudged down the center aisle of the church, clutching a mishmash of autumn flowers to her breast. Excited whispers followed in her wake.

"His face is so horrid that to look upon him is to go insane."

"He consorts with witches and demons."

"His last wife threw herself from the highest tower rather than spend one night in his bed."

"He's a beast!"

Harsh comments turned her blood to ice. All her life, she and her maids had exchanged terrifying tales of Dauer. When they grew older, the tales were of his perverse sexual needs—dark passions involving restraints and ravenous hunger. They speculated his staff was bigger than a stallion's and thoroughly insatiable. Larra never admitted to anyone that the twisted stories left her aroused despite her fear. However, that had been when he was just a boogeyman, a creature of myth and salacious fairy tales. To see him now, waiting for her at the altar, knowing he would soon have the right to do anything he pleased with her . . . Larra stumbled, righted herself, and continued plodding along the aisle.

Covered in a gray cloak, Dauer overshadowed the diminutive Father Ealthen with his sinister presence. Even the bright afternoon light pouring through the stained glass windows disappeared in the darkness of his massive form.

A desire to turn and run possessed her, but she knew escape was futile. Her sister had posted guards all over the church.

"You'll marry him now, or I'll imprison you until you do."

Her sister's brutal edict still rang in Larra's ears. She knew she was only a pawn in her sister's lust for power, but she never thought Andace would stoop this low. Dauer had had multiple wives, none which ever lasted more than a few weeks before a tragic death. Larra was convinced her sister prayed for her timely demise so that all of their father's riches would be exclusively hers. What little she gave in dowry to Dauer would barely dent the vast family wealth. Even when Larra swore she would retreat to an abbey, thus refusing any part of their inheritance, Andace refused.

"You do me no good there." Andace had tossed her the mangled bouquet. "Now go."

When Larra had hesitated, Andace had shoved her toward the door, ripping the back of her ivory dress and pulling out a hank of her brown hair. Her dearest maid had pressed her lips together to stop herself from crying, her whole face twisted in genuine sympathy. Such was the look of most people in the pews.

Andace hadn't even bothered to line the church with fresh flowers, so the air was heavy with the sweat of villagers too poor to afford finery or even to bathe. Andace had allowed Larra to wash—cold water and no perfumes, but at least on her wedding day she was clean. So greedy for any speck of wealth, her sister had removed Larra's delicate gold filigree earrings, saying that Dauer would provide for her now.

Heart racing, palms sweaty, Larra trudged up the final steps to the altar. Father Ealthen looked as stricken as she felt. He mumbled his way through the ceremony. Behind her, the villagers sat with perfect stillness; no shuffling of feet, no coughing, not even one fussy child. Too mesmerized by the spectacle before them to even breathe loudly, they simply observed. As much as they might want to intervene, they couldn't without suffering vicious reprisal. Andace ruled Relmon through might. She commanded an army of hardened soldiers and used them to enforce her edicts.

Purple silk trembled in Father Ealthen's grip when he said, "Lift your hands."

Larra froze, expecting to see a mangled claw extend from Dauer's woolen sleeve. Before she could retreat, he clasped her right hand with his left, lifting them together. His grip was firm but not crushing. Dauer's massive hand seemed normal enough despite the black leather glove, yet her heart raced at his touch. The heat of his flesh bled through the animal hide, warming her icy fingers.

While Father Ealthen wrapped the silk around their clasped hands and intoned the sacred words, Larra tried to see within the gloom of Dauer's hooded cloak. When she saw nothing but blackness, she shivered and turned her gaze away. Perhaps it was for the best she didn't look too closely. She would see his horrible visage soon enough, looming over her in the dark while he did unspeakable things to her body.

Quivering again, this time with a curious blend of dread and desire, she inadvertently squeezed his hand. To her surprise, he squeezed back. Did he understand her trepidation? Had he asked for her specifically, or had he been willing to take any woman?

Together they turned and faced the pews. Larra thought he must look like the grim reaper with a doll clutched in his fist rather than his scythe.

As they exited the church, Larra had to take two steps to his one, and no whispered comments greeted her ears. The people of Relmon wouldn't dare incur Dauer's wrath. Larra vowed she wouldn't either. She would follow his orders, and when he came to her at night, she would close her eyes tightly so she couldn't see him. If she did, she might live longer than a few weeks.

His horse-drawn carriage waited at the bottom of the church steps. Larra expected it to be black, but it was white with accents of yellow and blue. She had forgotten those were his family colors because she always thought of him in black, as befitted his reputation.

Dauer entered then helped her inside. He settled her next to him with their bound hands nestled between their bodies. By ritual, they would stay bound until they reached his home.

Once she closed the door, the carriage took off, and the ride was unnaturally smooth, as if they skimmed across ice. She found this odd, but was too worried about her proximity to Dauer to give it much thought.

Heavy blue fabric shrouded the windows, blocking most of the light. Her own breathing sounded loud and fast, but Dauer's was slow, calm, like an animal stalking prey. If he had a tail, it would be twitching in anticipation.

Trapped in the enclosed space, Larra tried to put some distance between them, but there was nowhere for her to go. She expected him to smell of corruption and death, but he smelled pleasantly of leather, wool, and wood smoke. She wanted to speak, to pelt him with a hundred questions, but a lump of fear prevented her throat from working.

When she glanced at him, his cloak lay open, exposing the thick leather belt around his waist. One of the perverse tales flashed through her mind.

In it, Dauer caught a young woman stealing from his garden so he imprisoned her. Each night he would force her to her knees, demanding that she suck him, but his cock was too big, so she always failed. As punishment, he clamped her tender nipples and whipped her bottom with a water-soaked lash until she screamed for forgiveness. Unheeding of her pleas, he then allowed all his men to plunge within her tender depths while he lurked in the shadows, stroking himself to fulfillment.

Picturing herself as that tormented woman caused Larra to tremble and wrap her arm around herself.

"Are you cold or frightened?"

His voice shocked her. She thought his tone would be shrill and keening like a seething beast, but his voice was smooth, dangerously low, rumbling like a winter creek clogged with ice. He had a beautiful voice. It clashed with everything she'd ever thought about him. How could a malformed monster possess the voice of a satyr?

"Both?" she finally answered.

Fire and brimstone laced his wicked chuckle. He pulled a blanket from under their seat and placed it on her lap. "This will help with the chill. As for the other, I'm afraid there is no cure for your terror."

"Are you what they say?" When the question left her mouth, she wanted to swallow it back, for it was as foolish as poking at a swarming beehive.

"Oh, I assure you, I am worse than what they say. I rape nuns and eat children. I drink virgin's blood and then suck their eyeballs from their screaming faces. I have the head of a bull, the snout of a pig, and the cock of a stallion. My lust knows no bounds and my perversion no limits. I am a beast through and through."

He paused for a moment then turned his head to whisper directly into her ear, "And now, I have you."

2

Dauer knew his words were cruel, and they only terrified his new bride further, but he couldn't help himself. Every day of his life he suffered his curse without complaint, but never had he done anything to deserve such abusive tales. Clearly, Larra believed what she had heard because she subtly inched away. If not for the purple silk binding their hands, she would have thrown herself from the carriage. Death would be preferable to marriage with him.

Gripping her hand tightly, he yanked her close. Squeaking with fright, she mashed into his side. He hoped she did not feel the padding under his cloak.

"Fear has a distinctive scent." He leaned near and took a deep breath. Larra smelled of rain in the sunshine, crushed autumn flowers, and tender dreams turned nightmare. "Yours is intoxicating, arousing all of my most beastly desires." He'd been fighting his lust since he saw her walking down the aisle. Andace hadn't lied about how beautiful Larra was. She was delicate, with rich brown hair flowing down to her hips, and wide, doelike eyes that shifted between brown and green. Freckles smattered her nose and cheeks, making her look younger than she was. Larra had a proud chin, a sensual mouth, and a most intriguing dimple on the right side of her face. The beast within wanted to taste her fear, wallow in her terror, and drink deeply of her dread.

"Are you going to kill me like all your other wives?" Her breathless voice was shockingly seductive.

All his other wives? He'd only had two wives, one before the curse and one after. Larra's question was only further proof of the malicious stories circulated about him. He had sworn that he would never take another wife, but loneliness and desperation drove him to try again. This time, he vowed to be more careful. He would not let his curse affect his bride.

"I do not intend to kill you." If he wanted her to give him a chance, he should stop terrorizing her, but the beast enjoyed such games, and the man had little control during the day.

"What one intends and what one does are often two different things," she said primly, stiffening her spine.

Rather than answer, he turned the question back on her. "What do *you* intend to do?"

"Me?" She turned to face him but quickly darted her gaze away when he lowered his hood so she couldn't see within. "I intended to spend my life in the abbey."

His human heart sank. She wanted to take vows? What unholy sin had he committed now? His remark about drinking the blood of virgins and raping nuns must have set her hair on fire. However, the heart of the beast was exuberant, drooling at the prospect of claiming her innocence. Knowing he could not undo what had been done, he said, "That is no longer an option."

Larra nodded then pushed the curtain aside.

"Don't." He winced back. "The light hurts my eyes."

"I'm sorry." She put it back into place, smoothing the edges so no light slipped through. "Is that better?"

"Much." Using his free hand, he nestled the hood of his cloak around his face. She seemed genuinely regretful that she had hurt him, even in a small way. No wonder she wanted to be a nun. If she could care about a bastard like him, she could forgive any sinner his transgressions. Would she ultimately be able to forgive him for what he intended to take from her?

Dauer knew he could not wait another night. Without physical contact, the curse would consume him completely. He'd told himself he would take her against her will if he had to, but now he didn't think he could. Why couldn't Larra be a greedy slut like her sister? If such were the case, all he would have to do is shower her with gems and furs and she would happily part her thighs, no matter what he looked like.

"I will be a good wife to you," Larra said softly. "When Father Ealthen wrapped the silk about our hands, he symbolically bound our bodies and also our souls." After a deep breath she continued, "I won't lie and say that I'm not afraid, because I am. I'm afraid you will be disappointed with me and then kill me in a rage because I'm not what you wanted."

Her tender admission touched his human heart. How could she think any man would be disappointed to have her in his home, his life, or his bed? Inside the beast raged; he wanted to harm her, destroy her, and hold her responsible for every wrong ever committed against him. Struggling, the man within worked his way free.

"I will be the best husband I can be to you," he said, knowing it was a lie. He couldn't be a true husband to any woman, not with his curse and the needs it placed upon him.

With their tentative agreement, they settled into a companionable silence. Dauer tried to keep his mind off her body and his hands to himself, but the beast found it impossible. Too long had he been alone. Too long had he waited to sate his perverse desires. Larra was here, now, right beside him, her breath hot and tasting of sun-drenched apples.

Unable to wait, Dauer leaned near, and the beast whispered, "I wish for you to tell me one of the tales."

"A tale about you?" Larra tensed.

"Yes, tell me one you have told many times."

Larra closed her eyes, took a deep breath, and then said, "While riding on a moonlit night, you came upon a lone woman. Her husband had cast her out."

Tentatively, he stroked his right hand along her face. With his hand clad in thin leather, he couldn't actually touch her directly, but even so, he felt her heat and the pulse of her heart when he caressed her neck.

"Why did her husband cast her out?"

"She was unskilled in his bed."

"Was she beautiful?"

"Golden hair and the face of an angel. When you saw her, you couldn't resist. You decided to educate her. She refused and ran. Gleefully, you gave chase."

Larra's nipples thrust against creamy lace. Lowering his face, he breathed to her ear, trailing his hand down to twist one then the other fragile peak between his fingers. She moaned, not with alarm, but arousal, which caused his prick to twitch below the heavy fabric of his trousers.

"What did I do when I caught her?"

"You told her if she pleased you, you would let her go." Larra's breath caught when he palmed her breasts, teasing the nipples between his fingers. Arching back, she added, "But only you knew it was a lie. You did not intend to ever let her go."

"What did I make her do first?" He wanted to take her hand and wrap it around his cock, but now was not the time for her to discover that particular truth.

"You ordered her to disrobe. Timid and shy, she removed her clothing until all she wore was pale moonlight. Silver kissed her slender limbs, contrasting the golden hair upon her head and the fair hair . . ." her voice trailed off as she searched for the right word.

"The fair hair on her luscious cunny," Dauer supplied, delighting the beast that thrived on salacious words.

Larra gasped at his crudeness, seemingly shocked he would toss such a word about so casually.

"Say it, Larra. I want you to say it for me."

"Cunny." She said it fast, spitting it out, then instantly her cheeks flushed pink.

Chuckling in her ear, he said, "Your blush is lovely. Tell me the truth; you've said that word before."

"Not to a man."

"Have you said it when you're alone at night, thinking of this tale and touching yourself?" Always, the beast could smell truths that eluded him, and this was no different.

Her deepening blush and a lowering of her proud chin confirmed the truth. Pleased to discover a wicked center to her prim and proper facade, he stroked his hand to her hip.

"Now that I have the golden one bare, what will I do with her?"

"You tell her to get on the ground, on her back. When she resists, you slap your riding crop across her bottom. The raised welts look purple in the moonlight. You caress them, telling her that if she listens and pleases you, you will let her go, even though you know that you are lying."

"Does she now do what I command?"

Larra nodded. "She's afraid but excited. She places her cloak on the ground then lies down. You tell me—her—to part her legs so you can kneel between them." Apparently warmed by reciting the tale, Larra pushed the blanket from her lap.

He took her slip, inserting herself into the story, as an invitation to explore. Sliding his hand down her hip, he worked her lacy dress up to her knees then halfway up her thighs. Freckles dotted her skin, youthful and charming, compelling him to tease his hand between her legs. When she willingly parted them, blood surged, thickening his cock.

"Now I'm kneeling between your beautiful legs. What do I tell you to do?" Encouraging her to become the woman in the tale only excited him more.

Larra bit her bottom lip. "You tell me to touch myself so you can watch."

"Touch yourself so I can watch." He exhaled a thick groan of sinful pleasure as he moved his hand to his lap.

Eyes closed, her head tossed back against the seat, she placed her hand upon her knee then smoothed it up between her legs.

"Part them more so I can see better."

She hesitated.

"Must I find a riding crop?"

Shaking her head, she parted her legs very wide. He lifted their bound hands so she had more room. When her thigh pressed against his thigh, his entire body twitched. The beast wanted to fall between her legs and feast upon her slick cunny then impale her upon his shaft until she screamed. The man within barely held him back.

Larra caressed the tender flesh of her inner thigh then nudged her fingertip against her luscious sex. Her moan was low, filled with need, shamed but determined to please.

"Slide your finger between your slick lips."

While she did as he bid, he parted his cloak and stroked his leather-clad fingers along his swollen shaft.

"Show me how wet you are."

Larra lifted her hand.

Before he could stop himself he leaned near, breathed her scent deep, then swiped his tongue along her finger. Her arousal filled his body with rampaging lust. Quickly he parted his trousers, gripped the base of his prick, and squeezed.

"Touch yourself again. Focus your attention on your stiff little clit."

She did, rolling her head forward with a gasp of surrender. Never had Dauer heard a sweeter sound. Larra slumped lower in the seat, spread her legs father apart, and gave him a better view of her sinful ministrations.

She seemed determined to find her pleasure as she worked her finger around and across her straining little nub. Clearly, this wasn't the first time she had masturbated. She appeared to know just how she liked to be touched—soft then firm, slow then very fast. How could this lustful woman even think of secreting herself away in a nunnery? Somehow, the thought of her chaste, hidden behind plain robes and surrounded by nothing but women, aroused the creature beyond his control.

"Fuck yourself with your finger. Plunge it deep inside your sweet little cunny."

With a strangled gasp of shocked satisfaction, Larra flung her head back and frantically worked her hand between her legs.

Tightening his grip around his shaft, he increased the intensity of his strokes, rubbing his thumb across the swollen head, slicking his glove with his own gratification.

He followed her pace until she clenched her legs together, trapping her hand as she rode her fingers to release. Her soft little moan caused him to climax in a swift gush. Their mutual peak washed over him, causing the beast to retreat a step.

Already he felt more human. Never would the creature within fully withdraw, but with a few more encounters, Dauer wouldn't fragment. Or so he hoped.

Over the winter, he'd discovered more and more occasions where he had done things as the beast but had no memory of them as a man. Panicked, he had tried to find a way to blend his separate halves and had realized there was only one thing both sides craved: pleasure. Greedy even after this wonderful encounter, both man and monster wanted more.

Larra rested against his shoulder, loosening her legs enough so she could withdraw her hand.

He tucked himself away, wondering how many other tales Larra would willingly tell. Or, if he was very lucky, act out.

3

On a cleft between the highest peaks nestled Hargarren Castle. Expecting thunderclouds, Lara exited the carriage to bright sunlight sparkling on snow. Blinking rapidly, she shaded her eyes with her free hand and gazed upon soaring white towers. Atop the central turret flapped a flag of white, yellow, and blue. Frigid air slashed against her gown, cooling the heat between her legs. Like a huge white cloak, snow surrounded the structure.

"Your home is beautiful."

Dauer barely nodded, keeping his head low.

Realizing the light bothered his eyes, she moved more swiftly toward the massive front doors. Her delicate slippers crunched through the frozen top layer of snow, and tiny clumps melted and soaked her feet. She would have plenty of time to explore the grounds later. While she did, she might figure out what happened on the ride here. It had started out as her telling him a story, but then she became the subject of the tale. She couldn't remember how that happened. She wasn't ashamed, only perplexed. Never in her life had she experienced such a shattering release. Dauer had been both kind and brutal, like two different people.

Once inside, he lifted their bound hands and carefully unwound the silk.

After so many hours with her hand clasped to his, sudden freedom washed cool air against her sweaty palm. Her wrist didn't hurt, but she rubbed it absently for lack of anything better to do while she glanced about the foyer.

This was now her home for as long as she lived.

Much to her surprise, everything was white, from the marble floor to the smooth stone walls. Cathedral ceilings at odd angles jarred her, for nothing was symmetrical. She expected something gloomy and dark, filled with a thousand creepy shadows, but this was bright, airy, and much warmer than Relmon Castle. Thick carpets covered the entryway, and two statues stood guard on either side of the door.

Curious, she approached the first. A naked muscular man looked over his shoulder. His expression was not one of fear but of resigned acceptance. The second was the same glorious man, but now a sneer of contempt twisted his lips. The more she gazed at him the more beastly his face became.

Larra shivered and stepped back, right into Dauer.

He steadied her, his hands on her shoulders, his body pressed against hers. His size and nearness terrified yet excited her. Leisurely, he rubbed his hands up and down her arms, as if inspecting his recently purchased goods. From his vantage point, she realized he must be able to see down her dress. Her nipples peaked, causing a shift in the rhythm of his breathing. His grip tightened, and suddenly he spun her around. Larra hung her head, too embarrassed to look up.

"You can't hide from me. I smell how aroused you are." He traced his finger from her lips to the edge of her bodice. "Is it my reputation or what you saw in the carriage?"

Confused, all she could do was bite her lips and shake her

head. She had no idea what caused her reaction to him. Never had she been so aroused and yet so afraid.

"I want to see you."

She thought he wanted her to raise her head, but he slipped his hands inside the top of her dress, forcing the bodice down until he exposed her breasts. A rush of air tightened her nipples almost painfully. The shock caused her to clench her thighs.

"Such a responsive little thing you are."

The cool leather of his gloves was more erotic than actual skin. He pulled and twisted her tender peaks until she gasped and arched her back. At once, she wanted him to stop but also to continue. In her mind rolled the story of how he clamped the woman's breasts to torment her while he whipped her bottom. Would he now do that to her?

His answer was a terrifying growl that shivered her down to her toes. He grasped a handful of her skirt, lifted it, and then ran a dagger through it, ripping and cutting the fabric until he exposed her right up to her belly button.

She darted her gaze wildly around the foyer.

With a chuckle, he tossed the ruined fabric and dagger aside. "None will come to see you or to rescue you." He stepped back, perusing her body.

Larra refused to cover her breasts or her exposed and vulnerable sex. Such an action might only anger him. She stood very still, her gaze on his boot-covered feet. When he stepped forward, she tensed.

He plunged his hand between her legs. "How wet you are." Rubbing his hand back and forth, he teased his middle finger between her lips then nudged it threateningly against her passage. "Slick with lust." He wiggled his finger inside and chuckled at her gasp. "Too big? Wait until you feel my cock stretch this tiny hole."

Trembling at his words and the visions in her mind, she turned her face away. Only from the corner of her eye had she seen what rested between his thighs during their ride. Monstrously large and terribly thick, she knew he wouldn't simply stretch her but cleave her if he plunged his shaft within.

"Your body doesn't lie. Show me how much you want me, Larra. Move your hips."

She did, slowly at first, then with more vigor as her movements worked his leather-clad finger inside. Her gaze fell on the second statue, and she swore he leered at her, pleased to witness her submission.

"Sweet little slut with a greedy wet slit." His entire finger was now deep within, his palm cupping her, rubbing her clit.

"I'm not," she gasped, trying to stop, to edge away.

"Yes, you are." He snaked his hand around to her lower back, pulling her against his rugged frame. "Say it, Larra, say 'I'm a greedy little slut.' "

She shook her head, pushing at his shoulders, but he refused to release her. His finger delved deeper, firm and insistent. What did he want from her? How could she say no to anything he demanded?

"Poor innocent, forced to wed a monster, but now, to your utter shock, you discover you lust after the beast. You don't want a man, no, you want a brute to use you, to force you, and to make you do things you swore you would never do." He thrust his finger in and out with rough brutality. "That's what you want. You want it nasty and fierce, you want me to compel you."

"No." Her voice was breathless and weak as she clung to his broad shoulders. For a fleeting moment, she wondered why his cloak was more heavily padded on one shoulder than the other was, but she was too appalled by her behavior to think on it now. "No." Her denial was pathetic, so feeble that even she didn't believe her defiance.

"Don't fight me. You save no face here, for none that you knew will ever see you again." He jabbed his finger in and out, dancing her on his palm, forcing her to ride him. "You belong to me. Say it."

Her entire body swayed back and forth as she danced upon his arm. Against her will, she moaned, "I belong to you."

"Again." Ruthlessly, he plunged a second finger beside the first.

"I belong to you!" Larra shuddered against him so close to climax she could taste release.

Abruptly he withdrew his hand and coldly said, "Get on your knees."

Falling to her hands and knees, she gripped the thick carpet in her fists.

He moved behind her and said, "Part them." His boot nudged her thighs.

When she did, he knelt and lifted the back of her dress to expose her bottom. He slapped each cheek once and chuckled at her whimper. She heard his belt jingle as he loosened it, then a shock of hot thick flesh was rubbing between her thighs.

"Oh, God," she moaned, digging deeper into the multihued carpet with her fingertips. The tales were true—he was as big as a stallion and harder than stone. How would her petite body ever accommodate him?

"You call out to God as the devil works his prick between your legs?" He laughed obscenely. Big hands gripped her hips, forcing her thighs together, clenching them more snuggly around his shaft. As he plunged back and forth, thick veins parted her lips, rubbing her clit.

The slicker she got, the faster he moved, until he was bucking against her, slamming his hips against her bottom, the buckle of his belt digging into her flesh. His breath was harsh and so hot she felt it through the fabric of her dress.

Panting with foreboding, waiting for the moment when he plunged within, she arched her back and wriggled side to side, desperate to get away before he did.

His fingers drilled into her hips to hold her steady. "You can't get away, Larra. Besides, you don't want to. You're so wet, it's dripping off me and onto the floor."

What he said was true. She'd never been so slick. Her scent filled the air around them, encouraging him to make animalistic growls and harder thrusts. Every stroke only tormented her more and caused her passage to tighten with need. How could she want him to fill her yet simultaneously dread that moment?

"I'm going to make you spend all over my cock." He reached around her waist and cupped his shaft, pressing firmly against her clit as he slowed his movements.

Larra almost screamed with ecstasy. Perverse dreams and wicked stories flashed through her mind, filling her throat with keening growls and begging moans. She wanted him, beast or not. She'd always wanted a man to find that secret place in her mind, where her most obscene fantasies resided, and bring them to life.

With one final shove that scraped his shaft along her clit, she climaxed, clenching her thighs around him. He bellowed, his hips jerked, and then he splattered all over her belly. She would have collapsed if not for his strong arm around her waist.

She heard him whisper something but didn't trust her ears because it sounded like he said, "My salvation."

He pulled her up against his body then stood, taking her with him. "Don't turn around." He was still hard when he withdrew. She heard him covering himself then felt his hand upon her shoulder. "I will show you to your room."

Similar to what happened in the carriage, once the moment was over, his mood abruptly changed. Her exhausted legs trembled as she gathered the edges of her skirt to cover herself. She followed him down an endless series of hallways and up twisting staircases. Asymmetrical arches and jarring angles confused her sense of direction. Even if her life depended on it, she didn't think she could find her way back to the entrance. Strangely, she had no desire to run. She didn't know exactly what Dauer hid below his peculiar padded cloak, but he hadn't forced her to do anything against her will. She'd reveled in his brute commands. Besides, where would she run? Her sister would only send her back.

Walking a few paces behind Dauer, she noticed that he had an odd hopping gate, as if his right leg were longer than his left. He stopped at a bare wooden door and pushed it open.

Plush decor in gold, green, and brown dotted a massive room. The color scheme was surprisingly similar to her room at home. Wood carvings lined every wall from floor to ceiling. When she first gazed at them, she saw nothing but smooth flowing lines, but the longer she looked, the more she saw faces bubbling out of the carvings. She blinked and they disappeared.

A crackling fire filled the space with light and heat, flicking shadows across a fabric-shrouded bed. Against one wall was a water basin and racks of clothing. Trailing her gaze along the dresses, she discovered that each was more elaborate than the last.

"I'll leave you to clean up and change for supper."

"Wait."

He stopped but didn't turn around.

"You said these were my rooms. Where are yours?"

He pointed to a door directly across from hers. Without a word, he left.

Peering around the doorway, she waited until he disappeared then darted across the hall and turned the knob. Locked. Disappointed but not surprised, she returned to her room and closed the door behind her.

Larra removed her ruined clothing, washed up, and then perused the dresses. Her eyebrows rose. All of them had plunging necklines, nipped in waists, and full skirts. He didn't want her to see him, but apparently, he had no problem looking at her.

She selected the most modest one in spring green with brown

brocade ribbon along the bodice. Struggling her way into it, she suddenly missed her maid. As she continued to pull the fabric around herself, she wondered if Dauer had servants. She hadn't seen any yet, but surely he couldn't run the entire castle by himself. Someone had stoked the fire in her room. Perhaps they made themselves scarce when he was in residence, or maybe they had known what he had intended to do with her in the foyer.

With the gown secure, she turned to the dressing table, and was puzzled by the lack of a looking glass. When she examined the frame, she found a few embedded shards. Why had he not replaced it? She checked around the room for some reflective surface but found none. She pulled her hair up and secured the knot with a decorative stick. In one of the velvet-lined boxes, she found matching earrings and slipped them on. She felt like a princess from a fairy tale. Her radiant smile faded. A princess should have a prince. Dauer was many things, but he was no prince. Their encounters in the carriage and the foyer were simply a prelude to what he would demand of her tonight.

"My first night as his bride."

Butterflies filled her belly, but was she anxious or anticipating? What happened between them had aroused her beyond comprehension. Having him order her about was immensely freeing, but still, she nibbled her lip, wondering what he would do next.

She decided worrying over it would solve nothing, so she left her room and went exploring. Most of the doors were locked. The few that weren't had only fabric-covered furniture and a thick layer of dust.

Half-expecting to find something sinister, she continued to try every door but was terribly disappointed. Nothing disturbing or even mildly creepy greeted her curious gaze. Perhaps there was no truth to the rumors. Dauer was simply a disfigured man who chose to live his life isolated within his castle. If people told such vile tales about her, she doubted she would want to mingle with them either.

A part of her heart broke, for she had delighted in telling tales about his brutality, his malicious disregard, and his evil perversions. When she didn't hear enough tales, she simply made up new ones and told them with breathless relish. A wave of shame crushed her when she realized she was responsible for circulating some of the worst stories about him.

Determined to make up for her misdeeds, she vowed to do anything he asked of her.

4

———————

Dauer found Larra wandering the halls and led her to the dining room. He had no doubts that she had been exploring every room, looking for proof of his vile reputation. He thought she would be smart enough to realize he would never leave confirmation laying about for her to discover. Wisely, he kept his dirty little secrets firmly buried.

That she chose the green dress didn't surprise him either. It was the most modest of the lot yet complemented her coloring perfectly. She appeared lovelier than a wood nymph. When she smiled up at him, the dimple on the right appeared then deepened with her blooming grin. Now that night had fallen, the beast retreated and the man stepped forward. He could appreciate her beauty without degenerating into thoughts of how he wanted to bend her to his lust.

"Do you always wear that heavy cloak?" Larra asked as he seated her at one end of the table.

"Yes." Out of respect for his servants' sanity, he disrobed only in the privacy of his room. He moved to the far end and sat. When he looked up, she frowned.

"Why are you sitting so far away?"

During day-to-day activities it was difficult to keep his hood low enough to cover his face, while eating it was impossible. However, her desire to be closer to him stirred a part of his heart he thought long dead. Apparently, whatever the beast had done to her in the foyer hadn't terrified her. All he could remember was ushering her inside, then everything went hazy.

"I wish to eat without having to worry about my hood."

"Oh." Embarrassed, she lowered her gaze and fiddled with her glass.

Determined to recapture a more pleasant tone for their meal, he lifted his glass and said, "A toast."

Larra lifted hers, anticipation shining in her eyes.

"To you, my wife. May you always grace my home with your beauty, your charm, and your sweet smile." He tilted his glass to her then sipped.

Blushing, she followed suit. Her eyes went wide. She dropped her glass and crystal shattered against the table. Sputtering, she slapped at the table for her napkin. In her haste, she knocked her plate and silverware to the floor. Once she found her napkin, she opened it and dropped her face into her hands.

Everything went silent so fast it was comical.

Against his will, he burst out laughing.

Mortified, she peeked over the edge of her napkin-covered hands.

"I apologize." He tried to stop, but he couldn't. For the first time in years, he laughed, not at her, but at the situation. His pretty, perfect wife was a klutz.

Larra considered the damage, shook her head, and then she too laughed. "I guess I won't be gracing your home with my grace." She stood and brushed the mess from her gown.

"Haven't you ever had brandy?"

"Is that what that was? I thought it was wine, so I took a

generous swallow. It stopped halfway down my throat then came right back up."

He continued to chuckle as he took another sip of his brandy. "Don't worry about the mess."

On cue, his butler entered and deftly cleaned up, replaced her tableware, served the first course, and departed.

"He's very proficient," Larra said, settling herself back to her seat. Dubious, she considered her fresh glass of brandy.

"Delicate sips, my wife." He couldn't stop himself from calling her that. He found the rhythm of it pleasing, the thought of her as his more so. If she could only understand his dual personalities, the difference between him as a man and as a beast. He wanted to tell her, but how could he explain?

After a deep breath, she tried the brandy again. Her face scrunched up, but she didn't gag. He found her willingness to try new things not only charming, but such adventurousness gave him hope. Perhaps this time he had wisely chosen a stronger woman.

Throughout the meal, she questioned everything she didn't recognize and discovered she did have a taste for fine brandy.

On the verge of cautioning her not to drink too much, he decided it might be for the best if she did. Intoxication would allow her to relax when he took her to his bed. No matter what qualms he felt, he was going to take her there. He needed her. Without the pleasure of her body, he would dissolve into the beast and never be a man again.

He was perplexed by the events of today. After their encounter in the carriage, he felt the beast retreat, but he couldn't remember anything from the foyer. He knew he had done something brutal, because he found a ripped part of her dress and a dagger. However, Larra didn't seem to be afraid of him. She wasn't cowering. In fact, she looked across the table with shy smiles and delicate blushes. While his butler, Morrow, de-

livered course after course, Larra became increasingly ani-
mated, chatting about a variety of subjects. He found her thoroughly enjoyable and regretted when the evening drew to a
close.

When he stood, a flash of worry darted across her face, but
she shook it away and plastered a determined smile to her lips.

"I won't hurt you," he soothed, offering his hand.

"I know." She clasped his hand but hers trembled. He would
give anything to remove her trepidation. Where the beast
sought to build her anxiety, the man inside wanted only her
willing capitulation.

Lighting their way through the halls with a lone candle, he
unlocked his door and pushed it open.

Larra gasped. "Why is your room so bare?"

All his room held was his bed and a washstand. He'd had the
decorative walls covered with blue fabric and the thick rugs removed. He hadn't used the fireplace in years.

"I find I need little in the way of luxuries," he said, but the
truth was he thought severity in dress and design was apt punishment. He set the candle on the washstand then closed the
door.

Larra fiddled with her earrings. Since there wasn't much of
anything to look at, she kept her gaze on the floor.

"You won't have to look at me." He blew the candle out and
pure blackness descended. Instantly more comfortable, he removed his cloak. He took his first fresh breath of air all day.
His entire body hummed with anticipation. He couldn't see
Larra, but he could hear her panting breath and feel the heat of
her body.

"What do you want me to do?" A desire to please overshadowed the terror in her voice.

"Do you remember the story you told me today?"

"Yes."

"I want you to remove your clothes then lie on your back on my bed."

With regret, he realized he should have put something softer on his bed for her rather than a scratchy wool blanket. He could do nothing about it now, but tomorrow night he would lay her down upon silk like a queen.

He heard the ruffling of fabric as she disrobed. Her scent wafted through the air, lovely with innocence and arousing with desire. Or was his need only fooling him? How could she want him? His last wife had thrown herself from the highest tower rather than share one night in his bed. Would Larra submit and then kill herself? He couldn't bear another tragic death.

In the dark, he heard a screech of wood against wood as she placed herself upon his bed.

"How will you watch me with no light?"

Her question eased his worries. "I will not watch you this time." He removed all his clothing then sat beside her. "This time, I will touch you. Lie still."

His bare fingertips traced along her face. Her skin was smoother than silk, giving and alive, so profoundly sensual tears filled his eyes. He hadn't directly touched another human in an eon. Trailing his hands over her forehead, down her nose, then to either side of her neck, he wanted to spend the night simply touching her. When he reached the delicate skin below her ears, he felt her pulse dancing wildly as her breath grew sharp.

"I swear I will not hurt you."

Larra took a gasping breath, but her body only tensed.

He couldn't imagine what this was like for her, alone in the dark with a man she had never seen. Her imagination must be running wild with horrible visions of his face. Longing to tell her the truth, he held tightly to his plan. He would never let her see him.

Reverently, he touched her from her shoulders, down her

arms, to the tips of her fingers. He wanted to follow his path with his lips but held back, afraid of doing too much too soon. If he went slowly, Larra would relax and realize he wanted only to give her pleasure. He traced lightly from her chin to her breasts then palmed them. Firm but pliable, he rolled them in his hands.

She arced up in subtle encouragement.

Dauer rubbed his thumbs across her nipples, marveling in the texture of the puckered flesh. He swore he could spend the entire evening simply exploring her breasts.

"Your hands are so soft," Larra whispered.

"Probably from wearing gloves all day."

"Why do you wear gloves? Your hands feel normal enough." She tensed. "I mean, I'm sure that you—that everything—"

He shushed her babbling with a finger to her lips. "Shhh. You worry too much. My hands are normal but very sensitive to sunlight. I'm not an ogre who is going to fly into a rage at everything you say."

She nodded below his finger. Her lips were plush, smooching around his fingertip. A desire to lower his mouth to hers consumed him. He hadn't kissed anyone since his first wife, but he couldn't demand that intimacy of Larra. Using her body to sate his lust was bad enough.

In a rush, he wanted to cover himself, relight the candle, tell her the truth, then fall to his knees and beg for her understanding, her acceptance. However, the last time he tried, his second wife threw herself from the tower, convinced he was a devil-worshipping warlock. Revealing his truth to Larra would serve only to salve his soul, not to make her trial any easier.

Hesitantly, he smoothed his hands along her body, but the lower he went, the more she tensed. When he dipped his finger to her belly button, she whimpered. When he went lower still, right to the edge of her downy hair, she bolted upright.

Shocked, he yanked his hand back, whacking his penis.

Growling in pain, he bellowed, "I told you to lie still!" Damnation. He'd told her he wouldn't rage at every little thing, and here he was doing just that.

"I'm sorry," Larra gasped. "Please don't be angry, but my sister lied to you."

Dauer cupped his hand to his smarting cock. "What did she lie about?" All Andace claimed was that Larra was beautiful, pliable, and would make him a good wife. He had no argument with any of her claims so far.

"I'm not a virgin."

Breathless, Larra sat tensely on the bed, as if waiting for him to erupt. Whatever he'd done to her as the beast, it didn't include penetration or she wouldn't be this petrified.

For the second time, he tried to smother his chuckle, but it quickly turned into full-fledged laughter.

Larra scrambled back, probably afraid he'd gone insane. He gripped her upper arm, not too hard, just enough to stop her from bolting off the bed.

"All this fear and trembling is because you are *not* a virgin?" He was profoundly relieved. When she told him she wanted to take vows, he simply assumed she was innocent. Besides, the beast had not smelled the truth. Or perhaps he had but decided not to share it with him. It would please the beast to make him think he had already stolen such a prize.

Confused, she haltingly asked, "You're pleased that I'm not chaste?"

His grip on her arm turned into a caress. "Larra, I was terrified that I was going to hurt you no matter how slowly I went. Believe me, I'm elated." He paused for a moment, considering a new twist. "Was it unpleasant?"

"My first time was awkward. Afterward, it was . . . nice."

It was not a rousing compliment to her lover, whoever he

may have been, but at least he hadn't hurt her. Dauer wanted to ask for details, but by refusing to invade her privacy, he might gain her trust.

"So you're not afraid of sex, just sex with me."

She moved to deny it but haltingly said, "I don't know you. In the carriage, I saw a glimpse of you, then in the foyer I felt . . . you swear that you won't hurt me, but I don't know how I can take your—you—comfortably." She shrugged below his hand. "I want to please you, to be a good wife, but I don't see how I can without pain."

Now he had some idea of what the beast had done. He'd slid himself between her legs to find his pleasure. The feel of his deformed penis must have frightened her beyond comprehension.

His hand captured hers and despite her resistance, he wrapped her fist around his shaft. "Feel me, Larra."

Tentatively, she explored him. Her hand was cool against his throbbing cock. Fighting desperately to hold still, he simply sat and let her touch him.

"I don't understand." Her voice broke, and he wanted to sweep her into his arms, but he couldn't.

"Your mind played tricks on you. Perhaps what I said in the carriage embedded itself into your thoughts." He knew it was a cruel deception, but he still couldn't explain without revealing a truth that might shatter her mind.

"But I felt the veins, the thick pulsing ridge—"

"With your thighs," he said, cutting her off. "I'm a man, Larra, not a monster."

"You were different today. Bossy and brutal."

He hung his head and softly asked, "Did I hurt you?"

"No." She hesitated then whispered, "What you did excited me."

Stunned, he tried to understand how the beast's excessive dominance could arouse any woman, let alone shy and blushing Larra. Rather than ask, he simply laid her back on the bed and continued his exploration. However, now he was concerned his tender sensuality would not engage her as fully. He felt at war with the beast for Larra's satisfaction.

He needn't have worried. Larra came alive under his strokes; her body writhed while her soft moans offered subtle encouragement. When he slid his hand between her thighs, she parted them willingly, allowing him to feel the heat and slick arousal hidden between. His mouth watered, demanding he taste her. Crawling onto the bed, he maneuvered himself between her legs, lifted her bottom with his hands, and then buried his face in her sex.

Larra gasped. She parted her thighs, balancing herself on her toes. Dauer slipped his tongue deeply inside, reveling in her pleasure, her willingness. Never had he known such sweet honey. Her honest desire inflamed him. Like a salve to his soul, her surrender restored a part of his broken humanity. Nibbling and chewing, he teased her until her legs trembled and her breath turned into gasps.

"Plunge your finger inside," she begged.

When he did, she bucked wildly, tightening around his finger as honey gushed onto his hand. Never had he known a woman to become so aroused, so wet, and to ask so boldly for what she wanted. Before her contractions stopped, he rose up and planted the head of his cock to her quivering passage.

Like a tiny sucking mouth, her sex begged him within, demanding and insistent. He eased inside. His eyes rolled back as her heat enveloped him. After hundreds of years of celibacy, this precise moment was epic, sublime, and no matter how much he wanted immediate satisfaction, he refused to rush. Bit by bit, he went deeper, feeling every texture within, every pulse of her heart, every fleeting quiver of her pleasure.

Below him, Larra shifted, rolling her passage around his shaft, squeezing him, compelling him. Against his will, he plunged deeper. Her whimper frightened him, and he abruptly withdrew.

"Please don't stop." Larra reached out, grasping his shoulders before he could move away. Her touch was magical. Her fingertips dug into his muscles, then her hands smoothed over his chest, flattening against his nipples. She explored his body with the same reverent curiosity as she had explored his penis. When she moved her hands up toward his face, he pulled away.

"I want to touch you."

"Please don't."

To his relief, she withdrew her hands. Angling her hips up by grasping her buttocks, he again descended slowly into her silky heat. This time when she whimpered, he took it as encouragement, slipping deeper until his balls nestled against her bottom.

He released a groan of profound rapture. The agony of denial evaporated with their union. Tears filled his eyes, and he blessed the darkness for hiding them from Larra. For a moment, he held still, simply enjoying the feel of her body wrapped around his. When Larra rose up to embrace him, she tightened deliciously around his shaft. In a moment of pure bliss, he forgot himself and kissed her.

Her mouth yielded to his, opening, welcoming, returning to him the gentle thrusts of his tongue. Devouring her with his entire being, he pressed her back onto the bed, lifted her legs around his hips, and thrust his hips to lock their bodies.

In a timeless moment he held her, flesh to flesh, so enmeshed within each other they were no longer two separate beings but one. Sensations he'd long forgotten enraptured him: the feel of her breasts flattening against his chest; the slender strength of her limbs along his powerful form; the soft, tingly spring of her curls against his much coarser hair; the scent of her skin; the taste of her mouth. For the first time in his endless life, he prayed to God that the sun would not rise. Let it be forever night so he could keep her bound with him in the dark, in this tender perfection.

Hours passed as he held her, occasionally kissing her lips, her face, and her shoulders. Eventually she grew restless beneath him.

"Move, please move," Larra implored, contracting her arms and legs around him in supplication.

Dauer buried his face in the hollow between her neck and shoulder. Tears flowed as he rocked to her, marveling at how she echoed his movements, how she clung to him, kissing his neck, gripping his buttocks.

Velvet blackness allowed a freedom he hadn't ever known. Even his first wife, lovely and perfect in his memory, had not taken such pleasure in their bed. Not like Larra. She whispered encouragement then punctuated her needs with demanding movements.

As he drew closer to climax, the beast pounded in his blood, demanding harder thrusts, willing him to ride fast and furious to find the pinnacle. Dauer refused. He allowed his gratification to build and build, taking Larra with him.

Locking his mouth to hers, he took her breath into his lungs, sharing his, their gasps mingling until the dam burst, spilling him into her as she clenched around him. Blinded by not only the dark but also by bliss, Dauer clung to her long after the shudders abated.

He didn't have to see outside to know that morning came despite his prayers. Bit by bit, the beast infiltrated his body. He always felt the change begin inside then slowly work its way to his outer shell. This time, the change was different.

Larra's fingertips trailed across his features. Her voice was a shocked whisper when she asked, "Why do you hide when all I feel is beauty?"

5

The wonderful heat and weight of his body vanished when he rolled off her. Lost in the darkness, Larra called out to him, but all she heard in answer was the ruffling of fabric, and she knew he'd donned his heavy cloak. Why did he hide himself away when all her hands discovered was smooth skin, a strong jaw, and thick hair that curled around his noble head?

Dauer wasn't a beast; he was beautiful.

Before she had touched him, she already knew because of his tears. She had said nothing, but she felt the gentle drops against her shoulder. A simple act of love wouldn't touch a monster. Only a man, a strong and secure man, would allow himself to feel so deeply.

"Dauer?"

"You may return to your room." His voice was so coldly dismissive, she shivered. When she hesitated, he bellowed, "Go now!"

Confused by his abrupt mood change, she scooped up her clothing. She didn't bother to dress but simply clutched everything to her chest. At the door, she scrabbled at the handle, twisting it frantically, but it wouldn't open. When he stepped behind her, she was so furious at his moodiness that she dropped everything, turned, and slapped him as hard as she could. Misjudging his height, she connected with the top of his head.

He growled. After grappling with her for a moment, he gripped her wrists and pinned her to the door.

Struggling, she tried to kick him, but he pressed close until he crushed her flat.

"Do you still think I'm beautiful?"

"I think you are a hateful brute!"

Laughing, he clutched her hands in one fist then shoved his other hand between her legs. She tried to clamp her thighs together, but she was no match for his strength. His leather gloves were cold but quickly heated.

"Let me go."

"You took such good care of him. Now you'll take good care of me."

Bewildered by his words, she stopped fighting. He spoke as if he were two different people. Was he truly mad as some tales said? Was he a recluse that finally cracked under the tide of loneliness and despair?

His hand left her, but then she felt something bigger nudging her thighs. When a ridge and veins pressed against her tender flesh, she screamed.

"That's what I wanted to hear! Scream for me, Larra. Shriek out your horror and dread. Music to my ears."

Here was the massive cock she'd felt in the foyer, the one Dauer assured her was only a figment of her imagination. Had he somehow switched places with another man? What vile amusement did they use her for? Perhaps he and another made sport of her. They tried to drive her mad with this evil game.

His thick cock was no illusion. Pulsing and hot, he forced it between her legs, pressing it right to her clit that still quivered from the tender encounter on the bed. But who was that man who held her, cried on her shoulder, and loved her so sweetly?

"Let me go!"

"Not until I've had my turn."

He tossed her over his shoulder then threw her on the bed. Before she could crawl away, he pounced, straddling her chest. She heard him fumble for something then felt silk wrapping around her hands. Shocked that he would use their marital binding cloth for his perversions, she nonetheless couldn't help a wild quiver of anticipation.

Once he had her hands secured, he flipped her facedown, dangling her legs over the edge of the bed. Two big hands grasped her buttocks, spreading them wide, and then something wet wiggled against her anus. It took her a moment to realize what she felt was his tongue. Too shocked to move away or even to protest, she simply lay there while he plunged his tongue inside her.

When her sex gushed and her nipples thrust against the rough wool blanket, she blessed the darkness for hiding her shame. No matter how she tried to deny the truth, she enjoyed his perverse behavior. How could she find two such different men entirely arousing?

Plunging his finger into her cunny, he lifted his head and exclaimed, "And here's the proof." Working one finger into each passage, he continued, "My eager little wench likes the nasty beast. You weren't this wet for him."

She refused to comment, afraid that if she denied his accusations, he would harm Dauer.

Chuckling, he pushed her up and now snaked his tongue into her passage. His head pressed against her, misshapen and strange, so she knew he could not be Dauer. As he drew her legs up onto his shoulders, one was much lower than the other was, forcing her legs to part wider for his grunting slurps.

He ate at her like a starving animal.

Larra buried her face in the blanket to hide her answering squeals of excitement. Why did his bestiality arouse her so thoroughly? Torn in two by the difference between them, by her reaction to both of them, she simply stopped struggling. If they battled for her body, let them, for she would willingly submit to them both. If they used her for sport, let them, for she would use them in the same manner. She would revel in the different pleasures they offered, and she refused to feel one more moment of humiliation. After all, one or the other was her sworn husband. It wasn't her fault she didn't know which one.

Lifting her head, she snarled over her shoulder, "Surely you can get your tongue deeper than that?" His hesitation empowered her. "What's wrong? It's no fun for you unless I fight?"

His answer was a lusty plunge that she countered with a howl. His tongue was flat and wide, deeply textured, more agile than any finger. When he wiggled it between her lips then lapped at her clit, she lifted her bottom to give him better access. Encouraged, he snarled and forced her hips higher. He bit her inner thighs, her nether lips, and then her clit.

A violent orgasm contracted her, clenching her thighs around his head, which only encouraged him to flatten his tongue and swipe it hard and fast until a wave of climaxes rendered her a gibbering animal.

"Dirty girl." He lifted her legs off his shoulders. "Let's see how filthy you are." Pulling her hips to the end of the bed, he rose up until his massive cock pressed against her still trembling passage.

In the foyer, she'd been terrified by his sheer size, but now she knew she could take him. Not only that, she wanted to. She wanted to feel him invade her, posses her, own her utterly.

"What are you waiting for?" she taunted. "Permission?"

"He fed you his cock slowly, didn't he?" the beast asked as

he teased his finger against her still slick anus. "He was gentle and sweet, loving and tender." His tone wasn't mocking, but curious. "Tell me, Larra, which do you prefer?"

Unable to decide she said, "Both."

She gripped the blanket with her bound hands, waiting for his initial thrust. Pulse pounding in her ears, she tried to relax, but anticipation tightened her muscles and shortened her panting breath until her lungs burned. Why was he hesitating?

With the thick head plugging her and his finger ready at her bottom, he just knelt behind her, mumbling something she couldn't understand. Shuddering, he pressed forward and her eyes went wide. Twice as big as Dauer, the beast's cock stretched her painfully despite her slick readiness. As the bulbous head nudged inside, she stifled a cry and heard snatches of what he was saying.

"You'll hurt her."

"I want to hurt her."

"There's no salvation if she's broken."

"She wants it."

Larra held very still. There were not two separate voices but only the beast talking to himself. Again, he used the word salvation, as he had in the foyer. She didn't understand how she could rescue him or even what she was delivering him from. A thousand questions swirled in her mind as he continued talking to himself.

His voice rose and fell from indecipherable mumbling to clear and sharp bursts. Suddenly he bellowed, "I want my turn!" With that, he pressed forward, stretching her beyond endurance.

Her scream of genuine pain shocked him so much he abruptly withdrew. She didn't think he had hurt her badly since she didn't seem to be bleeding. More than anything, he'd frightened her with his impulsive thrust. Now she knew she simply could not accommodate him, no matter how much she wanted to. He must have realized this truth as well. When she rolled over and sat up on the bed, she tried to find him in the dark. After a moment, she heard him in the corner, crying. His sobs broke her heart.

Making her way to him, she settled at his side and placed her bound hands on his shoulder. He flinched.

"Go away!"

He sounded like a cranky child. At a loss for words, Larra used her teeth to remove the silk cloth from her hands. "I know you didn't mean to hurt me."

"I hurt everyone! No one likes me; they like him."

So there were two different men. She couldn't fathom why they would play this game, but it did explain the strange stories about Dauer. Perhaps they were brothers, forced to live this outlandish bound existence to claim their inheritance. Or maybe Dauer felt sorry for him and allowed him to live here. She longed for her most trusted maid; together they would be able to arrive at an explanation.

"I like you," Larra said, leaning against his shoulder.

"Then why did you scream?"

"Because it hurt."

"I knew it would. I wanted to hurt you."

"Why?"

"All those stories they tell that aren't true—I wanted to make someone pay."

Brutal, vicious stories of perverse pleasures and dirty deeds must have burned his ears. Larra was glad the darkness hid the hanging of her head. How could she repay them both for the gossip she had eagerly spread?

Larra wrapped the silk binding cloth around the tip of his penis and stood. Silently, she drew him back to the bed. Grunting, he followed but refused to lie down when she nudged him to do so.

"I don't want you to be in charge."

She giggled. "Don't you want to try something different?"

"I want to be inside you." He'd lost the harsh edge to his voice and now sounded wistful.

With regret, she explained that he was simply too big, but there were other ways for him to find his pleasure.

After a long stretch of silence, he said, "I want to see you, but I don't want you to see me."

Inspired, Larra wrapped the binding silk around her eyes and had him relight the candle. In the next instant, she felt him lifting her up over his shoulder.

"Where are you taking me?"

"To the dungeon."

Larra shivered from his words and the cool air rushing over her naked body as he strode down, down, down to the very bowels of the castle.

"Are you going to punish me?"

"Yes. Are you afraid?"

She didn't answer because she was yet she wasn't. In a way, she wanted him to punish her for spreading the vilest of stories. In another way, she was terrified he would explode and go too far, causing her permanent damage—what if he sought to disfigure her so she matched him?

He placed her on her feet and moved away. She stood in the center of what must be a vast room because every sound echoed. The air was damp and smelled of fetid water and rust. Somehow, not seeing him made the moment more erotic than terrifying. She heard a ruffling of fabric and then caught a whiff of sweat and some spice, not vile or unpleasant, but unusual and entirely unidentifiable. Even though he was a beast, he was clearly a clean beast. She wondered if, in anticipation, he had prepared himself for her. That he cared about her perception of him pleased her and altered her view of him. She decided not to think of him as a beast but merely a tragically disfigured man.

From behind, his rough calloused hands gripped her shoulders then slid down her arms, exploring her with forceful excitement, in direct contrast to how Dauer had touched her. Twisting, he peaked her nipples, causing her to gasp and curl in. He grunted approval. His breathing was rough and hot against her neck. When he picked her up and placed her facedown on some type of device, she didn't struggle. Fear and anticipation hammered her heart. A padded surface cradled her from chest to hips. He bent her legs, placing her knees into cups. Metal wrenched against metal as he adjusted the machine to hold her legs apart. Next, he secured her arms above her head with manacles. Shuddering and groaning, the machine shook below her as he lifted her up and inverted the table so her bottom was higher than her head.

Bound and exposed, a curious freedom possessed her. Why she took pleasure in her helplessness, she didn't know, but she refused to rebel or to plead when she knew he would not listen. Just the prospect of being at his mercy aroused her beyond her wildest fantasies. And, too, she deserved his punishment.

Once he had her settled, the dungeon became unnaturally quiet. When he slapped her bottom barehanded, the smack echoed off the stone walls, matching how her body shivered in response. She bit her bottom lip not to cry out.

Unable to see him, she felt him when he leaned close and growled, "I want to hear you scream, Larra. That is the point of punishment."

He retreated and again smacked her butt. This time, she let out a whimper. Apparently, it wasn't enough because he whacked her again, twice as hard. Her flesh stung and she struggled against her bonds. When she howled, he chuckled approval.

After a thorough spanking, when without even seeing herself she knew her bottom was bright red, he withdrew. For a moment, all she heard was his sharp breathing mingling with hers.

"Now tell me the truth. Confess that you told those awful tales about me. Confess that you embellished them with your own nasty needs."

Larra nodded, unable to speak. Something hard and flat plowed across her buttocks, bringing her so much stinging pain, she screamed out, "Yes, yes! I told stories about you. I'm sorry. Please forgive me."

Refusing her plea, he paddled her until she dissolved into tearful confessions and begging absolutions. He poured a lifetime of pain into spanking her, and perversely, she thought she ought to have even worse. From her mouth came the most horrible tales, and once she said them, she couldn't take them back. When her flaming cheeks could take no more, he stopped, flinging the paddle aside.

Metal groaned as he settled himself behind her, angling the machine so she was almost horizontal.

"Now tell me one of the tales, as you did in the carriage." Hot breath caressed her bottom, soothing some of the pain. She decided he was sitting between her forcefully spread legs.

Hesitantly she told him the tale she found most titillating, the one where he caught the girl in the garden and punished her in a most arousing fashion.

"Would you like that, Larra? A hundred hungry cocks ready to fuck your bound body?"

When she nodded, he smacked her butt. "Speak!"

"Yes!"

"I would enjoy that too. Watching them pound away at your insatiable cunny." He placed his face close between her spread legs so that his breath caressed her quivering nether lips. "Perhaps they would widen you enough for me."

Silently, she begged him to touch her. Her sex was so hungry, it tightened unbearably, causing her to wriggle restlessly against the machine.

He laughed. "I have something for you." With that, he

moved away. She heard him shuffling things around, dropping items that clinked against the stone floor.

Anticipation flooded her with a thousand lusty ideas, each more wicked than the last. Bare feet shuffled against the stone floor as he returned to her. After a few adjustments of the machine, he placed something against her, something that simultaneously slid up her bottom and her slit. Cold at first, the unfamiliar material warmed to her body. He secured the device to her with a series of straps that wound around her hips.

Before she could ask the purpose of the device, the two cylinders moved together in a slow plunging rhythm. Her eyes went wide behind her blindfold.

"You enjoy my invention, don't you?"

Larra couldn't speak. Never had she felt anything like this. It was as if two cocks filled her at once. Hot, flexible shafts that weren't too stiff or too soft. What magic did he possess to create this spell? Was this the same magic that caused his carriage to glide with unnatural smoothness?

"I can increase the size," he said, and suddenly both cylinders grew thicker. "Or I can increase the speed," both plunged to her with lightning thrusts. "Or both." Now they were thick and fast, causing her to gasp in delight as she clung to the bar above her head. If this was the evil witchcraft her maids had warned her about, she was more than happy to be subjected to something so delightfully wicked.

Toying with her response, he continued to change the tempo and dimensions of his device. Larra writhed. Waves of ecstasy washed over her until she drowned. Below her, the machine shifted, drawing her legs together. Behind her, another shaft slid between her clenched thighs. Thick and crisscrossed with veins, it rubbed lazily against her swollen clit. All three worked together, building in pace until she reached the peak of pleasure.

"He can never give you this." Unrelenting, he continued his

delicious torment until she came again and again. Finally, in a great thrust, he climaxed. He collapsed against her, balancing his weight on the machine as he recovered.

Lost in a haze of pleasure, replete with satisfaction, Larra was barely aware of him removing the device and releasing her. He then cradled her in his arms. She sensed movement upward then found herself nestled in her own bed.

Tenderly, he tucked her in. "You have pleased me greatly, Larra." With that, he placed a soft kiss to her forehead, and left before she could remove the silk and catch a glimpse of him.

6

Dauer surfaced as soon as night fell. He was in his room, in his bed, nude, and reeking of sex. Panicked, he fumbled to light the candle. A flicker of pale brightness revealed that Larra was not with him. He breathed a sigh of relief but lost his composure when he remembered how viciously the beast erupted when morning came.

What had he done to Larra?

His head throbbed as he tried to remember. The line between them had fragmented over the years, but he thought Larra would be able to resolve the fissure and draw the two separate halves together. However, they were now so far apart he had no recollection of what the beast had done.

A snatch of conversation surfaced, where he begged the beast not to break her, but he lost hold as soon as he grasped a thread. Frustrated, he shook his head, determined to remember but unable to do so.

Rather than binding his two separate halves, Larra seemed to be pushing them further apart. He had no idea why, but if things continued down this path, he would have to get rid of her.

His heart clutched painfully at the mere thought of her leaving. Last night went beyond his wildest expectations. Pliable, willing, adventurous—Larra was more than he could have hoped for, and far more than he'd ever dared ask for. A sweet completeness in her arms ensnared his mind, body, and soul.

He wanted her all for himself.

That the beast had touched her revolted him even though the original idea was that by sharing her they would realign. Now, jealousy and possessiveness turned him against himself. How could he protect her from a beast he had no control over?

Grabbing his cloak and gloves, he dressed then crossed the hall, cautiously opening her bedroom door. Low embers lined the fireplace, giving just enough light for him to see a lump in the bed. Holding his breath, he approached. After a painfully long moment, he saw a gentle rise and fall. Strands of dark hair tangled across her face and the pillow. In sleep, reposed, she had the aspect of an angel. So delicately ethereal, he hated to wake her. Her hand was up, and as he leaned close, he noticed a dark band around her wrist. A bruise.

Fury consumed him. Always he'd felt the anger in the beast, but he never thought he would actually injure Larra. Dauer rolled the covers down and found the same spicy scent of sex on her. He winced when he saw her chapped, red, and slightly bruised buttocks. The beast had a lust for spanking, but this was evidence of a beating.

Enraged, he vowed to destroy everything in the dungeon. He'd been vaguely aware of what the beast did there, but he'd thought it harmless, for who could he torture with his inventions? Now he'd found a target. Dauer had to protect her, but where could he send her? Not back to her sister. Perhaps he could send her to his stronghold in the east, but what if he sent her away and the beast only called her back?

With a sigh, Larra rolled over. Blinking, she wiped the sleep from her eyes. "Why didn't you tell me?"

At a loss for words, he sat on the edge of the bed and simply gazed at her from under the hood of his cloak. How could he explain?

She reached out and placed her hand on his thigh. "I don't mind that there are two of you. At first I thought you were moody, your attitude changed so fast, but last night, I realized the truth. What I don't understand is why you didn't tell me."

He realized she thought he and the beast were two separate people. Caressing her bruised wrist, he softly inquired, "Did he hurt you?"

"Yes and no." A smile laden with delicious secrets crossed her face, infuriating him more deeply than the thought of her being hurt. Had the beast given her greater pleasure than he had? She stretched, utterly oblivious to her naked body and the effect it had on him. "But why only one wife when you could have two?"

She wasn't terrified, she wasn't angry; she was simply curious. Baffled, Dauer struggled to find a plausible excuse. "If you saw him, you would understand why he couldn't find a woman of his own."

Considering, she sat up and winced a bit when she put weight on her bottom. "I didn't see him. However, I could feel him, how tragically deformed he is. You are very kind to share me with him."

Kind? Under his cloak his eyebrows rose. Just about the last thing he felt right now was kind. He alone was responsible for what had happened to her. It was his idea to find a wife to provide them with pleasure in the hopes it would restore their balance. Sadly, all he had done was splinter them further.

Larra utterly amazed him. His last wife hadn't even spent a few hours in his company before she flung herself from the tower. Heartbroken, wallowing in guilt, he vowed never to subject another woman to his curse.

Angry and cheated, the beast took up residence in the dungeon, crafting weird punishment devices to extract vengeance while Dauer channeled his drive into inventions that would ultimately benefit all mankind.

Cravings overwhelmed them both, compelling them to try again. Here, with Larra, they found a willing woman, but what would her reaction be when she discovered they were not two separate beings? Would she accuse him of witchcraft or some other such nonsense then kill herself rather than face another moment in his presence?

Trailing her hand up his thigh, she smiled when she found him hard. Coyly she whispered, "What a lusty pair you are." After a squeeze, she added, "However, I simply must eat if I'm going to survive so much vigorous activity." With that, she flung back the covers and climbed out of bed. Naked, she moved fluidly, without modesty or seduction.

Struck mute, Dauer remained on the bed while she poured water to wash up.

"Wait." He wanted to do something special for her. To show her without words how much he cherished her open spirit.

She hesitated, the moistened cloth held in her hands.

Within her rack of clothing, he found a robe and helped her slip it on.

"Follow me."

Giggling, she grasped his hand. "Are you going to let me eat and wash before you subject me to you hearty advances?"

"How would you like to do all three at the same time?"

Tilting her head, Larra smiled. "Do you have magic like he does?"

Challenged, Dauer confirmed, "My magic is stronger than his."

He guided her through the darkened hallways and up to the second-highest tower. When he pushed open the door, she emitted a delighted laugh.

"It's beautiful!"

The snow-covered glass dome above them glowed as moonlight glittered on the pure white crystals. All around them, the winter-hardy plants bloomed, reaching up majestically toward the gleaming ceiling. A waterfall of jagged marble anchored the center of the room, spilling down into a small pond.

Dauer had spent years designing his atrium, dragging bucket after bucket of dirt up the narrow steps. The beast thought the project silly, preferring instead his metallic creations in the dungeon, but this was the only place Dauer found solace. Here, even in winter, lush green plants and blooming vines greeted his world-weary eyes.

Larra skipped to the edge of the pond and tentatively draped her toe across the water. "It's warm." She slipped off her robe. He remembered part of the tale she'd told the beast in the carriage, about how all she wore was pale moonlight. Silver kissed Larra's slender limbs like a caress. Her hair cascaded over her shoulders, so dark it appeared black, but her eyes glowed bright.

Shyly, she turned to him. "Can I get in?"

"Of course."

Hunting for holds with her feet, she discovered he'd lined the bottom with smooth rocks that sloped toward the center. When the water was up to her midthigh, she plunged below, emerging a moment later, floating on her back.

She purred. "I am never again going to wash up with the basin."

He hadn't designed it with bathing in mind but discovered he, like her, preferred it to a wet cloth. "You are free to come here whenever you wish."

"That's if I remember how to get here." She rolled over to her belly, causing the moonlight to glide across her tortured buttocks. "Aren't you going to join me?"

"I am going to do as I promised." He went down to the kitchens. As usual, Morrow had several covered platters waiting for him. He filled one large plate. When he returned, Larra was in her own world. Splashing and singing, she reminded him of a water sprite. The smallest of comforts delighted her, causing Dauer to wonder how badly her sister had treated her.

When she saw him with the plate of food, she swam to the edge of the pond, wriggling against the bank like a hungry fish.

Playfully, he held out a bit of roast. Lifting herself up, she took it from his fingers with her mouth then settled back into the water. He repeated the motion, enjoying the way she wrapped her lips around his fingers to suck the tidbit inside. He fed himself too but found he wasn't as hungry for food as he'd thought. Simply watching her aroused him.

"Well, that takes care of two out of three." Her smile was pure seduction. "Now it's time for you to join me."

He shook his covered head. "I don't want you to see me."

She let out a disappointed sigh. "What is it with you two? I mean, with him it makes sense, but you—what are you hiding from?"

How could he explain that his face was just as terrifying as the beast's? No matter what form he was in, anyone who saw him went mad. The beast didn't terrify his last wife, he did. Frustrated by his refusal to remove his hood, she'd yanked it aside. When she had seen his face, she had gasped in wonder, in delight. Then she had looked further. Her mouth had fallen open. With a scream, she had run. Before he could catch her, she'd flung herself from the highest tower. Nevermore had he or anyone gone in there since that tragic day. Blood streaks marred the surface of the castle for months afterward, like a black mark on his soul.

"I've touched you and found only beauty." Larra's voice was softly plaintive, begging and becoming all at once.

That was the problem. His beauty blinded. So perfectly formed, so strongly etched, he was not simply handsome but exquisite. A dangerous godlike magnificence caused those who looked upon him to go insane. When the curse was fresh, he'd been trapped in a mirror, enraptured by his own reflection. Luckily, the beast eventually emerged, took one look at his misshapen head, and proceeded to smash the mirror. Ever since, he'd smashed every mirror he encountered.

Annoyed, Larra grabbed the tie from her robe and covered her eyes. "There. Now I can't see you." She tilted her head, listening. "Well? Get in. I promise I won't peek."

Hesitantly, Dauer removed his cloak and slid into the water.

When she reached for her blindfold, he grasped her hands, infuriated that she lied.

"I wasn't removing it, simply adjusting it."

He settled the fabric firmly over her eyes. "I ask one promise of you." Grasping her hands, he kissed each fingertip. "You must never try to see me or him."

Her brows lowered ominously. "You won't ever let me see either of you?" Resentment, devastation, exasperation—he couldn't describe the emotions that crossed her face.

"No." Teasing his fingertips across her lips, he tried to coax a smile, but she flicked her chin, drawing her face away from his touch. "Please understand how important this is to me." He refrained from grasping her shoulders and bellowing that his request was only to save her sanity.

"How can I go my whole life without ever seeing my husbands?"

Her melancholy voice surged guilt. How could he ask this of her? Overwhelmed, he wrapped her up in his arms. "I'm sorry. I truly am sorry. But I swear, this is the only promise I will ever ask of you."

She held stiffly away from him. "You want me to provide pleasure to you and another. You didn't ask; you simply did what you wanted."

"I should have asked. I'm sorry." He nuzzled her neck. "Do you wish to return to your rooms?"

"If I said yes, would you let me?"

"Yes." However, he didn't think she wanted to.

"I want some aspect of normalcy. I'm willing to be a wife to two husbands, but how can I only imagine you?"

"You don't have to imagine." He lifted her hands to his face. "Touch me, Larra. I'm real." Cupping his face, she traced all his features as if memorizing every aspect of his countenance. "What can I do to reassure you that I do not ask this of you lightly? My request is truly life or death."

She pondered for a long moment. "If I cannot see you directly, then may I see a painting of you?"

"There are none." Besides, they would show him as he was before the curse. Inspired, he kissed the tip of her nose and said, "Do you remember the statue in the foyer? That was cast from my image."

She shivered.

Unwilling to explain where they came from or why one changed the more one gazed upon it, he smothered any further questions by kissing her. "Promise?"

Reluctantly, she promised.

Mindful of her tender fanny, he wrapped his arms around her waist, floating her against him. Delicately, he slid her legs astride his hips, but he refused to enter her. Too afraid of hurting her since her encounter with the beast, he swore this night he would only hold her.

"Why do you tease me?"

"Aren't you sore?"

She didn't answer. With surprising agility, she grasped his shoulders and slipped his cock into her silky heat.

Exchanging a mutual sigh, they simply clung together in the water.

"Someday I will ask a favor of you." Larra crossed her arms over his back and rested her face against his chest.

"Consider it done." He paused then added, "As long as you ask for something within my power."

Her laugh rippled her passage along his shaft. "I will not ask for the moon."

"Ah, too bad, because that I can give you."

Bobbing in the water, Dauer allowed all his worries to wash away. As he held Larra, he knew what he had to do to protect her from the beast. Morrow would have to help, but he'd requested bizarre services from his butler before.

"I have never known two men who are so different."

"How so?"

"He is rough, demanding, and," she lowered her voice, "quite perverted." Kissing his chest, she said, "While you are gentle, sweet, and deliciously languid." She rolled her hips against his. "Tell me how two so dissimilar souls ended up together."

Hedging away from the topic, Dauer lowered his mouth to her ear and whispered, "I don't wish to speak of him while I have you in my arms." He kissed his way along her neck, nipping and biting her sensitive skin. Teasing his tongue across her collarbone, he eased her back, exposing her breasts to cool air and his hot, hungry mouth. When her nipples peaked, he sucked them, pulling harder when her whimpers urged him on. Involuntarily, his hips bucked.

Gasping, she flung her head back, trailing her hair in the water. Strands draped across her shoulders. Sucking warm water into his mouth, he gushed it back over her breasts, causing her hair to tickle along her sides. Giggling and groaning, she grasped his head, teasing her fingertips through his hair.

Angling her up, he withdrew and balanced her with his hands so she floated on her back. Rather than being upset by his pulling out, she had a look of curious expectation on her face. Pleased, he wanted to do everything in his power to bring her shattering ecstasy.

Lowering his lips to her luscious sex, he parted her folds with his tongue and flicked up the length. When he latched onto her quivering clit, she arched back, dunking her head underwater. Sputtering, she scrambled for a handhold. He floated her back to the edge, where she lifted her hands and clung to the side.

Urging her to the surface, he again lapped at her sex, gushing water over her clit until she squirmed. Circling the stiff flesh caused her to buck and breathe his name. Below the water, his cock throbbed in time to her contractions, and a primal need to mount her consumed him. The intensity of the desire was stunning. The beast sought only to satisfy himself, but that was not his way, and he wondered if she was melding them together after all.

She clamped her thighs around his head, digging her heels into his back. Sweet cream gushed over his lips, prompting him to lower her and impale her on his aching shaft. Hot, slick, she was so profoundly pleasurable he grasped her shoulders to force himself deeper. He tried to be gentle in light of her tender bottom, but he couldn't stop thrusting. Longing to hear her cries of pleasure, he grasped her waist to hold her steady for his brutal movements.

Tender words of encouragement turned to demands for more. Water sloshed around them, spilling beyond the banks of the pond. No matter how he dug his feet in, he couldn't plunge as hard as he wanted. Frustrated, he lifted her out of the water and sat her on the edge. Now he could move more vigorously, and he did. Mindless and animal, he forgot everything in his drive to climax.

Digging his fingers into her buttocks, headless of her startled sob, he poured his prick into her with ruthless abandon.

"I need," he gasped. "I need more, Larra. I don't mean to hurt you. Forgive me."

She struggled, but she wasn't trying to get away; she was attempting to pull him up onto the bank. As she crawled backward, he followed until they ended up on the soft moss.

"You're not hurting me." Larra wrapped her arms and legs around him. "Give me more."

Brutally, he battered his hips against hers. His toes dug divots into the moss and his knees crushed tender plants in his haste to reach his pleasure. Every muscle in his back and buttocks tensed as he rode her. Sweat trickled down his chest as he worked, but the pinnacle hovered just out of his reach.

He shook his head, trying to dislodge the truth from his mind, but he realized exactly what he was after. He wanted to wipe the memories of the beast from her. That secret smile when she mentioned his perverse behavior—his subconscious realized what his conscious just now understood. She wanted more than sweet lovemaking. Wicked, dirty, and ravenous sex excited her. It wasn't the beast spurring his actions but his own jealousy, his own competitive spirit.

A series of depraved scenarios filled his mind, and he whispered them to her ear. She writhed in response, adding her own lusty suggestions.

"I'm going to dangle straps from the ceiling and then use them to bind your arms and legs. That way I can do whatever I wish to your helpless body." He rolled onto his back, keeping her meshed with him. "I'll cover you with scented oils then tease you for endless nights until you beg me to fill you."

Balancing herself with her hands against his chest, she rolled her hips in intriguing circles. "But you'll refuse."

"Oh, I'll fill you all right." He pulled her against his chest and slid his hand between her cheeks. Pressing his finger against her rosebud, he said, "Here."

She tensed.

"Are you afraid?"

She nodded against his chest.

"But you see, you wouldn't have a choice. I can do anything to you, my sweet wife. Anything at all." He fumbled for the plate of food, found a bit of fat, and then smoothed it around her puckered hole. Now his finger slid easily inside. Her bottom sucked at his digit as if to pull it farther within while her cunny clenched his shaft. "Ride me, Larra."

She moved awkwardly. He had her turn around, so that she faced away from him. This way, he could tease her ass while she was sitting up, balancing her weight against his thighs. Her wet hair spilled down her back like ink, echoing the shape of her nipped in waist and flaring hips. Nestling down, she took his finger fully then caught her stride by moving back and forth, working herself into a frenzy.

He sat up until he maneuvered her to her knees. He slipped a second finger into her. Her panting was music to his ears.

"Tell me how much you want this."

"I do, I want you." She thrust back.

He shoved forward, his weight ramming his fingers deeper. He knew what he did was wrong. To use her so violently after the beast had done so went against everything he believed in, but he couldn't stop. Knowing it was wrong only added another layer of stimulation. Excitement mounted, lifting him higher until his breath was a harsh wind across her back. As he hit the peak, he shuddered, blinded by the intensity of his orgasm. Wave after wave of rapture caused him to pulse deep inside, filling her with his seed.

She would have collapsed if he hadn't wrapped his arm around her waist.

Breathless, he inquired, "Are you all right?"

"Yes." Her voice was weak.

He drew her into the water. Guilt consumed him as he

cleaned her delicate, limp body. His aggression had been too much for her. He'd always worried about a woman's sanity if she saw him, but what if they somehow fucked her to death? What woman could handle two such demanding lovers?

Lifting her out of the water, he dried her off, and then carried her to her bed. Rolling to her side, she fell instantly to sleep. He removed the blindfold, pulled the covers up, and vowed that she would suffer no more at his or the beast's hands.

7

Larra didn't know if it was morning or night. All she knew was that her body hurt in ways she had never experienced. Her breasts ached, her bottom was chapped, and both her passages were tender from Dauer's passionate thrusts. When she sat up, she winced and stood with all the grace of an elderly woman. She wasn't sorry for a bit of it. Who knew that she would find the men of her dreams within the strange walls of Hargarren Castle?

Beside the recently stoked fire, a small tray held a modest meal of roasted meat, bread, and a small tankard of ale. While she ate, she dressed, knowing that whatever she wore would not stay put for long. She wondered which lover would come to her first, and she grew wet at the prospect of taking them both at once.

"Overnight, I've become a lusty wench!"

When she left her room, she realized night was falling. How had she slept the day away? Snow swirled against the windows, forming odd shapes, some like melted faces peering in. Snow came early here to the mountains. Winter would not take hold in Relmon for another month or perhaps two, if they were lucky.

Severe angles jarred her sense of place, but she eventually found her way to the foyer. In the gloaming, she examined the statues that guarded the door. The one to the right of the entrance, the one of the man looking back over his shoulder, riveted her attention.

Every muscle in his back, buttocks, and legs was rigid, showing off coiled tension. She glanced around, ensured she was alone, and then tried to wedge her head between the statue and the wall so she could examine his privates. There wasn't enough space. Disappointed, she stepped back.

Dauer said it was of him, so she studied the perfect symmetry of his face. Sharp angles gave him a noble carriage, as if the world lay willingly at his feet. His chin broadened out below his mouth, and the subtle lift of his brows conveyed a compelling mix of power and compassion. His nose was straight, long, and nestled between stone eyes that were incredibly expressive, telling of a deep regret and profound sadness.

Tears sprang unbidden to her eyes, shocking her with their intensity. She wanted to wrap her arms around him and whisper that everything would be fine. Closing her eyes, she reached up and traced the face, feeling the truth that this was his likeness.

Then why would he not let her see him directly?

Regretting her promise, she still clung to her agreement. Once she gave her word, she would hold to it. She would have to content herself to gaze upon his stone image rather than his actual visage.

Puzzled, she moved on to the second statue. The sneer of contempt grew until a dark malevolence ensnared her soul. A scream stuck in her throat. The more she looked, the more misshapen his head became. One eye melted down to his cheek, the other bulged out. His mouth opened so wide she feared she would fall in.

A blast of cold air flung the entry door open, nipping her exposed skin and swirling snow against her bare feet. The shock was enough to draw her gaze away from the statue. Using all her might, she shoved the door closed, latching it securely.

Outside, the wind howled like the call of lonely wolves.

Shivering, not from the chill but from a deep-rooted apprehension, she practically ran from the foyer. At one point, she glanced over her shoulder, convinced the statues would be right behind her, ready to pounce and force her to submit, but she was alone in the hallway.

Clutching her hand to her pounding heart, she slowed her steps and uttered a dismissive laugh at her childish behavior. Still, her mind wondered over what she'd discovered, for if Dauer was the one on the right, the other had to be the beast.

She stopped midstride.

The two statues looked alike at first, but then the one on the left changed. Was the beast Dauer's brother? If so, what was his name? She vowed to ask, for she refused to continue calling him the demeaning title of "The Beast." Yes, she had been frightened but blamed her own overactive imagination, for when she'd been with him, she did not feel that depth of evil, not as she did in the foyer. He was brutal and rough, but only because she allowed him to be. Last night, Dauer himself had shown those same tendencies when she encouraged him.

All the stories she'd told of them rushed back, and she understood her own bizarre lust. She found tepid men dull. Her first lover had been courtly and kind, kissing her hand a hundred times before he'd ever dared to kiss her lips. Even then, he held his passion back as if she were spun glass that would shatter from a stronger embrace.

After seemingly endless years of courting, his slender penis had entered her with barely a sting of pain. When she told Dauer it was nice, that was all she could really say. It wasn't painful but it hadn't engaged all her senses, not like her encounters with her two strangely different but oddly similar husbands. When her intended died in battle, she'd cried for his loss, cried for his family, but she hadn't shed a tear for her loss because she had never loved him. Sweet, kind, and gentle, he would have been a solid husband but not a thrilling lover.

Wandering the castle, Larra made her way to the dining room but found the candles cold and the table empty.

"Can I serve you?"

Jumping, Larra turned to find the butler. "Morrow?"

He bowed deeply.

"Where is Dauer?"

"He sends his regards."

When she questioned him, he refused to elaborate. When he offered her supper, she declined. Lonely, she examined more of the castle and spent the evening in the music room. She'd never had the patience to learn how to play an instrument as a proper young lady should, but perhaps now was the time. Quickly she grew bored but continued to make noise in the hopes one of her husbands would show.

They didn't.

Eventually she went to bed. All night she waited for the door to open and one of them to slip into her bed. Debating incessantly over which she would prefer, she fell asleep undecided.

She slept alone.

Endless days and nights drifted past without a word from either of her husbands. None of the servants would tell her anything. They fed her, stoked the fire in her room, brought her whatever she requested, but remained closemouthed.

Convinced she had offended Dauer or his brother in some mysterious way, she spent her time trying on all her dresses, her jewels, and teasing her hair into elaborate styles, using the windows to check her image, for she could not locate one mirror in the entire castle. However, she took no pleasure in such things and realized her appearance probably didn't matter.

During this time, she noticed other odd things about her new home. Of all the paintings, not a one included people. No proud displays of ancestors dotted the walls but only bucolic settings.

Anger finally gripped her as firmly as snow gripped the land around her. Determined to find a way to occupy her time, she covered herself in thick furs and went out into the courtyard off the dining room. White crystals covered long-dead gardens, sculpting them into elaborately beautiful shapes.

Inspired, she found huge basins that she filled with water then allowed to freeze overnight. Servants would pop the ice from them so she could carve the blocks with whatever tools she could find. After a week of frustrated efforts, Morrow gave her a set of carving tools wrapped in red velvet.

"A gift from your husband." He executed a perfect bow, placed the bundle into her frozen hands, and then whirled away before she could ask any questions.

With better tools, what she saw in her mind's eyes came to life. She carved Dauer in repose, his beautiful body reclined, his cock hard and ready for her. Also, she sculpted his misshapen brother, but with his face turned away, his malformed body aligned so that he was as normal as she could make him. Always she tried to show them as they were; sensual, unusual, unique, and utterly male.

Larra didn't care what the servants thought, for she created what came from her heart. The more she slaved over her cold creations, the more she became enchanted with them. Hot spikes of desire consumed her when she crafted her husbands in ice. She remembered hearing a tale about a man who fell in love with a statue he created, and she fancied herself in love with her own works. But in truth, she simply missed them. Never in her life had she spent so much time alone.

Wintry nights marched past as she kept a lonely vigil in her bed. In her dreams, she found release. Each man took a stance in front or behind her and then teased himself against her until her body dissolved into pleasure. Two thick cocks filled her passages until her body succumbed to shattering orgasms. Night after night, she envisioned the statues coming to life and performing wicked acts that had her howling stronger than the wind.

A pathetic cry of endless torment awoke her afternoon slumber. Without company, she'd become a creature of the night, preferring to wander the hallways and gardens alone rather than suffer the sympathetic glances of the silent staff.

Flinging back the covers, she fumbled for her robe, secured it around her silk chemise, and then entered the hallway. Silence greeted her ears. Convinced it was only a part of her dream, she turned back to her room. A wail of torment stood the hairs on the back of her neck on end.

Cautiously, she followed the sound down, down, down until she found the hidden door to the dungeon. When she pushed the metal door open, it creaked horribly.

"Let me loose, you bastard!"

Larra entered and found Dauer's brother strapped to a table.

A thick cloak covered him, but his pale and gnarled hands fought against iron manacles. His hands were so hideous she wanted to run, to shield her eyes, but his cry compelled her forward.

"Who has done this to you?" She rushed to his side, fumbling at the restraints.

"Larra?"

"Who has done this to you?" she asked again. Struggling with the chains, she realized padlocks bound him. Without a key, she could do nothing. "I can't free you without the key."

"Find Morrow, he has it."

Baffled, she asked, "Why would he restrain you?"

"Because Dauer told him to!"

Flinching back at his tone, Larra turned and ran back up the steps. When she found Morrow, he only bowed politely. When she demanded the key, he refused, saying that he followed his master's orders. With that, he refused to say any more.

Defeated, she returned to the dungeon.

Screaming and bellowing, the beast railed to no avail.

"Calm yourself." Larra pressed her hand to his chest. "I will find another way to free you." She searched through the room but found everything in disarray. Even the machine he'd used to restrain her was bashed and mangled. "What happened in here?"

"Dauer destroyed everything."

And now she thought she understood. Dauer had been furious that his brother harmed her, so this was his punishment.

"Will you tell me your name?"

He hesitated, and then said, "Bauer."

"Dauer and Bauer. So you are brothers."

"Of a sort. Will you stop asking me questions and find a way to free me?"

His demanding tone annoyed her. "I would think you would speak more kindly to me when I am the one who could free you."

The only answer he gave was a frustrated growl.

Everything she tried failed, and he grew more agitated.

"Go and use your charms on Morrow. Toss him a good suck, and he'll gladly give you the key."

His vulgarity rankled. Did he honestly think that was all she was good for—tossing a man a good suck or a randy fuck?

Smartly she said, "Perhaps I will. I'm sure Morrow can entertain me far better than you can. I'll just leave you to your punishment." She swirled away.

At the door, he called out to her. "Wait! Larra, please don't go."

"Apologize."

He hesitated for a moment then mumbled, "I'm sorry."

Deciding that was all she was likely to get out of him, she returned to his side. "Is there anything I can do?"

"I can smell you." He took a deep breath. "I can smell your sweet cunny."

Right back to vulgar, but his rough voice turned her instantly wet. Defensively, she drew her robe more firmly around herself.

"I can smell your reaction, Larra. He hasn't come to you either, has he?"

"No. Where is he?"

"Oh, he's around. Closer than you think."

Were they only playing a new game with her? She held very still, listening, for even the tiniest sound would echo in the room. All she heard was Bauer's deep breathing. When she glanced at him, his cock rose up like a leviathan from the deep, pushing against the fabric of his cloak.

"How the tables have turned." She teased her hand over the heavy bulge. Now she had a chance to see him, and he could do nothing but protest. "Maybe I'll just open your cloak and—"

"No!" He twisted so violently she jumped back. "Please don't, Larra." Misery laced his voice. "I couldn't bear for you to see what I am."

Touched, she soothed him with her tone and a caress to his shoulder. "I won't." She placed the tie from her robe over her eyes. "Here." She leaned down so he could feel the blindfold.

He relaxed when he realized she was not going to look at him but then tensed when he asked, "Are you going to get me back for what I did to you?"

Clearly, she heard the trepidation in his tone. A surge of power infused her when she realized she could do anything to him. Anything at all. Rather than calm his fears, she remained silent.

"Larra?"

She pushed his hood back, stroked her finger along the slick heat between her legs, and then rubbed her scent across his lips.

"Ambrosia." Snaking his tongue out, he sucked the juice from her finger with a hearty growl. "I want you to kneel right over my face."

Laughing, she removed her robe and her silk chemise. Tossing the robe on the floor, she flung the silk over his legs then clambered up onto the table. Below her, he shifted as if to grab her, but he couldn't. Power and pleasure combined, causing her to sweat despite the damp air. She knelt backward over him, as if to do as he asked and lower herself to his face. She held herself just out of reach. His frustrated snarl caused her only to gush and long to torment him further.

Lifting his cloak exposed his spicy scent. When she leaned over to take a deep breath, he thrust his hips. She took her chemise and wrapped it around his cock.

"This is what I feel like inside, like sweet hot silk." She tightened the fabric until it created a snug sheath around him. Gracefully, she moved her hands up and down, heating the fabric and creating gentle friction.

Mad with desire, he rocked his hips, sliding his shaft within the fabric and her hands. When she lowered her mouth and breathed out against the silk-covered tip, a low animal moan rumbled his chest. Her breasts swelled with want, and her nipples thrust against the rough fabric of his cloak.

He pleaded with her to lower herself onto his face, but she held back despite how he strained and begged. When she sensed he was on the verge of climax, she settled lower, allowing him to lap at her dripping sex.

Roughly textured, broad and flat, so agile was his tongue she lost her breath. Plunging his tongue deep within her then twisting it had her writhing atop him within moments. She ground against him, mashing her clit against his chin. She tried to imagine what they looked like and the vision pleased her. Her wanton atop the bound beast, her using him for her needs while ministering to his. Her hands worked faster against his throbbing cock until she imagined the pale blue silk was only a blur.

He came in such a burst he pushed through the fabric, spattering against her lips. So wonderfully wicked did she find his flavor, she released her own climax to him, which he happily swallowed, encouraging her to give him more until she collapsed on his chest.

This was better than her dreams. She must find Dauer and tell him that his brother had not hurt her, that she wanted them both. He owed her a favor, and now she had something to ask for. She wanted them in her bed at the same time, four hands to tease her and please her, one mouth at her sex, one at her bottom, both feverish to bring her to climax.

When she started to move away, he begged, "Don't go. Stay with me for a moment."

She turned and rested her head against his chest.

"Why is it you alone don't find me repulsive?"

Below her cheek, his heart made a lazy *lub-dub*. "Because you are only a man, not a monster."

"I have done monstrous things, but with you, I feel almost human."

If he could have wrapped his arms around her, she knew he would have. Her acceptance of him softened his soul and opened his heart.

"What have you done?" she asked.

He didn't answer and she didn't push. She might be better off not knowing.

"Why will you not let me see you?"

"Despite what you say, I am a monster. None can look upon me without screaming."

Her reaction to seeing just his hands had her reconsidering her desire to see him fully. "I would not scream, for I know the man inside."

"You must swear that you will never look at me, Larra. Please. It is all I will ask of you."

She nodded against his chest, puzzled, for Dauer had said almost the exact same words. Determined to extract a payment in kind she said, "I will do this for you if you promise to do something for me."

"Anything. Just ask."

"I will tell you soon enough." She lay beside him on the table for quite a long time.

"You should go now."

Reluctantly she climbed off, covered him carefully with his cloak, and then removed her blindfold. She hated leaving him bound, but she promised to get the key from Morrow. She slipped her robe on and grabbed the sticky silk chemise.

Bauer seemed anxious for her to go. Did he fear Dauer was coming and would punish him more if he found her here? Protectiveness stole over her. She was not going to let them fight over her. Brothers should be best friends, not enemies, not at eternal crossroads the way she was with her sister.

"Go, Larra. See if you can find Morrow."

The tone of his voice struck her strange. He was beyond desperate for her to go, and she didn't think obtaining his freedom had anything to do with it. She opened the door, squealing the metal against metal, but did not pass through. She closed the door only to make him think she had.

Hesitating in the doorway, she witnessed Bauer's chest roil, as if waves washed through his flesh. Pressing her lips together to hold back her screams, she watched his gnarled hands smooth, elongate, and turn a light burnished copper. Perfect hands with highly buffed fingernails extended beyond the gray sleeves. Her hand flew to her mouth but not fast enough to stifle her gasp. In that moment, she realized there were not two brothers, but one man with two faces.

Larra had taken two steps toward him when a strong arm wrapped around her waist and a massive hand cupped over her mouth. Pressed into the body of an unknown man, a stench of foul sweat enveloped her. She gagged and tried to scream, but his gore-flecked fist allowed her only to utter a high-pitched keening.

"Larra?"

Dauer's voice sounded terribly far away. He continued calling her name, his tone more confused and strident as someone yanked her up the stairs. The brute held her firmly to his chest so all she could see was a green sleeve with red accents, but she felt the hilt of a dagger digging into her back as his ale-breath washed over her neck.

When she struggled, he shook her so hard her head snapped back into a metal plate on his shoulder. Her vision slid sideways. Before she lost consciousness, she saw Morrow crumpled in the upper hallway.

8

_____

Dauer called out repeatedly for Larra. Shuffling footsteps were his only answer. Who had taken her away? Had one of his guards decided to save her from him? He felt more fear than anger.

Struggling against his bonds, he bellowed for Morrow. True panic settled in when he realized without the key, he would die strapped to a table. Was this his ultimate punishment? To perish alone, slowly, tormented by all he'd done in his past and what he'd done to Larra. Her beautiful brown-green eyes were curious, open, and so eager to embrace her new station despite his restrictions and demands. She gave her body to him and the beast with a willingness that touched them both. Astounding how such a simple act could have such a profound impact on his soul. He'd tried to stop taking advantage of her by binding himself as the beast, but still, he'd used her for his own ends. No man of God could absolve him of his sins.

He truly didn't care if he died, for he deserved to die, but he could not bear to allow Larra to be hurt. Where a part of him wanted to give up and suffer what he deserved, a stronger part demanded he rise up, face this problem, and restore Larra to her proper place. He wanted to keep her here but knew it was wrong. If he found a way to rescue her, he had to give her up.

Torn between self-pity and a desperate need to rescue Larra, he scrabbled at the manacles even though he knew they would not release. His thoroughness to contain the beast now worked against him. Drawing deep breaths, he forced himself to calm. Above him was a wooden ceiling that formed the floor for a storage room. All around him were stone walls buried deep into the ground. Craning his head backward, he saw the metal door was open. Rather than wasting his voice calling out, he grasped the metal chain from the manacle and banged it rhythmically against a metal strap on the table.

Hours passed and his hand cramped, but still he bashed away, hoping someone would hear him, if anyone was alive. He stopped for a moment, listening. Dead silence shivered his spine. Dauer didn't mind dying for his sins, but he would be damned a thousand times before he would let anyone harm Larra.

Within his flesh and his mind, he felt the beast surface, berating him for his foolishness in binding them to the table. They argued the point until both stopped in sudden realization; they were both fully, consciously aware of the other for the first time since they married Larra. Not only were they aware, but also they were able to converse without the shimmering wall that usually separated them. A profound relief washed through them both, for they thought Larra was only fragmenting them, when in fact, she had restored them. Jealousy had held them apart. Now that they both faced the prospect of losing her, they merged, willing to work together to save her.

Dauer started to bang the chains again. When he grew tired, the beast pushed him to continue. He had no idea what time it was when Morrow stumbled into the room. Holding a hand to his bloody head, he fumbled for the key.

9

Larra woke but didn't open her eyes. She had no idea where she was or who had abducted her, but she didn't want to alert her captors that she was awake. Below, a velvet couch cushioned her body, and above, a dusty fur tickled her nose. She gritted her teeth not to sneeze. Her hands were not bound, nor her feet, but why would they bother when all she wore was a robe? If she ran into the night, she would freeze to death. In the air around her, she smelled wood smoke, dust, stale cooking odors, and the smallest whiff of a floral perfume. If she had not spent so much time blindfolded, she would have missed it. Once she smelled that scent, she knew exactly who her abductor was.

"I know you're not asleep." Andace's voice came from across the room, near the crackling fire.

Larra sat up and blinked at her sister. A bloodred dress crushed in her waist and lifted her breasts. The bodice plunged deeply between her alabaster mounds while the skirt flared around her hips then spilled to the floor. Orange flames danced across her features, distorting her eyes into the unblinking glare of a predator. Midnight black hair fluffed coquettishly around her heart-shaped face in direct conflict with her smirk of contempt.

Andace was beautiful—of that, there was no doubt—but she possessed a cold, hard beauty, like a gemstone. Glittery and stunning as a diamond, Andace sparkled but had no warmth. At times, Larra was convinced she had no soul.

"All he could afford was a robe?" Indigo blue eyes raked her from head to toe. "Or is that how he kept you; barefoot and scantily clothed?"

Still smarting from her shocking discovery about Dauer, Larra refused to discuss him with Andace. "What do you want?" Larra stood with the grace of a queen. Suddenly she did not fear her sister. A childhood of torments faded away. Head high, she considered the food on the table near the fire.

"So you tamed the beast."

Larra deliberately turned her back and sampled the array of treats. One bite of the roast caused her belly to rumble. She wasn't sure how long she'd gone without eating. A sudden flash of Morrow crumpled in the upper hallway caused her almost to choke. Dauer was strapped down, utterly vulnerable. What had her sister done to him?

"If he would have killed you, it would have made this so much easier."

When Larra turned, Andace was considering her scarlet nails with studied disdain.

"You wanted Dauer to kill me?" Her sister had never liked her, but she didn't want to believe her hatred ran so deep.

"Of course." Andace rolled her eyes, tossing her hair back. "Then I would have the perfect excuse to avenge your tragic death by taking over his lands." Clapping her hands together, she lifted them in an expansive shrug. "With you still alive, I'll have to improvise."

Larra desperately wanted to ask after Dauer but didn't dare.

If her sister knew she'd developed feelings for him, she would do something cruel and vicious. Calmly, Larra asked, "What do you want with Dauer's lands? You already have all of Relmon."

"Honestly, you are an idiot and far more stupid than Father's jester. Your puny share of Relmon was never my goal." Andace snapped her fingers. A nude woman entered, her head craned so low her blond hair covered her face. Her breasts were large and firm, the nipples capped with rosy points. In her hand, she carried the end of golden chain affixed to a collar around her neck.

Andace snapped her fingers once and pointed at the floor beside her feet. Obediently, the woman knelt beside her and handed Andace the end of her leash. Fondly, Andace traced her fingers through the woman's thick honey-blond tresses. There was something familiar about the woman, but Larra couldn't put her finger on exactly what.

"Didn't you ever wonder how I knew your deepest thoughts, how I always managed to tease you about the things that mattered to you the most?" She chuckled. "Did you think I had magical powers like one of your pathetic story creatures?"

Larra *had* thought Andace possessed some unnatural ability, for she knew just how to wound her the deepest, but she said, "I assumed brutality came naturally to you."

One edge of her mouth curled up. "And stupidity to you." With a sudden jerk, Andace pulled the woman's hair back, exposing the face of Larra's most trusted maid.

Larra felt her eyes widen with shock. "What have you done to her?" The normally chatty, vivacious Keale trembled and kept her eyes downcast.

"Get up." Andace yanked on the leash, causing Keale to rise. "Now tell Larra the truth."

Keale kept her face low but rolled her eyes up. A viciously cruel smile crossed her rose petal lips. "I was never your friend. Every secret you told me, I told to my mistress."

Devastated, Larra struggled to keep her composure. Keale had been her closest companion since Larra was seven years old, but she was determined not to let Andace know how deeply she had hurt her. Andace would only rejoice.

"I should have been born a man." Andace fondled Keale's nipples. "If I were a man, none would question my blood-thirsty ways." With one vicious movement, she twisted Keale's nipple until Keale moaned low in her chest. "They would revere me and give me a powerful name to match my conquests. As a woman, I have to suffer name calling of a different sort."

Larra was shocked that Keale stood there enduring Andace's harsh treatment with no shame that another witnessed her submission. In fact, both of them seemed to enjoy having an audience. When Larra looked away, Andace twisted Keale's nipples until Keale screamed.

"Stop!" Larra took one step forward, as if to rescue Keale.

Andace laughed. "She enjoys this. Show her the truth."

"Yes, mistress." Keale squatted down, parted her thighs, slipped her hand between her legs, and then lifted her slick fingers for inspection.

"She likes pain." Andace shoved her down so hard Keale's knees cracked against the wooden floor.

A flush of embarrassment washed across Larra's cheeks when she thought of the pleasure-pain the beast bestowed on her. The beast that she now knew was actually Dauer himself. Was she so different from Keale? She decided that she was, because Dauer never attempted to control her in any other way. Clearly, there was far more between Andace and Keale than bedroom games.

Eyes glittering, Andace noticed her reaction. "That's why he didn't kill you." She laughed long and loud.

Larra thought she would melt through the floor.

"How your mother would die of shame if she weren't already dead. Her perfect daughter is a pain slut. Had I known, I would have made you my slave."

Genuinely shocked, Larra recoiled. "You're my sister."

"By marriage."

Larra's widowed mother and Andace's widowed father married when they were still young girls. Larra had been thrilled to have an older sister, but her joy had quickly faded when Andace resented her on sight. No matter what Larra did, Andace rejected her. Still, the thought of having any kind of relationship like that with her, sister or not, was nauseating.

"Oh, calm yourself. Keale told me you showed no interest in women."

Keale lifted her head a fraction to peer up and blow a kiss in Larra's direction. All the times Keale crawled into her bed on the pretext of comforting her now took on a decidedly sinister air. Suddenly cold, Larra wrapped her arms around herself. One way or another, she had to get out of here and make her way back to Hargarren Castle.

Intent on finding something to wear in what she thought was the back bedroom, Larra brushed dismissively past Andace, who grabbed her hair and yanked her back.

"Where do you think you're going?"

Straightening herself, rubbing at her smarting scalp, Larra said, "To get dressed." She wanted to turn and hit Andace as hard as she could, but Andace had always been bigger, stronger, and so mean that Larra didn't dare.

Only once had she struck out at her sister. Shortly after Andace had come to Relmon, she had accidentally ruined a small painting of Larra's deceased father. Heartbroken, Larra's mother convinced her to forgive, which she did, but then Andace continued to ruin everything that her father had left to her. All by accident, Andace would say, with a barely perceptible smirk on her face. Determined to protect her things, Larra had hidden them away, but Andace found them and destroyed them all, that time without apology. That time, she stood over the broken items with a smile of triumph, twirling a broken doll in her hand. A haze of fury had overcome Larra, and she had charged, knocking her sister flat, but Andace had expected the attack and beat Larra so severely she was bed-bound for many days. After that, Larra avoided her new sister as much as possible. Anything of sentimental value she had, Andace would destroy, so Larra never took a fancy to anything of value. She had no keepsakes of either her mother or her father, but she decided it didn't matter, because she had their memories locked in a place Andace couldn't reach. One thing she had that Andace didn't was patience. The right time to flee would present itself, and Larra was determined to be ready.

Andace nodded to Keale who scampered away then returned with an armload of cloth, which she threw at Larra's feet.

"Wear this," Andace said, toeing the pile.

Larra pulled the item up and discovered her moss green dress—the one that Keale said the laundress had destroyed. She didn't want to even speculate why Keale and Andace would want one of her dresses.

"I'll need some kind of underclothes."

"Think of the salacious tales that you were found tossed from the tower without any." Andace arched her brows suggestively. "Now hurry." Andace clapped her hands, but Larra deliberately slowed her pace as she turned to remove her robe.

Snickering, Andace mocked, "I'm not interested in watching you, not with your pale skinny body."

"Dauer seems to like my figure just fine."

"It's hardly a tribute to your allure that the beast of Hargarren wants to mount you," Andace said snidely.

Over her shoulder, Larra said, "You're the beast, not him."

A brief spark of fury crossed Andace's face, but she lifted her chin. "I may be a beast, but I get what I want."

Not this time, Larra thought. Chained, Dauer couldn't possibly come after her. All she had to do was wait for Andace and Keale to fall asleep, and then she could escape. She didn't know where she was, but it didn't really matter. Follow any road long enough and it would lead her somewhere. Eventually, it would lead her back to Dauer.

When she finished dressing, she turned.

"What is that little smile on your face about?"

Indigo eyes missed nothing. Whatever joy Larra had felt slid away when Andace stepped close, looming over her.

"Tell me."

"I don't know anything."

Andace shoved her back. Larra hit the floor with a dull thud. Andace climbed onto her chest, wrapped her hands around her throat, and squeezed. "You either tell me what you're hiding, or I'll kill you now."

10

After a heated debate, Dauer put his best man in charge of the castle then left through the tunnels. If he rode out with his fastest horse and all his men, his home would be vulnerable to attack. Whoever had invaded took only one thing: Larra. Which could mean only one thing: They expected him to follow to get her back. He hadn't lived a thousand years without learning to trust his gut, and his gut told him someone deliberately choreographed this event.

Dauer emerged from the tunnels in the low-lying farmlands. In a paddock, he found a sturdy horse, mounted, then made his way into the forest. Pale moonlight glistened on snow as his horse crunched a path through icicle-decorated trees. He paced the main road so as not to disturb the recent hoofprints. If someone sought to follow him, they would not find him merrily prancing down the main path.

No one is following us. I would smell them.

Dauer heard the beast clearly in his mind for the first time in decades. When he took a deep sniff a hundred scents assaulted him—his horse, the trees, the very smell of snow. He lifted a hand to his face and touched his own nose, but it had the power of the beast's nose.

Stop calling me that. Larra calls me Bauer.

Dauer refused to argue with himself in his own mind. All he could think of was Larra's gasp of shock when she witnessed the transformation. A sudden scent of her fear and shock invaded his memory. He blamed the beast and shook his head, trying to rid himself of it.

The only way we'll find her is if we work together.

Furious, he accused Bauer of hurting Larra and only wanting her back to harm her again.

I overreacted. She forgave me. I won't do it again.

Dauer pushed his hood back to get a better view of the road.

Stop. Bauer commandeered his nose, sniffing wildly. *She didn't go that way. Go back.*

Dauer continued to pace the main road despite Bauer's commands. They argued briefly and struggled for control of their body.

If you want to save her, we must go back!

With that, Bauer wrested control and turned their mount around.

"She doesn't love you. She'll never love you." Why Dauer said this he didn't know. Perhaps to remind himself that such a thing would never be, not for either of them. Larra would never feel for him what he felt for her, not after witnessing his transformation. No woman could love a man such as he.

Stop your whining. She's no fragile child. I smelled her fear, her shock, but also her curiosity. Larra is smarter, and for that matter, stronger than you will ever know.

"Don't lecture me—"

Wait, I have her scent. Bauer urged the horse across the road. Dauer peered down at the smooth snow-covered trail.

"It hasn't been used for months."

Her scent is here.

Bauer twitched their nose and now Dauer could smell Larra too. As they edged the pathway, sudden tracks sprang up.

"They went to a lot of trouble to hide the proof of their passage."

I can smell Larra, her sister Andace, and . . ."

He trailed off, sniffing, and Dauer opened his senses. He discovered an odd scent that was both male and female.

It's either a man in women's clothing or a woman in a man's clothing. Either way, that person is extremely agitated.

Having a disturbed person in charge of Larra broke something inside them both. For the first time in decades, Dauer didn't feel alone. Larra lit up his world with her presence. He had to get her back.

You're just all warm and sweet because of the sex.

"Is that all it is for you?"

Bauer considered for a moment. *No. There is something special about Larra. She made me feel almost human.*

"You are human."

You know what I mean.

Dauer did indeed understand. He didn't feel so much like a freak anymore. For the first time since the curse, he felt that he might actually be worthy of love. A part of him cringed away in genuine fear. Love could be dangerous, deadly even.

Love is what got us into this mess.

"No. Our love wasn't strong enough to overcome our lust. That's what got us into this mess."

They rode in silence, contemplating their punishment. The tracks were easy to follow as they led deeper into the shadow-thick forest. Trees crowded together so densely that barely any moonlight slipped through. Since his eyes were better, Bauer pulled back so Dauer could commandeer their sight.

Despite his fears that Larra had driven a permanent wedge

between them, she'd actually integrated them beyond his wildest expectations. True, he was in Dauer form, but Bauer could use his senses without struggle. They no longer simply occupied the same body, but they were able to share the same form. He couldn't believe he'd been contemplating sending her away. She had been gone for only a few hours, and already he missed her tremendously.

Dauer ignored the cold nipping at his fingertips and toes with Bauer's help. If Andace had harmed one hair on Larra's head, he would skin her alive.

I can think of worse.

Dauer could too but deliberately turned his mind away from such thoughts. If Andace wanted to kill Larra, she would have done so. She wouldn't have had her kidnapped. Andace wanted something, and once he found out what it was, he would kill her.

Slowly, painfully, with a lot of blood and screaming.

"I hardly think Larra will appreciate us torturing her sister."

Depends what she's done to her.

As he continued down the path that would take him to Larra, he wondered if she would forgive him for his lies, and if she could, perhaps not love him, but at least like him just a bit. Just enough to stay with him.

When the clouds rolled over him like a giant gray blanket, he pushed back his hood to better see the trail. When the wind picked up and flurries of snow pushed their icy fingers into his open cloak, he pulled it tighter. When the snow fell, swirling in the wind, blinding his eyes, he pulled the hood over his head and navigated by Bauer's nose. When the horse could no longer carry his weight, he climbed off and led the poor beast.

Leave it for the wolves.

"Is that how you would repay a creature who helped us? I thought Larra made you feel human?"

Neither he nor Bauer spoke for a long time.

Just when he thought he could not go on, Larra's scent intensified. So sweet and compelling, her essence washed away his exhaustion and dread, infusing his form with energy.

A horse, over there.

Bauer pointed their mount in the direction of the open paddock, whapped his butt, then gave him a gentle shove. With a whinny of appreciation, the horse moved off while Dauer strode toward the windowless cabin.

Larra, her sister, and another woman are within.

"Let's not stand on ceremony." Dauer pushed the door open. The scene before him was so shocking he stood immobile.

Larra lay on her back on the floor. Andace straddled her chest with her hands wrapped around Larra's throat while Larra flailed ineffectively, trying to push Andace off. His entrance caused Andace to glance up and relax her hold on Larra.

"Dauer!" Despite her surprise and a nasty burst of fear scent, Andace only redoubled her efforts to throttle Larra, who stopped struggling.

Bauer reacted on gut instinct. He lunged toward them, wrenching Andace's hands away. Screeching with fury, she tried to scratch his face but managed only to flip back his hood, exposing his face.

When Andace looked right into his eyes, her eyes bulged and her mouth quivered. "You're not a beast, you're beautiful!" She shook her head as if to rid his vision from her mind, but she couldn't look away. "Too beautiful." Her face roiled as her mouth opened wide. A scream of horror erupted as she lifted her hands in a desperate bid to stop looking at him. When that didn't work, she clawed at her own eyes.

Gibbering, she slid off Larra and crawled into a corner.

He barely got the hood over his face before Larra regained consciousness.

"Dauer?" Her voice was raspy, and she winced after she spoke.

"I'm here." He pulled her into his arms. Having her back in his embrace gave him a sense of homecoming. Fear shattered his tranquility because she could leave him at any time. This thought compelled him to hold her tighter. "Forgive me. I should have told you."

She shook her head and struggled to sit up. Letting her go caused a flash of burning tears to blur his vision. For once, he thanked his hood for hiding his face. At least he wouldn't suffer the indignity of having her watch him cry. Mercifully, Bauer remained silent.

Larra struggled to her feet then staggered to a table before the fire. She grabbed a cup and drank greedily. Wincing, she touched her throat. Dark finger-shaped bruises bloomed across her milky skin. When she darted her gaze around, she discovered Andace mumbling in the corner.

"What happened?"

Dauer stood, brushing the dust off his cloak. "She saw my face."

Larra nodded thoughtfully, a frown of concern darting across her features. He could practically read her mind. If that was what looking at him would do, why would she want to be anywhere near him?

When her eyes went wide, he whirled around. A nude blond woman hefted a dagger in her fist. She lunged toward him. He stepped aside, grasped her wrist, and deftly twisted her arm behind her back. She dropped the blade but continued to struggle.

Larra stepped forward and slapped the woman hard across the face. "I won't tolerate any more of either of you." She took a deep breath and pushed past the pain of her tortured voice. "Stop, or I'll put you both outside."

As if in warning, a howl sounded against the door, pushing a puff of snow through the bottom crack. All the fight drained out of the woman, so he let her go. She went to Andace and tended to her wounded face.

Before he could stop him, Bauer said, "You can't seriously expect me to let them live."

Larra tossed the naked woman a blanket from the couch. "I do."

"But they tried to kill you."

"And you stopped them." Larra gave the two women a sad shake of her head. "Whatever you did has rendered Andace harmless."

"Just because a sword lays idle doesn't mean it's harmless," Dauer countered.

"No matter how evil Andace is, she is still my sister." Larra spoke with finality.

When Bauer sought to argue further, Dauer held him back with great effort, reminding him that Larra would not condone the death of anyone, no matter what crime they committed.

Because she's a woman, and women are too soft to do what is necessary.

"Killing Andace will solve nothing and only further alienate Larra." Dauer mumbled so Larra would not hear.

"I must return to Relmon," Larra said, her voice tight, her shoulders forcefully thrust back. "There is none left but me to lead my people."

Her words were as stones dropped into his belly. Logically, he knew she could not leave her lands without guidance. He could do no less himself. Even now, his men waited anxiously for his return. Dauer had thought he would ride through his gates, triumphant, with Larra riding pillion before him. Once the congratulations were over, he would take her to his room and lose himself in sensual bliss. Later he would have Larra compose the story of his heroic rescue, with a few embellishments, and tell it to everyone so it would spread across the land, replacing the dark tales of him with something daring and grand . . .

Now, he would return alone, lonely, tell his men he saved Larra only to have to let her go. After their commiserations, he would go to his rooms and lose himself in sleep, where in his dreams he could hold Larra close. There, she could look right into his eyes and tell him how much she loved him. It would be only a dream, but it was better than what he had now, which was nothing. What broke his heart more than anything was that she had not even bothered to ask for an explanation about his transformation. Perhaps such information wouldn't matter. She saw her opportunity to escape him and welcomed it with open arms. What woman in her right mind would want to stay with a man such as he? A man she could never look at. A man who would outlive her. A man who couldn't even father her children.

"Once the storm breaks, we will set off for Relmon." Larra added a log to the fire. She kept her attention on the dancing flames, almost as if she couldn't bear to look at him.

He considered the two women still huddled in the corner. "Do you wish for me to bind them?"

Larra shook her head. "They will cause us no more trouble."

"I will check the horses so that we can be ready." He exited the snug cabin. Biting cold was a welcomed diversion. He clomped his way through thick drifts of snow. Inside the stable, his horse and the other munched contentedly on hay. A sluggish stream provided water. On the other side was a small carriage of supreme quality. Andace would travel in nothing less than the best. He shook his head. He would have to put them all inside while he sat up top to guide the horse. Leaving Larra alone with two evil women wasn't his idea of a good solution.

Perhaps they could die in the night.

"Don't even think it. I'll just bind them before we go."

And if Larra complains?

"I'll bind her too."

They laughed, but it sounded empty.

We can't just let her run off to Relmon. She is our wife.

"What do you suggest; we force her to come with us?"

When Bauer purred with the lusty pleasure only a true beast would know, Dauer rolled his eyes, mainly because he found the image just as appealing. It seemed less and less separated them now. Perhaps all they needed was one more nudge, one more step, one more burst to fully integrate.

Inside the cabin, he found Larra alone by the fire. She had blocked the bedroom door with a chair so the two women within could not come out. At first, he was irked because they had the only bed, but then he realized Larra probably wouldn't want to sleep with him again, not after what she'd seen. And they were safer in there, away from the fire. When Larra nodded to the empty space beside her, he sat on the thick braided rug. Without her saying anything, he knew what she wanted to discuss.

"I used to be a normal man." He tossed a log onto the fire and fussed it into place. When the bark burst into flames, he swore he felt the fires of hell calling to him even though no inferno could burn away his sins. "A thousand years ago, I was a normal man, but then I killed my wife and child."

11

Larra couldn't believe what she'd heard. Dauer killed his own family? She shook her head, convinced either he had misspoke or she had misheard.

"I did not intend to kill them, but the gods have a fickle way of punishing a man with no soul."

His voice was hollow, weary, and his body slumped as if the thousand years he spoke of crushed down on his shoulders all at once.

Questions popped into her mind in a rush, but her tortured throat made voicing them difficult. Also, she was afraid if she spoke, she would only sputter in shocked disbelief. She'd always known Dauer hid something dark but nothing as pitch black as this.

"Long ago, when I was a boy, I followed in my father's trade of fisherman. It was a dangerous life as the sea could be sweet or cruel, but I enjoyed my life, as meager as it was. When I came of age, I married a woman from my village. Her family made fishing nets, so it seemed a logical choice. She was very shy, but so was I. Eventually we grew to care for each other."

Larra waited patiently while Dauer fiddled again with the fire.

"Her belly was rounded with our child when all able-bodied men were called to arms. My father convinced me to offer my services for our family. I did well in training. So well that I came to the attention of our king's commander." He sighed and shook his head. "I won't horrify you with tales of what it takes to turn a normal man into a killer, but that's what he did. After his brutality, I had no heart, no soul, and I lived for only one thing: to kill those who stood in the way of my king."

Larra shivered. She remembered a time when she had watched the training of Relmon solders and despaired to her stepfather about the brutality and austere conditions. He'd tried to calm her. While drying her tears he had explained that that was the life they chose—there was nothing to be done about it. "Would you wish for them to go into battle with nothing but pillows and poetry?"

She didn't understand until she was much older, but still it broke her heart to think of Dauer under even more severe conditions.

"My king claimed all the land from the sea to the mountains as his. With that, we set off from the sea, hacking our way through every village that refused to fly his colors. I don't know how long it took to make our way to the mountains, but when we did, we simply split our army along the foothills and swept around and down, back toward the sea."

"You killed everyone?" She understood what Relmon soldiers did in times of war, but even then, they didn't kill women or children, only men. Or did they? She had no idea under what instructions they operated. Now that she ruled Relmon, what would she order them to do? Would showing mercy make her lands vulnerable? Could she make the decisions that she must to protect her lands and her people? A new and terrible weight of responsibility pressed against her shoulders.

"Our orders were to kill until those in charge surrendered. If they refused to submit, we killed everyone." He took a deep breath. "We decimated entire towns. Streets ran with blood like sluggish rivers. At times, gore would cover me from head to toe, and all I could see was a haze of red. I just kept swinging my blade until I ran out of people to hit. That's how I killed my wife."

Larra almost asked him to stop, to not tell her this horrible tale that she would never be able to rid from her thoughts, but she knew if she stopped him now, their future together would be lost.

"It was just another small settlement of fishermen who refused to submit to the king. Negotiations fell apart, and they sent us in. We quickly dispatched their handful of soldiers and then turned our killing blades on the others. Rage consumed me, for they should have yielded. Angered by their foolish pride, I hunted down the stragglers long after the rest of the army moved on to the next village."

Dauer's voice broke on a gasping breath. When she placed her hand on his back, he turned his head away.

"Don't comfort me. I can't bear kindness for such a despicable act."

Larra promptly returned her hand to her lap. A thousand years had passed, but for him, the event was still raw. Even after all this time, he could not absolve himself. Her forgiveness only sprinkled salt in his wound.

"She had hidden in a dark pantry corner under half-empty grain sacks. Only a wisp of brown hair gave her away, but it seemed short, and I thought her a man. I thrust my sword repeatedly, spilling bloody grain everywhere. When I triumphantly yanked the bags back and saw her face, I dropped to my knees. Terror glazed her eyes, but right before she died, she recognized me. She issued a curse so vile it haunts me to this day. When she fell back, I saw what she'd been protecting in her frail arms: our son. I nearly cut him in two—"

"Stop!" Larra could not bear to hear any more. Her dinner roiled in her belly, a belly that right now could hold his child. Protectively, she placed her hand low.

Dauer climbed dejectedly to his feet. "You see now why I didn't tell you." He shook his head and gestured to her stomach. "Fear not, Larra. I am not capable of such a feat. Part of my curse seems to be the inability to have any more children to inflict my wrath upon."

In a flash, she rose to her knees. "How dare you presume to know the workings of my mind?" Despite her rough voice, her tone was clear and strong. "I don't fear having your child, I only wondered if such were so."

"And if it were, you would welcome my spawn?"

He practically spit the word at her, as if giving birth to his offspring would bring the devil to flesh. She did not realize until this moment how much he hated himself. It wasn't shame or disgrace—Dauer loathed his very existence. How could he ever love anyone when he detested himself so greatly?

Larra exhaled and took another slow breath before she spoke. "A child would be difficult with so much facing us, but yes, I would welcome him or her." Lifting her hand to his she asked, "Wouldn't you?"

Abruptly, he laughed.

Shocked, she withdrew her hand.

"What does it matter now?" He pushed the couch closer to the fire. "You will sleep here."

She had no idea what he meant by his remark. Had his feelings mattered at some point but no longer? Every attempt she made at further conversation, he refused. In frustration, she settled on the couch while he took the floor. He didn't bother to cover himself with a blanket. He simply swaddled his enormous cloak about his person. A terrible thought occurred to her: He had lived a thousand years bound by heavy fabric so none would see his face. Whatever crime he committed, surely he had paid enough.

Watching the rise and fall of his chest, tears fell unfettered from her eyes. She had never known the man he was, the man who lived only for killing. The man she knew was the man he was now. A man split in two, forced to hide his face of ugly and his other of beauty, a man who treated his servants kindly and treated her both as a ravenous sexual partner and the most exalted lover. Had the curse rendered him a man of extremes, or was that who he really was? There were elements of both that she craved: Bauer's naked lust, his rough language, his almost childlike inventiveness; Dauer's soul-shattering passion, his educated tongue, his intense devotion.

As she fell into a tortured sleep, she wondered if she could do anything to help him. Was she his salvation? If his first wife had cursed him, perhaps his current wife could save him. However, the question was, did Dauer really want to be rescued?

12

By the time they reached Relmon, the sun hung low, skimming an orange glow across snow-covered lands. When they emerged from the forest and joined the main road, Dauer discovered a hoof-churned path. Andace had moved hundreds of men before the storm. He was able to traverse the mess only because everything had turned to ice, capturing a part of Andace's evil scheme for a moment in time.

He didn't marvel on it long.

With a sigh that plumed his breath, he lifted his shoulders, flicked the reins, and urged the horses along.

Thatched houses dotted the farmlands. As he drew deeper into the valley, tight clusters of closed shops lined the main road. Overlooking the valley at the top of the winding path was Relmon Castle. Larra's home. Where his castle looked forbidding, hers seemed almost welcoming, with two wings flung out like wide-open arms. Even from a distance, he saw lights flickering in the windows. Welcoming lights in so many windows sparkled brighter than the heavens. He glanced at the night sky, shrugged, and then turned his gaze to Larra's home. Speculatively, he wondered how many servants bustled about in ready for her homecoming. With that many lights burning at only the blush of night, surely, the fore-guard had noticed their coming, since they were the only travelers on the road. With his unmistakable form at the reins, it wouldn't take a genius to figure out Larra was within the carriage.

Even without confirming their mistress, nay, fresh ruler, sat within his conveyance, the entire castle sprang to life in the *hopes* that Larra rode within the carriage Dauer, "The Beast" of Hargarren, commanded. Just the anticipation that Larra *might* be inside compelled every man, woman, and child within Relmon Castle to their feet in welcome.

At the front entrance, a handful of servants eyed him warily. Did they think he returned the dead body of their mistress to them? He felt the fear and suspicion in their gazes, but he refused to offer any explanation. As he climbed down, they opened the doors of the carriage, gasped, and then removed the gibbering Andace.

"Put her in Lonin's old room," Larra said, stepping down with the aid of a sturdy footman. "Keale will care for her."

Keale nodded briefly with her head lowered. Dauer had no idea what they'd discussed on the ride here, but Keale clearly wasn't about to argue with Larra's orders.

Larra slammed the carriage door and dismissed the servants without a breath of explanation. Apparently, she didn't care to enlighten them any more than he did. Silently, he followed her within. No man should walk behind his wife, but if he dared precede her, he feared a bolt to the mangled shreds of his heart. Besides, following behind Larra was no sacrifice for his eyes. Truly, he would follow her anywhere. Watching her walk was a treat and an enticement. Her backside compelled his gaze, but he followed because he couldn't wait for her to stop, turn, sit, or any movement that brought her facing him.

Warmth and rich cooking smells greeted him as soon as he

entered. Tapestries softened rough-hewn walls, and thick rugs warmed the stone floors. He had never set foot in Relmon Castle before. He had conducted his dealings with Andace through messengers, but he found the home suited Larra. All the colors of the forest echoed her coloring, drawing his eye to her rich brown hair cascading down her back as she moved through the great hall. Every servant's face split into a genuine smile when she appeared. Larra took care to acknowledge each of them with a touch or a few words. When she lingered and drew them aside, he stood silently, a statue in his encompassing robe.

She belongs here, his mind whispered, here in a normal home with people who care about her, where she didn't have to cater to the lusty whims of a beastly husband nor the tortured conscience of a cursed man. He'd been a fool to think he could capture her heart when he had none to offer in return. Suddenly, he wanted it over. He wanted her to turn and dismiss him so he could make his way back to his lonely vigil on the mountain.

"We'll have supper in my rooms," Larra said over her shoulder then slowed her pace until he caught up. She snaked her arm through his. "Why do you drag your steps? I assure you, nothing evil awaits you in Relmon."

Dauer nodded, but every servant they passed cast him a dubious gaze, recoiled from his path, or whispered behind their hands. Larra wanted him here, but her people certainly didn't.

Oblivious to their reactions, Larra continued to her rooms, and once there, she closed the door. "Finally we are alone." She turned and wrapped her arms around his chest.

Her gesture was so unexpected he stood still for a moment then embraced her. He tilted his hood back so he could smooth his cheek against her hair and breathe deeply of her scent.

"I gave instructions for our troops to be recalled from your borders."

He nodded and held her tighter.

Two sharp knocks pulled them apart, and he hastily replaced

his hood. Attuned as she was to his needs, Larra set the sides of the table so that, when seated, they would face opposite directions. This way, he could remove his hood and eat without mishap.

Larra made small talk that he answered distractedly because as she faced the door, he faced her bed. Heaps of silk pillows in green, brown, and yellow littered the head of an enormous fabric-shrouded bed. He hardly tasted his food because all he could see, hear, or smell was Larra within those covers. Once the last of the sun faded from the sky, he swore he would have his wife writhing and breathless within the covers of her virginal bed.

By scent alone, he confirmed that no man had ever been in this bed. He had no idea where her liaison had taken place but certainly not here. His heart skipped a beat when he realized that his senses and thoughts were a blend of both halves. Never had they been so close, so aware of the other. Curious, he pealed back his sleeve, confirming that his form was still that of the beast. If he left Larra here and returned to Hargarren alone, would his awareness reverse to separate halves? A rush of despair gripped him because all he'd wanted was to be one cohesive whole.

His gaze shifted to the lone window where the sun slipped behind the mountains. Rather than a painful shift, his body changed slowly into his other form. He felt his shoulders align, his skin grow taut, his eyes level. A smooth transition rather than one filled with fighting and struggle.

To distract himself from his wayward thoughts, he gazed around the room. Stacks of books and half-written pages littered a large desk. Tapestries of mythical creatures covered the walls while fanciful statues and carvings of sprites took up every spare bit of space. No wonder she delighted in telling tales. She had surrounded herself with nothing but story creatures.

When he looked closer at some of the statues, he discovered

someone had carefully glued them back together, multiple times. Several of the tapestries had been meticulously restored. When he asked, Larra quietly sighed and said, "Andace."

Her sister had tried to destroy her dreams, but Larra simply rebuilt them, time and time again, until Andace grew tired of tormenting her. Larra may not have been able to fight her sister physically, but she had persevered with her strength of spirit. He admired her doggedness and her ability to forgive. Anyone else would have killed Andace for what she'd done, but Larra let her live. Perhaps it was the worst punishment of all. A life of gibbering insanity wasn't much of a life.

He replaced his hood when the servants came to clear off the dishes and light the candles, which quickly filled the air with the sweet smell of honey. Fading radiance from the sunset mixed with the golden glow, creating a sensual atmosphere. His gaze returned to her bed no matter how he tried to look elsewhere. When the servants filled a bathing tub with steaming water, his cock swelled at just the thought of her naked body, pink and warm, sliding into bed, pressing against him. He gripped the back of the chair so forcefully he cracked the wood.

Larra's hand at his back drew him to the tub. She closed her eyes to undress him, but he stopped her.

"You first."

Larra slid off her dress, a slight smile deepening the dimple at the side of her face. Hungry eyes ate up every bit of slowly exposed flesh. Once the garment pooled around her feet she released her bound hair and stepped into the water.

Kneeling, she lifted a small cup and poured water over her shoulders. Glistening drops caught the light, drawing his attention to the swollen tips of her breasts.

"Close your eyes."

When she did, he removed his hood and gloves then settled beside the tub. He poured water over her hair until the brown strands slid around her back and shoulders, hiding her from his gaze. He worked a fragrant soap into her hair but took far more time to work the suds along her skin. When he cupped her breasts, she rolled her head back with a purr of pleasure, which only deepened when he worked his hand between her legs. How could he even think of letting such a beautiful, sensual creature go?

"I think I'm clean enough." She playfully pushed his hand away, rinsed quickly, and then stood. He wrapped a sheet around her as she stepped out. "Your turn," she said, fumbling her fingertips along his cloak, seeking the fasteners without opening her eyes. A musty smell of wet wool and leather drowned out her sweet scent.

The danger of her undressing him without a blindfold only heightened his excitement. Intellectually, he knew Larra was far too smart to do something so hazardous as to peek at him, but the thrill of it caused his heart to beat wildly in his chest.

Once she had him stripped bare, he stepped into the water, knelt, barely fitting into the tight little tub. Larra dipped the cup and poured it over his head. Night-black strands sluiced down into his eyes. She used a different soap on him, something masculine and strong. Not a bit of him escaped her nimble touch. When he rose out of the water, she slipped her slick hand around his shaft, teasing the length, then slid her fingertips across his balls. She repeated the motion to rinse him. He lost sight of her hand when his chest rose, and he uttered a groan of longing.

She chuckled lightly, enjoying her power to arouse him.

"I need you." He reached for her, pulling her to his chest.

"I wasn't finished." Her protest was lost against his claiming kiss.

Lifting her into his arms, he carried her to the bed. Once there, he settled her against the pillows. Ravenous to taste her pleasure, he kissed his way from her lips to her belly in mere moments then parted her thighs. Candlelight turned her pale skin tawny gold and sparkled in the wisps of her tight curls. He lowered his head and ate her passion like ambrosia.

Larra opened herself willingly to him, trailing her fingers through his hair. She clutched the covers when his talented tongue drove her to climax. He wanted to pleasure her again and again, but his body screamed for its own release. When he rose up, she wrapped her arms and legs around him, pulling him into her, welcoming him with such wanton abandon he lost control and climaxed with hardly a thrust.

Disappointed because everything was over so fast, he rolled to his side, pulling her with him while keeping himself within her snug heat.

"Tell me a story." One of her lusty tales would stoke his fires anew. Her stories were the most powerful aphrodisiac he'd ever known.

With a contented purr, Larra snuggled her head against his chest and said, "I forgive you."

He held still for a moment, thinking she forgave him for such a short bout of lovemaking, but then he realized she forgave him for killing his family. Her mercy rubbed raw against what was left of his soul. He tried to move away from her, but she clung, hard and fast.

"If your first wife cursed you, perhaps your last wife can save you."

"Oh, Larra." He lowered his head to the hollow between her neck and shoulder. "She did not curse me. I cursed myself." Afraid the shock of his confession would compel her to open her eyes, he pressed her head close to his body. "Her vile words put the idea in my head, but it was my words, my crushing horror and disgust with myself, that split my soul apart."

He pulled the covers around them, nestling her close as he explained. "I didn't even realize what I had done until hundreds of years later. When I cursed myself, I split into good and evil. By day, I was a hideous malformed beast that delighted in wreaking havoc. By night, I was a beautiful angel who sought only to ease the suffering of all I encountered. However, I couldn't commit much evil in daylight and none wanted my help at night, especially when I couldn't show my face. My curse made me an outcast. I took refuge in caves, reverting to an animal. I lived that way for hundreds of years, unaware of my separate halves. The part of me, the man, was dead and only the two extremes remained. Slowly, over time, they became aware of each other, and part of their elements merged, giving birth to me again."

He took a breath, unable to convey how painful his rebirth had been. Tearing his way between the mother and father of good and evil only to emerge tottering and frail, unable to comprehend what had happened had almost killed him.

"There was a small part of me that knew the two halves. I did my best to control them, or at least to find outlets for their needs. Once I channeled their efforts, I prospered and founded Hargarren."

His castle became his prison. There, he hid himself away from the world as much as he could, but loneliness and desperation drove him to seek companionship. He could not have asked for anyone better than Larra. She had done what he needed, and she accepted him for what he was.

"I accept your kindness, but you cannot fix me, Larra."

She was quiet for a while, her breath moist and sweet against his flesh. Softly she said, "When I promised to never try to see what you looked like, you swore that you would do anything I asked." She paused for a moment, as if to gather strength. "Well, now I know what I want. I want to hear you say three little words."

He knew what words she needed to hear, and he would happily shout them from the highest turret. He hadn't been sure he could love again, but now he knew he loved Larra. He would say it to her whenever she wished.

"I want you to say, 'I forgive myself.'" When he pulled back, she rushed on. "It doesn't matter if you don't believe what you're saying, I just want you to say the three little words once in the morning and once in the evening."

"No." He refused without even considering her request. He could never forgive himself for what he'd done.

"You swore you would do anything I asked if it were in your power. Are you a man of your word or not?"

"I can't." Saying the words, even just to placate her, chaffed against his conscience.

With a sigh, she slipped from his embrace. "Then there is nothing left for us to do except say good-bye."

Dauer rode out at first light. He was home before sunset. He told his men-at-arms to stand down and had his stable boy return the borrowed horse. Morrow asked after Larra, and Dauer went straight to his room without an answer. All he had to say were three little words and she would have been his for a lifetime.

Winter settled in with an icy grip that matched his cold demeanor. He took no pleasure in anything he did. His servants avoided him as best they could. He and Bauer began to split into separate halves again.

One night, trapped in a haze of longing, he went to Larra's room. Dead embers lined the fireplace, dust gathered on her dresses, and any trace of her scent had long ago dispersed from the air. When he sat upon her unmade bed, he caught a whiff of her essence. Pressing his face to her pillows, he filled his lungs with her unique perfume.

Overwhelmed with need, he shot to his feet, determined to find Morrow and have the room scrubbed from ceiling to floor. Perhaps if he removed any trace of her existence, she would cease to haunt him. A scrap of silk stopped him in his tracks.

Tossed so casually among her potions and perfumes, as if it

were just another part of her normal life, was the purple binding cloth she'd used as her makeshift blindfold. Willingly she wore it just so she could be in his bed. Willingly she swore to not see what he looked like. Willingly she forgave him for his past.

"And all she asked of me in return was to say three little words." Powerful emotions shook him, causing him to clutch at the bedpost for support. He took a deep breath and whispered, "I forgive myself."

Strangely, he felt better, not that he believed the words, but that he had done what Larra wished. He rolled the words around his mouth again. "I forgive myself." Peace settled over his shoulders as softly as Larra's embrace. Dimly he felt Bauer within. Had she found the solution? Could something so simple be the last push to fully integrate his separate halves?

He wanted to return to Relmon, sweep her into his arms, and say the words again. Turning to the window, his heart sank. Ice and snow crusted the glass. Howling winds heralded another vicious storm. Nothing moved under the thick blanket of snow. He wouldn't be able to reach her until spring. As he sank down to her bed, a plan formed. For the first time in hundreds of years, he felt hope.

13

When the fore-guard told Larra that Dauer was coming, every lonely chill of winter left her as if the entire land turned suddenly to summer heat. Larra couldn't issue orders fast enough as she hurried to her rooms to bathe, dress, and ready herself for Dauer's visit.

She knew there were plenty of reasons he could be coming back to Relmon, but in her heart, she knew he came for her. During the chilly nights of winter, she often sat at her window, looking toward the mountain that held his castle, wondering if he missed her, wondering if he found any solace in his isolation. In the dark of her lonely bed, she thought of him too, but those thoughts set her body on fire. Her wandering fingers only stoked the flames.

For a time she regretted asking him to forgive himself when he clearly wasn't ready, but then she decided if she left it up to him, he would never be ready, and they couldn't be together until he let go of his past to embrace the future.

Her heart beat wildly in her chest as her maid fussed over her dress and hair. With her laces bound tight, Larra almost lost her breath as she ran down the stairs. She wanted to be ready to greet him when he arrived. Unable to sit still, she paced the length of the great hall until she heard the *clop-clop* of hoofs on the stone entranceway.

She pushed open the door, flew down the steps, and almost knocked Dauer off his feet. His great gray cloak swallowed her up when his arms came around her waist. All the advice her friends had given over the years to play coy and aloof with a man went right out of her head. She missed him terribly, and she wanted him, and everyone else, to know.

Proudly, she turned, and that's when she noticed the suspicion and dread on the faces of her servants. She could talk him up all she wanted, but they would never accept him until they discovered, on their own, that Dauer was not the monster tales said he was. Chagrined, she realized her stories had painted that picture. Her moping since he left probably didn't help matters either.

"I would ask if you missed me, but the answer is obvious."

Larra laughed, grasped his leather-clad hand, and pulled him inside. She gave strict orders that they were not to be disturbed. Once she had him in her room, she closed her eyes, pushed back his hood, and leaned in for a kiss. Her lips felt only air.

"I'm still in my beastly form."

"I don't care." She leaned in again, but all she felt was his finger against her mouth. Exasperated, she kept her eyes tightly closed but scowled at him, or where she thought he was standing.

"I need to tell you something."

His serious tone of voice caused her to lower her head. Had he ridden all this way just to tell her there was no hope?

"Open your eyes."

Trembling, she did, but kept her gaze lowered.

"Trust me, Larra."

Trusting him implicitly, she shifted her gaze up, and then blinked rapidly as her mouth fell open.

"I forgive myself."

His words barely registered as she stared at his face. He wasn't as beautiful as the angel statue or as hideous as the beast statue. In fact, he looked almost ordinary. If she passed him in the hall, she would find her gaze only drawn to him for his impressive height and his strong, angular features. She wouldn't run screaming or fall at his feet babbling. He was simply a handsome man smiling at her. Deep brown eyes crinkled at the corners from his wide and open smile as strands of night black hair curled across his forehead. Dark stubble dusted his square chin while sleek brows rose questioningly.

"Am I ugly?" he asked, honestly baffled by her reaction.

"No!" She shook her head. "You're very handsome. I just can't stop looking at you because, well—"

"You've never seen me." A slight blush made him only more attractive. "I'm not used to being looked at."

She glanced away, but a finger below her chin brought her gaze back to his.

"I don't mind that you stare." He stroked his finger across her lips, his entranced gaze tracking the motion. "It's because of you that I've changed."

Her wide and curious gaze must have asked the question.

"Every morning and every evening, I said three little words. At first, I didn't believe what I said, but eventually the sentiment sank in, and ever so slowly, the last fissure between my separate halves melded until I became the man I was so long ago, before the war, before . . . before my war lust overcame my ability to love."

Tenderly, he cupped her face, drew her close, held his mouth right to hers, and said, "I love you, Larra."

She could barely see him through her tears. "I love you,

Dauer." Finally, her lips touched his, but she didn't close her eyes. She couldn't. Seeing her striking husband for the first time astounded her.

They spent the day and night exploring and loving each other until they fell into exhausted sleep.

It took a while for Dauer to become comfortable without his protective cloak, but with time, and gentle nudging, he soon left the heavy fabric behind. Once he did, it didn't take long for the servants to warm up to him. Larra explained away the cloak by claiming he was shy. Dauer implored her to give the tale a more heroic spin, but nothing else made as much sense.

"Besides, I've done enough for your heroic image with my other tales."

"I suppose." Dauer nipped the tip of her breast with his teeth then smiled up at her. "Tell me a story, Larra."

And she did.

His to Reclaim

Shelli Stevens

1

"*Gemma!*" The shrill scream pierced through the woods, filtering past the aged walls of the log cabin. "Oh my God! I can't believe this. *Gemma!*"

The sound of feet pounding down the path mingled with the alarmed whimpers and short breaths of the approaching woman.

Gemma's fingers clenched around the brush in her hand, her pulse quickening as she turned to face the door. *Was it too much to hope that it was nothing more than the caterer having encountered a problem?*

The door flung open, smashing into the wall. Her younger cousin Megan stepped into the room, eyes wild with panic.

"He's really coming."

They were just three words, but they were enough. The brush dropped from Gemma's hand, and her body went numb with shock.

This was really happening . . . No! The room spun and she gripped the vanity table to keep from falling to her knees. *No. Was he insane?*

"There's no time." Megan closed the door, hands shaking. "Shift and then run. Run fast. It's the only way you can possibly escape him."

"How far away is he?" Gemma's voice came out remarkably calm as she fumbled to undo the buttons on her wedding dress.

The cold fear began to subside, and a hot burn of rage blazed through her. How dare he? After five years, how *dare* he?

Megan grabbed her arm and tugged her toward the door. "A mile. Maybe. And he's not alone, Gemma. He's brought friends. You must hurry! There's no time to change out of your dress. Run, and I'll find Jeffrey and tell him what's happened."

"My dress will be ruined during transition—"

Crash!

The door broke in half, and splinters of wood shot into the interior of the cabin like tiny missiles.

Heart in her throat, Gemma retreated, her body trembling as she stared at the man who now filled the doorway. The man who'd just made good on the appallingly dark promise he'd made just days ago in an e-mail. She'd been half-convinced it was a joke—someone toying with her heart—and had told Megan as much.

But it wasn't a joke. The proof was standing in front of her eyes. Maybe a couple of years ago she would have wished for this, but not now. Dammit, not now!

Sweat clung to the hard muscles of Hunter's nude body—it was clear he'd just shifted back to human form. A familiar heat crept through her body, and she hardened her jaw, refusing to acknowledge it. The same way she'd refused to acknowledge it for the last five years.

It was hard not to, though, with his dark hair and tan body. He was tall and broad, a mass of muscles and ridges. Her gaze dropped, and her cheeks burned hot. She swallowed hard, unable to tear her gaze from his hard thighs and the thick cock that rested between them.

The blood raged through her veins, and she closed her eyes to count to ten. When she opened them again, her gaze was firmly back to his face, unwilling to let her eyes shift any lower than his shoulders this time, for that would be a guaranteed diversion from finding a way out of this situation.

Unfortunately, five years had done nothing but enhance Hunter's raw sex appeal.

His eyes, burning like dark blue crystals, met hers. And like the devil come to collect his due, he advanced into the room, his face a mask of fierce determination.

Oh, God. She needed to act. Now. Swallowing against the thickness in her throat, Gemma glanced around the room, looking for anything that might be used as a weapon. She grabbed the chair from her vanity table and lifted it above her head with a grunt.

Hunter lunged forward and knocked it from her grasp, sending it crashing to the ground behind her. Before she could draw in a startled breath, he'd circled her wrists with one of his massive hands and pulled her body firmly against the rock hard wall of his chest.

"*No!*" She growled and lifted her knee to tag him in the groin, but he blocked the shot.

Instead, he pulled her tighter against him and forced his thigh between hers. His thick cock brushed her hip and she stilled, barely able to breathe as her heart slammed against her rib cage.

His soft laugh feathered warmth against her cheek. "You should have listened to your cousin, angel." He leaned forward and said softly against her ear, "You should have run."

The blood drained from Gemma's face, and she heard Megan whimper from the corner of the room.

Megan. Hope flared.

"Megan, go find Jeffrey!"

Her cousin lurched away from the wall and toward the doorway but fell back with a shrill yell.

Two more men—though these ones were clothed—filed through the broken entrance.

"It appears we will have to take the younger one with us as well," Hunter ordered with a sigh.

"Me?" Megan squeaked in alarm. "No! You can't—"

Her words were cut off by the hand that slid over her mouth, then the burly man slid another arm around her waist to lift her off the ground.

Panic renewed in her gut, and Gemma tugged at her imprisoned wrists, her mouth in a tight line. "Let her go, Hunter. She has nothing to do with this."

"We will, angel. Tomorrow. We don't want her running off to tell Jeffrey the minute we leave, now do we?"

"*Bastard.*"

His smile came slow. "Now you know my mother well enough to know that's not true."

Of course he would throw that at her. She bit her lip, trying to hold her temper. It wasn't easy as she watched helplessly as the two men carried her cousin, kicking and screaming, out the door. Megan's muffled sounds were ineffective at bringing them the help they desperately needed.

Gemma drew in a slow breath. "You know, Hunter, I always suspected you were a bit certifiable. Congratulations, you've just confirmed it."

He caught her chin with rough fingers, lifting her face so she had to look at him. A shiver ran down her spine; unfortunately it may not have all been because of fear. His eyes narrowed until the blue irises were just slits of blue. They burned hot as his gaze scoured her face.

"Am I? You were the one about to marry a human." His gaze darkened. "I gave you fair warning. Call off the wedding or I would do it for you."

"I'll *still* marry him."

"I wouldn't count on it."

"Oh! I'll say it again, Hunter. You're certifiable," she repeated and tried to twist her chin from his grasp. His hold just tightened. "In fact, I'm sure you won't mind if I just call you Certi from now on."

"Angel, I don't care what the hell you call me." His head lowered until his mouth was just a breath above hers. "I'll just look forward to hearing you call it when I'm riding you in bed."

Shock ripped through her, widening her eyes and snatching her breath away. Heat rushed through her body. Curling thick down through her blood before gathering heavy in her pussy.

His nostrils flared, and she knew his were–senses meant that he could smell the dampness between her legs that his image had created. Heat flooded her cheeks.

"Like hell that will happen, Hunter."

"You want me, angel." It wasn't a question. And there was no asking when his lips crushed down on hers a second later.

Gemma went rigid in his arms, letting out an outraged feline growl that was all jaguar.

He answered with a deeper growl, plunging his tongue past her compressed lips to take control of her mouth.

There was no fighting him. With each bold stroke of his tongue against hers, a little more common sense got swept away. He plundered her mouth, leaving no inch unexplored, controlling her tongue and mind with ease.

The heat built in her body; her breasts swelled, the nipples tightening to scrape against the lace bustier beneath her dress. Five years dropped away, and once again it was Hunter holding her, kissing her. Making her forget everything but his touch and the way it made her feel.

His cock pressed hard into her belly, a tangible reminder of his promise to fuck her.

With a groan, he released her chin to plunge his hand into her bodice. He cupped her breast in the palm of his hand, squeezing just enough to send another rush of moisture straight to her panties.

Her head fell back, a gasp ripping from her lips. The calloused pad of his thumb swept across one tight nipple and her knees wobbled.

His mouth lifted from hers, and he pulled her breast above the bodice. His head swooped down, and he wrapped his lips around the hard tip. Hot breath and a moist tongue teased her before his teeth raked against her flesh.

"Oh, God." She trembled, minutes away from hiking up her wedding dress and begging him to fuck her.

Wedding dress . . . ? Jeffrey! The name of the man she was supposed to marry in two hours resounded in her head. *Who's certifiable now, Gemma?*

Already, Hunter reached for the hem of her dress, lifting it over her legs to cup her ass.

Now, Gemma. Act now! Knowing she had an advantage—just barely—she grabbed his hair and stepped back enough to slam her knee into his stomach.

He stumbled back with a curse, eyes flashing with dismay and rage. It was only a second, but it was the only break she needed.

Gemma moved past him and sprinted out the door to the cabin that she'd been using to get ready for her wedding. She leapt off the porch and landed on the dirt path.

Her heart slammed in her chest, her body trembling with adrenaline. Increasing her pace, she growled and willed the change to speed up. It didn't take long. Her twenty-thousand-dollar designer dress exploded into a mass of pearl buttons and lace as her body shifted into its jaguar form.

Seconds later she was on all fours, charging through the resort in a desperate attempt to escape Hunter. The thrashing of branches and trees behind her signaled that it was going to be one hell of a challenge.

Dammit. How could he have been so stupid as to get distracted by Gemma's sweet body?

Hunter snarled and dodged between two trees that appeared on one section of the trail.

He shouldn't have lost focus. As an ESA agent, he was better than that by nature. Their job was to protect and defend all shifter species from threats of corruption, danger, and violence. The Elite Shifter Agency hired only the best of the best. You had to be tough, intelligent, sharp, quick-minded . . . *definitely not lose your focus over a nice set of tits, you idiot.*

His fellow agents would laugh their asses off if they knew he'd gotten completely muddleheaded by a woman.

He hadn't been able to stop himself from touching her, but it had been a costly delay. He should have had her in the vehicle by now, and they could've been halfway to White River. As it was, Joaquin and Brad were probably wondering where the hell he was.

Hunter paused and breathed in the air, careful not to lose Gemma's scent.

She wasn't even following the human-made trail anymore. His gaze darted around the lush forest. He listened for the sound of her escape. The sudden flash of yellow and brown between the trees was a dead giveaway to her location. Unlike him, Gemma's jaguar form didn't have the luxury of dark brown fur that hid his spots. Though she was desperate in her attempt to escape, she didn't stand a chance.

His resolve softened a bit with pity before he hardened it again. He couldn't afford such a weakness. He gave a low growl and took off after her. Not that he could blame her for running. Not after what he'd done to her so many years ago. But what Gemma didn't seem to quite understand was the cloud of danger lingering over her life right now. And at the center of that vortex was none other than her husband-to-be.

Jealousy, like a hot brand iron, stabbed sudden and deep, twisting inside him. His paws hit the ground hard as he quickened his pace, jumping over bushes as he gained on her.

She shouldn't have been marrying Jeffrey Delmore in the first place. She was his. She'd sworn it. It didn't matter that she'd barely been twenty at the time. It was one promise he intended to see she kept. Gemma belonged to *him*.

Guilt twisted his gut; he was completely out of line, but he refused to acknowledge it. Not now. Right now, his primal side was in dominance, and the chase was on to reclaim his woman.

He was only about twenty feet behind her now, and she must have realized she couldn't outrun him much longer. He could hear her agitation in the growls she emitted while continuing to dodge through trees and beneath low brushes.

And then she blew it, giving him the final advantage he needed. Her back legs caught on a tree root protruding from the ground, and she stumbled, losing her balance before falling onto her side.

She tried to get back up again, but the damage was done. Hunter used her moment of vulnerability and jumped on her. The weight of his body pinned hers to the ground.

Fur flew as she swiped at him with her claws. Jaws snapped at his neck but missed. They rolled on the hard earth, fighting for dominance.

He locked gazes with her. *Stop fighting me*, he said with his mind.

Rage flared in her gaze, and she continued to struggle beneath him.

With a growl of frustration, he caught her neck between his teeth, using just enough force to warn her she'd better yield. Relief washed through him when she stilled beneath him.

Shift back, Gemma. Please, I don't want to hurt you.

She tried to swat him again with a paw, but he reared back, avoiding her attempt.

Realizing fighting was futile, her eyes closed. The fur on her face slowly receded to show smooth ivory skin. She had chosen to obey. Quickly, to avoid crushing her, he rolled off her and shifted back to his human form.

"You have no right," she rasped.

When he turned to look at her, his heart clenched a bit. She sat on the ground, her knees drawn up to her chest as she glared at him.

Her pale skin seemed luminescent against the greens and browns of the forest. The tawny curls of her hair—which had always fascinated him—tumbled over her shoulders, shielding her breasts from him.

His mouth pursed. *Too bad.* He hadn't seen her naked in years, and it was quite obvious her body had changed since then. Her curves were bolder, where as before they'd been slight.

He lifted his gaze to hers, wincing slightly at how her brown eyes condemned him.

"Let's not make this any more difficult than it needs to be, angel."

"Oh, I think it was too late for that the minute you decided to obliterate my wedding day."

His jaw hardened, and he stepped forward. "You will walk with me now to the vehicle."

"What's option B?"

"I'll carry you."

Her nostrils flared, and the arms around her knees tightened.

"Let me think," she murmured and then continued to watch him for a moment.

Her lips parted a second later, but words didn't come out. Instead, the piercing scream she issued was guaranteed to raise the dead. *Or bring her groom running.*

2

———————

"Shit!" Hunter pulled her to her feet, planting his palm firmly across her mouth to muffle her. "I should have gagged and bound you, angel. But I had hopes you might have been happy to see me."

She grunted her annoyance and tried to kick him again. He gave a bitter laugh. Of course she hadn't appreciated his last comment.

With his hand still over her mouth, he wrapped an arm around her waist and lifted her off the ground. Her feet continued to swing back at him, but fortunately he'd trapped her arms against her side. It probably would have been easier to bite her in jaguar form or to knock her out. Carrying her unconscious would have been much easier.

But even as he ran, collecting bruises from her jarring kicks, he knew he could never have hurt her. Not willingly. Not even if it would've been for her own good.

"Go ahead and fight me, angel. I want you nice and tired tonight when we finish what we started in the cabin."

She went rigid and then screamed her fury, slamming her

head back toward his. He pulled back, easily avoiding a hit. His fingers brushed the underside of her breast, and his cock jerked, his throat tightening. *Shit.*

He rushed to the waiting vehicle, relieved to see the door already open. Joaquin sat behind the wheel, and Brad sat in the backseat with Gemma's cousin restrained on his lap.

"Damn, Hunter, took you fucking long enough." Joaquin cast him an uneasy look and gunned the engine on the SUV.

"Sorry about that." With a grunt, he forced Gemma into the back of the vehicle and then climbed in after her, slamming the door shut and pulling her sideways across his lap. "The bride had a bit of a prewedding meltdown."

He released his hand from her mouth and realized immediately it had been a major mistake.

"Prewedding meltdown, you asshole?" she shouted. "I'll *show* you a meltdown. When I get through with you, your own mother—"

"Leave my mother out of this. If she could hear the language you use today, she'd die of shock."

Joaquin laughed softly from the front seat.

Guilt flashed across Gemma's face before it disappeared and she lifted her chin.

"Whatever you say, *Certi.*"

Brad glanced over at them. "What did she just call you?"

"Certi. It's short for certifiable," Gemma snapped before Hunter could answer. "In fact, you all should be given the nickname."

Instead of being offended, Joaquin and Brad just laughed outright, which seemed only to infuriate Gemma more. Her face turned red and her eyes bugged.

Hunter stared hard at Gemma for one moment before looking away. There was no reasoning with her. At least not right now.

"Head back to White River." He gave the quiet order to

Joaquin and then glanced sideways to see how the younger woman was faring.

He'd met Megan only on a couple of occasions, but the impression she'd given was that she seemed more fragile than her cousin, a bit naive, and prone to drama.

Right now, she looked ready to keel over. Maybe from the sheer fact she'd probably never sat on a man's lap before.

Against her pale face, her blue eyes were wider than what seemed possible, and her lips trembled. She kept her hands clenched into fists and stared at Gemma with a pitifully hopeful expression. As if her cousin was the answer to the way out of their situation. Not gonna happen.

The SUV bounced out of the woods, spitting up dirt as it turned onto an old logging road.

"I'd rather sit on the floor," Gemma muttered. "Anywhere else."

She squirmed on his lap, bringing the soft curve of her ass in contact with his cock. He hardened further against her, his pulse quickening.

The hand he'd wrapped low on her waist splayed across her belly, and with each bump of the vehicle, his fingers brushed against the springy curls shielding her pussy.

She let out a soft gasp and arched her body away from him.

That's right, angel, keep moving on me like that and you'll get a hell of a lot more than you bargained for. I don't care how many people are around us.

She went rigid, her eyes widening with alarm and something else. He almost missed it, but it had been there. Desire.

A small amount of relief swept through him. After all the years that had passed, she still wanted him. But then he'd known that in the cabin, when the juices of her pussy had teased his senses with the most seductive perfume.

She'd wanted him in that cabin. Had he taken a moment to explore the folds of her sex with his fingers, he could have discovered the tangible proof. Five years. For five years, he'd dreamed of touching her again, thought about her body and sweet moans as he'd pumped his cock with his fist. And now he had her again.

He tapped the swell of her pussy with two fingers, and she sucked in a quick breath, whimpering.

Be prepared, angel, for tonight you are mine.

This was utter and complete madness. Gemma tried to ease away from Hunter's intimate touch, but his arm tightened around her waist.

She was on the verge of either an orgasm or a complete meltdown. Probably both.

If she thought there was even a slight chance of escaping these three overgrown brutes, then she might have tried to jump from the vehicle. But with the speed they were going, the fall would likely hurt her enough to slow any chance of escape. Not to mention she'd be leaving Megan all alone.

She glanced at her cousin. Megan sat, her spine rigid and jaw tight, on the other man's lap, staring out the window.

Blinking back tears, Gemma tried to come to terms with what had just happened. Tried to accept the fact Hunter had forced his way back into her life as if the past five years hadn't existed. But they had. No matter how much she may have wished otherwise.

She closed her eyes, going back to that place in her mind she had no desire to visit. But the memory of their last night together rushed her mind before she could halt it. . . .

Her pulse raced, her panties already drenched from her desire for him. He never failed to affect her this way, even the first time she'd met him at his mother's deli and he'd been passing through. He'd approached her right away, flirting shamelessly.

And before her sandwich order had been filled, he'd asked her out.

They hadn't even been together a month, but staring up at him now, she knew it didn't matter. Hunter was the one for her. Body, mind, and soul.

"Hunter," she whispered, grasping his chin in an attempt to lift his head from her breast.

He sucked on her nipple one last time before raising his head with a wry grin.

"I'm sorry, Gemma. I'm going too fast."

"Actually, you're not." She shook her head and stroked her fingers through the strands of his short dark hair. "In fact, tonight . . . I don't want you to stop, Hunter."

Hot possessiveness flashed in his gaze even as he said quietly, "I won't rush you."

"You haven't rushed me. You've waited almost a month and have been more than patient." She gave a light laugh and wrapped one leg around his hip, trapping him between her thighs.

His cock jerked against her hip, and he gave a hoarse groan. "You're an angel. My angel. You have no idea what you've done to my life. How did I get so lucky to find you?"

Her lips curved into an impish grin. "Mmm, we both love the roast beef sandwiches at your mom's deli, and one day our paths finally crossed?"

Hunter laughed and then drew in a ragged breath as she touched the tip of his cock, unable to stop herself anymore.

"Gemma . . . are you sure?" he rasped with obvious uncertainty. "Once I start . . ."

"I've never been surer about anything in my life. I've never met anyone like you. Never felt this way about anyone else." She trailed her fingers up and down the hard ridges of his back. "I just know this is right. Take me, Hunter. Now."

With a growl, he closed his mouth over hers. The weight of his body fell heavy on top of her, pressing her deeper into the mattress.

Her shirt and bra had long since been disposed of, and he made quick time tugging her skirt and panties from her body.

Then he was between her thighs, his hot tongue probing her pussy and clit as he prepared her for his cock. Devouring and eating her until the pleasure threatened to explode in her head.

Only when she writhed and begged beneath him did he kneel between her thighs. He cupped her ass in his large hands, and with one smooth thrust, buried his cock deep inside her.

Pain and pleasure exploded as her body struggled to accept the thick invasion of his body.

"Gemma."

With the discomfort fading to a dull throb, she could finally register the shock in his voice and that he'd gone still inside her.

"You're a virgin?" he choked out.

"Yes. I thought you knew?" She ran her tongue over her lips and hesitantly wrapped her legs around his waist.

The movement brought him deeper inside her, stretched her, and she drew a ragged breath in.

"No, angel, I didn't know." He gave a soft laugh and lowered his head to lick one of her rigid nipples. "But I will say it's a very nice surprise."

Warmth spread all throughout her body, from her toes to the top of her head. She ran her fingers through his hair and gave a soft sigh.

"You're so tight. So creamy. God, Gemma, you feel incredible." His face pinched, and he began to move inside her, slow and gentle at first. She matched his thrusts, learning the rhythm he so patiently taught her.

Pleasure built inside her, twisting higher and higher still. Her mind spun with the sensation, her heart heavy with emotion.

"*Hunter, please,*" *she cried out, not even sure what she was begging for.*

"*Yes, angel.*" *His fingers bit into her ass cheeks as he lifted her to move faster inside her. His gaze held hers, a possessiveness that seared her to her soul.* "*Tell me. Who do you belong to, Gemma?*"

"*I'm yours, Hunter. All yours.*"

"*Yes, Gemma.*" *He pressed deeper inside her.* "*Mine forever. Say it.*"

"*Forever,*" *she agreed wildly.* "*I'm yours forever, Hunter.*"

He pulled out of her and buried his face between her legs again, his tongue seeking her swollen clit.

The orgasm ripped through her, rocking her all the way to her core. With her body still quaking from release, he entered her again with his cock, pounding inside her faster and harder until he screamed her name and she felt him spurt hot and thick inside her body.

"*You are mine, angel,*" *he whispered, before his weight fell heavy on top of her.* "*Forever . . .*"

The van hit a pothole, and Gemma fell backward against Hunter's chest. His arm tightened around her waist, and his lips grazed the nape of her neck. Hot shivers raced through her, but she ground her teeth together and jerked away.

Apparently forever had the same definition as the next morning in Hunter's world.

The memory of that last night she'd spent with him faded back into the dark recess of her mind. The same place she'd tried unsuccessfully to store it all these years.

Her stomach churned with the familiar pain and bitterness. He'd left after that night with a promise to see her the next day, only she'd never seen or heard from him again.

That had been five years ago. *Five years.*

And then last week he'd sent her the cold, toneless e-mail. Her jaw hardened with anger. *Certifiable.* Because he'd actually done it.

Not for the first time, she had to ask herself how well she'd really known Hunter. She'd known he helped out at his mom's deli every now and then and taught martial arts. Yes, they'd talked about anything and everything. Their fears and dreams. Fantasies. She'd thought she knew him, but *had* she?

They'd not even been together for a month and at times he'd seemed to be hiding something. That something had always eaten at her. Even today. Was he married? Had he been seeing another woman? What was he hiding?

It didn't matter. None of it did. Not anymore, at least. And she had to stop trying to analyze and solve a puzzle that should have been put to rest years ago.

Hunter had obviously slipped off the deep end with the stunt he'd pulled today. Gemma shook her head. She'd find a way out of this for her and Megan. She had a good future with Jeffrey, and damn Hunter for trying to take that from her.

When Gemma pulled away from him again, this time Hunter let her go. She moved to the seats behind him and folded her arms across her chest, her shoulders rigid.

He watched her closely, trying to gauge just how much she hated him right about now. The answer wasn't encouraging.

"We need to put clothes on you two before we reach the main road," Joaquin said suddenly from the driver's seat.

Hunter gave a terse nod. His people had no issue with nudity, but humans—though having grown less apprehensive and more tolerant of their kind over the years—weren't comfortable with the frequent display of nakedness. And right now, they couldn't afford to draw extra attention to themselves.

"I have no clothes," Gemma reminded him acidly. "My dress

is now scattered around the forest in enough tiny pieces to deck out an entire community of squirrels."

Hunter bit back a soft laugh, knowing that she wouldn't appreciate his amusement.

"We brought extra clothes. Figuring Gemma might try and run." Brad grinned and glanced closer at Megan. "Fortunately we got you, little lady, out of there before you got the chance."

Hunter noted the spark of interest in Brad's gaze as he stared at her and made a note to talk to the man later. Megan was off-limits. She'd just been in the wrong place at the wrong time. Not to mention she was just too young.

Hunter reached behind the seat and grabbed the nylon bag sitting next to Gemma. He unzipped it and handed her a cotton dress.

"Put this on."

For a minute, he thought she'd refuse, but then her eyes narrowed and she tugged the dress over her body, smoothing the fabric down her curves. She probably appreciated the fact that she didn't have to be naked in front of him anymore.

Hunter changed into the clothes he'd worn earlier—before he'd gone after Gemma.

A few minutes later, they turned onto the major highway, putting more distance between themselves and Delmore's luxury resort.

He glanced behind him again, and the air locked in his lungs. Even with the dress on, her body still tempted him. The urge to suck on those soft pink nipples, stoke the fire between her legs, and bring her pleasure until she begged him to fuck her rode him hard.

He wanted to hear her promise that she was his again, but he knew the chances of that were slim to none. Leaning more toward none.

Hunter couldn't fault her for getting on with her life. And as far as he knew, Gemma still had no idea that he worked for the Elite Shifter Agency. *He* knew what had happened after that mind-blowing night they'd spent together. But he also realized that from her point of view, she'd given herself to him entirely, and then he'd vanished from her life. Talk about taking the asshole of the year award.

Regret twisted in his gut. He wished things could have been different. That he could have found a way to tell her . . .

But he hadn't and she'd moved on. And he knew deep down he shouldn't begrudge her for that. He might have even accepted her new life easier if she hadn't moved on with Jeffrey Delmore.

His eyes narrowed, and he glanced out the window of the SUV.

It was obvious Gemma had no idea what kind of man she was marrying, that her future husband was a low-life filth who headed up a sick underground trafficking ring that ended in death. He knew Gemma well enough to realize she'd never have gotten involved with such blatant evil. And it was evil.

They'd been trying to get the proof on Delmore since they'd first begun to suspect him, but the man was slick. This weekend, they were trying a new route, though. Sending in bait. And hopefully the bastard was stupid enough to take it.

Thank God he'd found Gemma before she could marry the creep. Hunter was determined to see that she never did.

3

Hunter ran along the river, his paws hitting the earth as he expelled his frustration and anger. After the morning he'd had and fighting the temptation of Gemma's body during the car ride, he needed this outlet.

Brad had, too, apparently, and joined him now in the run. They followed the river for a few miles before turning back toward the safe house. Instead of going inside, Hunter dove into the slow-moving river and swam for a bit in jaguar form before shifting back to human a few minutes later. He cooled his overheated body and washed off the sweat.

A splash next to him was notification that Brad had decided to swim for a bit, too. His friend emerged from beneath the water a minute later. He shook his head, sending water droplets flying.

"Fuck, I needed that," Brad said, leaning back to float next to him. "How you holding up?"

"Doing fine."

"Hmm. She's a feisty one, huh?"

Hunter glanced at him. "Which one?"

"Gemma." Brad gave a soft laugh and shook his head. "Not Megan, that's for sure. She's too scared. But she sure is a sweet little thing."

"She's too young for you," Hunter warned quietly.

"She's eighteen."

"That's too young. And she didn't ask for any of this. Don't traumatize her more by trying anything."

Irritation flickered in Brad's gaze. "You know me better than that, Hunter. I agree she's too young. I'm not going to lie and say I haven't noticed her. But I know where to draw the line."

Relief had Hunter easing onto his back, drifting slowly with the current.

"I have to ask . . . do you?" Brad asked, kicking with his feet to float another few inches away.

"Do I what?"

"Know where to draw the line with Gemma?"

"Gemma's a different story. We have a history."

"She was supposed to be getting married today. I'd say that history is pretty much—"

"You have no idea what we had," Hunter snarled, finding his footing on the bottom of the river again. "And don't bullshit me with pretending her fiancé was some kind of saint. We both know what kind of scum he is."

"Look, I'm not going to disagree with you there." Brad paused. "But are you sure she doesn't know about Delmore's dealings?"

"She doesn't know."

"If she ends up being involved with the ring, you know we have to bring her in and have her prosecuted—"

"She *doesn't know.*"

"But if she *is* involved—"

"Then yes," he snapped. "We prosecute her with the rest of the bastards."

Brad watched him steadily and then shook his head. "I hope you're right about her. We took one helluva risk with this little abduction today. The bigwigs at ESA aren't thrilled."

"I'm right about her. And you know as well I do that having her out of the way makes it easier for us to go in and do the sting." Hunter dunked his head underwater then emerged, shoving the wet strands of hair back off his forehead. "Besides, now I can question her. Find out if she is involved. Though, like I've said, I doubt it."

"Does she know you work for the ESA?"

"No. I plan on telling her tonight." He hesitated, debating how much to confide to his friend. "We had a relationship five years ago. It was getting pretty serious, and then the McGowan case hit."

Brad blinked and then gave a short laugh. "That's some fucked up timing. Did you ever get a chance to explain to her? Give her a message?"

Hunter shot his friend a hard look. "You know the answer to that. There's no way I could've. My own goddamn mother didn't even know what happened to me."

Brad was silent for a moment. "I'm sorry, man. It sounds like she really meant something to you."

"She did. Still does." He shook his head. "And I'll get her back."

"Well . . . good luck with that. I've got to say, she didn't seem too thrilled to see you."

"No, I don't think she was." Hunter laughed softly, a smile curving his lips. He swam toward the shore of the riverbank, Brad following behind him. "I'm going to see her shortly. Talk with her, explain why I took her today, and tell her who I am. Why I disappeared five years ago."

"I don't envy that conversation, man. I'll say it again. Good luck."

"Thanks. Why don't you put a feeler out on Megan? See if she might know anything about Delmore."

"Already got it covered." Brad grinned. "I'm relieving Joaquin and having dinner with her in about an hour."

Hunter cast his friend a warning look. "Remember what I said. Hands off."

"Hey, I already told you. Any fantasies I may have about the girl stay right up here." He tapped his head, and then a devious look crossed his face. "Well, for a few more years at least."

Hunter closed his eyes and then shook his head with a soft laugh. "You're trouble."

"So I've been told."

"I'll catch up with you later tonight. We can discuss anything we learn from the women."

"Sounds like a plan."

Gemma paced the room, no longer searching for a way to break down the door. Hopefully Megan was faring well, though her poor cousin was probably beside herself with fear.

Hunter wouldn't allow anything to happen to her, though. She knew him well enough to realize that. Megan was likely lounging around in perfect comfort, watching television—while, of course, being guarded by one of Hunter's friends.

She paused in front of the window, looking out over the mountains that surrounded them and the river rushing by below. She spotted Hunter and Brad walking back from the river. They were naked but fortunately too far away for her to see their bodies clearly.

Still, her body responded to the memory of Hunter's incredible physique. How it had looked, felt, tasted. A warm shiver ran through her, and she bit her lip, folding her arms across her chest. She couldn't go there. Wouldn't go there.

The past was behind her. Where it belonged. Hunter had made his choice five years ago.

And now she'd made hers. She would have given anything to be safely wed at this point. It would have been another wall put up between her and Hunter. And she needed that wall. Especially now that he was back in her life. *Why was he back?*

Her gaze lifted to the horizon again. The sun had set moments ago. If her day had gone as planned, she'd have been Mrs. Jeffrey Delmore right now.

The window was locked, but even if it hadn't been, she was too high off the ground to jump out.

Like a princess in a tower . . .

Only she wasn't a damn princess, and her prince sure as hell wasn't going to rescue her. No, if anything, her prince was the one who'd put her in here.

"He is *not* your prince," she whispered fiercely to herself, knowing she couldn't let herself feel anything but hatred for Hunter. "You are not a naive virgin anymore. Your prince was standing at the altar a few hours ago, wondering where the hell you were."

Her stomach rolled, and she pressed her hand against it. Poor Jeffrey. The man had been nothing but patient and tolerant with her. He'd pursued her for years before she'd forced herself to give up on Hunter and move on with her life.

Walking to the bed in the corner of the room, she sank down onto the plush mattress.

She may have given up on him in her mind, but her heart never had. As she let herself acknowledge that depressing truth, her lips twisted into a bitter smile and her eyes misted.

As if her thoughts had summoned him, the door unlocked, and Hunter stepped into the room.

Dammit. Of course, he'd have to catch her like this. Defeated and with tears on her cheeks.

He closed the door, watching her intimately. "I know you must hate me a little right now."

"A little?" She gave a harsh laugh and brushed the tears off her face. "That's the understatement of the century."

Something flickered in his eyes, and for a moment, she thought it might have been pain. But that wouldn't have made any sense. She'd probably just wounded his ego.

"I've come here to talk." His gaze once again turned unreadable. "I want to explain why I did what I did."

"I'm sorry, would that be kidnapping me on my wedding day? Or the part where you fucked me five years ago and forgot I existed."

He was across the floor, pulling her up from the bed before she could blink.

"I never forgot you, angel," he said thickly, his face pressed close to hers. "Let's just clear that up right here and now."

Her heart tripped, but she pushed back the hope that threatened. She couldn't afford such weakness.

"Forget I said anything. It doesn't matter anymore." She swallowed hard, forcing herself to say, "I'm in love with another man, or have you forgotten?"

His nostrils flared, and he shook his head, mouth thinning. "Don't lie to me, Gemma. I know you better than that."

Was she really that transparent? Frustration boiled in her belly. It wasn't right that he could read her so easily!

"Apparently you don't know me that well." She lifted her chin, forcing her gaze to be deliberately hard. "You have to let me go at some point, Hunter. So know this. Once you do, I'm going straight back to Jeffrey, and there's not a *damn* thing you can do about it."

He blinked, the only indication that she'd gotten to him was the slight tic in his jaw.

"Angel, what makes you think I'll let you go?" he asked

softly. His gaze moved over her body. "You promised me forever, and I don't take well to people breaking their promises."

She stopped breathing. Her legs weakened and her mind spun. He was screwing with her head. Of course she knew it. There was no possible way he could literally keep her hidden forever. But it still didn't stop her gut reaction and desperate panic.

She clenched her fists. She couldn't love him again. Wouldn't love him again. Gemma reloaded with the only ammunition she had and then took her shot.

"You were not my only lover, Hunter."

He flinched, his face tightening as if she'd hit him. But he recovered all too soon, saying stealthily, "But I was your first, Gemma. And I intend to be your last."

The sheer arrogance of his statement had her reacting without thought, swinging her palm toward his cheek.

He caught her wrist, eyes burning.

She finally broke, everything inside her crumbling. There was no fighting him.

"I hate you, Hunter. Do you have any idea what you've done to my life?" she choked out, tugging at her wrist. "I was going to start over today with a decent man. I'd put you behind me. And in one day, you've demolished every step I took to get over you."

"First, Jeffrey is not a decent man by any means."

"Oh! What gives you any right—"

"And, second," he ground out. "I don't want you to get over me. Ever."

She swung at him with her other hand, but he captured her second wrist just as easily as the first.

He dragged her body fiercely against his until her curves were squashed against every hard inch of his body; his cock jammed fully erect into her belly.

Heat flared in every inch of her body, and tingles of awareness seared her blood.

His mouth hovered above hers, his breath hot against her face. "You haven't forgotten me any more than I've forgotten you, angel. Admit it."

"But I deserve to," she whispered. "I have every right."

"Yes." His forehead touched hers, his voice unsteady as he said, "But thank God you didn't."

He crushed her mouth with his, the ruthless invasion of his tongue leaving no doubt in her mind that he meant to claim her again tonight.

She struggled, knowing she had to or else she'd be sucked into the vortex of familiar passion between them, knowing she would lose everything she'd fought to gain by trying to love Jeffrey.

She almost succeeded in overpowering her own emotional draw to Hunter—almost made it convincing that this kiss was one-sided. And then he changed the tide.

His lips softened against hers, moving in a gentle caress. This time, when his tongue entered her mouth, it was to tease hers with soft flicks, to coax a response from her.

She gave in all too easily. Her body turned pliant against his; her nipples tightening into hard points as moisture gathered heavy between her legs. Hunter caught the cry of surrender that escaped her mouth.

He released her wrists, but only to slide his hands under the back of her knees to pick her up.

Cradled in his arms, he never broke the kiss as he crossed to the bed.

He laid her gently on the mattress, taking off the cotton dress she'd put on earlier, leaving her once again naked and vulnerable to him.

His gaze scoured her from head to toe before he let out a

strangled groan. He shed his clothes, exposing a body that she could never forget no matter how much she wanted to.

Golden skin, broad shoulders, wonderfully defined muscles on his chest and abdomen. And then lower, strong thighs with a long thick cock between them. He was ready for her. Not that she'd had any doubt.

"Gemma," he whispered, crawling onto the bed next to her. "I need you. You have no idea how much I need you."

Beyond reason and living only for this moment, she lifted her arms to reach for him again.

4

Hunter's chest tightened with emotion. She'd stopped fighting him, if even for just a moment. He hadn't come here with the purpose to make love to her. He'd planned to talk. Needed to make her understand.

But he'd lost it when she'd goaded him about Delmore. Had lost all reason and kissed her. And now, with Gemma giving her body to him readily, he couldn't back out. Only a fool wouldn't take what she offered.

Not willing to let the mood change again, he claimed her mouth once more, tasting her sweetness and drawing forth her fervent response.

Moving his hand off her shoulder, he slid his open palm downward. Cupping a breast, he lifted and jiggled it in his hand, testing the weight.

She was fuller here now than she'd been at the beginning of her womanhood.

He scraped his thumb over her nipple, and she drew in a quick gasp, her tongue sparring faster with his.

Lifting his head, he glanced down at her breasts, observing

the hard, dark pink tips. His mouth watered to taste her. Everywhere. To taste and touch the woman who'd dominated his thoughts for the last five years.

His head swept down, and he closed his mouth over her nipple, his tongue running over the tiny ridges and sucking on her soft flesh.

Beneath him, Gemma moaned and dug her fingers into his hair. Her body arched.

He transferred his attention to the other breast and closed his mouth over it, gorging on her tits like a man starved. He caught her nipple between his teeth, tugging on it just enough to make her cry out. God, she tasted sweet.

"Hunter," she gasped and wiggled out from under him, rolling onto her stomach. She crawled toward the headboard, pleading, "It's too much. Wait—"

"It's not enough." Her ass was now waving in his face like a red flag, and he growled and grabbed her hips, stalling her retreat.

She groaned, her head falling to the pillow, but made no further attempt to escape. In fact, the position she'd just put herself in raised her ass and pussy more prominently for his use.

Coming up behind her on his knees, he rubbed his cock against the slit of her sex. Discovering the slick cream between her swollen folds.

"Stay like that," he ordered, his voice rougher than he intended. "Just like that, angel."

He brought two fingers to his mouth and licked them before placing them between her legs. He toyed with the slit, parting the folds and swirling around the evidence of her desire for him.

Gemma let out a ragged moan, and he watched her head twist on the pillow.

Hunter leaned forward, kissing the middle of her back at the same time he slipped one finger deep into her silken heat. His cock tightened, and his blood pumped harder. Hot. Wet. So snug.

He added a second digit, stretching her and readying her body for when she'd ultimately take him.

"Hunter," she whispered, clenching the bedspread, thrusting her hips back so he sank deeper. "Please."

He pulled his hand from her to cup an ass cheek in each hand, leaning down to kiss the swell of one side.

"You always had the best ass," he muttered, squeezing her cheeks and giving her a gentle bite on one side.

With his fingers still wet from her pussy, he pushed one against the tiny rosebud between her buttocks. Her body went rigid.

"Relax, angel." He pressed with enough pressure to sink deeper into the dry, tight hole. "I'll take you here. Not tonight, but soon."

"Hunter . . ." Her muscles clenched around him.

With a soft laugh, he pulled his finger from her body and focused his gaze lower again.

"But right now, I need to taste your sweet pussy. Remind myself what I've been deprived of all these years."

He drew his tongue down the curves of her bottom to lick the swell of her pussy. She whimpered, her ass clenching in his hand.

"I know you like it when I do that, angel. Would you like me to fuck you with my tongue?"

Not waiting for an answer, he slid his hands down to part her labia and hold her open to him. Leaning forward, he breathed in the musky scent of her, let the perfume of her arousal intoxicate him. His dick pulsed harder for release.

With a hoarse groan, he speared his tongue deep inside her. Her guttural scream in response sent a surge of triumph through him. Good. He wanted her to lose control. Wanted her to be insane with pleasure.

Her juices coated his tongue, a combination of tart and sweet, making him want to taste more. He retreated and licked his lips, savoring the sharp flavor of her before he went back for more.

He moved into her channel deeper this time, and then faster. Setting a rhythm in which he tongue-fucked her. Knowing it might not be enough to bring her release—though it was damn close to bringing him his—he reached beneath her to find her clit.

He discovered the little nub hot and swollen. It was the fuse to her orgasm. The minute he touched it, she went off like a firecracker.

"Hunter!"

Her thighs shook, and the muscles of her channel clenched around his tongue.

Not giving her a chance to recover, he came to his knees behind her and gripped his cock. Sucking in a quick breath, he placed his cock at her entrance and drove himself into her.

The hot spongy walls of her gripped him, still pulsating from her orgasm. He sank deeper, each inch into her body bringing him closer to nirvana.

"Gemma," he whispered, closing his eyes to savor the feel of her. "Oh, God, Gemma."

Too damn long. It had been too long since he'd been inside her. The last time being when he'd taken her virginity. His throat tightened with emotion. With regret. And then with anger. Anger that the bastard Delmore had touched her.

Never again. Never again would he allow that to happen.

Mine.

He gripped her ass and slowly pulled back out of her. Poised at her entrance, he teased her for just a moment, rubbing his cock against her clit, before plunging back to the hilt.

Gemma pushed against the mattress with her hands, rising up so she was balanced on her knees.

Hunter wrapped an arm around her waist and leaned back, pulling her with him. She almost sat on his lap now, riding him in a way that gave him access to the front of her body.

He brought his hands up to cup her breasts, squeezing her nipples as he lifted his hips to impale himself into her again.

"Oh, God, yes," she breathed on a sigh and reached her arms behind her, curling them around his neck and pushing her tits more firmly into his palms.

He pushed harder into her. Faster. The rhythm he'd tried to set became more uncontrolled and desperate. Each thrust into her resounded the word *mine* in his head.

Pinching her nipples now, he kissed the back of her neck. It grew harder to breathe, to bring in more air than he was expending. He gasped in short breaths, his sac tightening with the impending climax.

"Hunter," she whispered, bouncing against his thrusts. "Please. Please, Hunter."

He released one of her tits to slide his hand down between her legs. Finding her clit again, he squeezed it just hard enough to make her cry out sharply.

Then her body clenched around him again, more of her slick cream covering his dick as she orgasmed. Her frenzied cry catapulted him to his own release. He buried his cock to the hilt and grabbed her hips, jerking her hard back against him.

"*Gemma.*" He clenched his jaw, closing his eyes. His hips jerked with each spurt of cum he emptied inside her, again and again, until he was empty, his body weak, and the fog from his climax began to lift from his mind.

It took a moment to remember his surroundings. To realize that he'd finally had Gemma again. And then to understand that her body had gone completely still, and she was breathing in small, short gasps.

"Angel?" He kissed the back of her neck and cuddled the one breast still in his hand.

She jerked away from him, and his cock slid from her body as she moved to the other side of the bed.

"Don't," she whispered raggedly. "Don't say anything."

His brows came together, his heart slowing. "Gemma—"

"If you thought I hated you earlier, it's nothing compared to how I feel about you now." She shook her head. "I just betrayed the man I was supposed to marry."

She pulled a pillow in front of her to hide her nakedness. But though she might hide her body, she couldn't hide the conflicting emotions in her eyes. The confusion, the guilt, the shock.

He latched on to the one emotion that gave him hope: the recognition in her eyes of the intimacy they'd just shared, how powerful it had been.

Sliding his legs off the bed, he drew in a slow breath. Annoyance brewed low in his gut.

He walked around to her side of the bed, keeping his voice firm. "I didn't force you to do anything, Gemma. You went willingly—"

"I didn't accuse you of forcing me. I let myself be seduced. Yes. But only because you touched me." She clutched the pillow tighter. "When you touch me I just . . ." Her jaw hardened and the shutters went down on her expression. "It doesn't matter. It happened, but it won't happen again."

He closed the distance between them. "Like hell it won't, angel." He caught her chin, his gaze burning into hers. "And the sooner you realize you belong to me, the better."

She drew in a sharp breath, and fire flashed in her eyes. "You've got gall."

"No doubt." His lips curved into a sardonic smile before he grew serious again. "We need to talk, Gemma. It's what I came in here to do in the first place."

"Funny how talking ends up to be fucking in your world." She shook her head.

He bit back another wave of frustration. "Gemma, you can't avoid—"

"I know you want to talk, Hunter. And I know you always get what you want. But *please*, give me this time to myself." Her voice cracked on the last words.

Watching the raw emotional vulnerability on her face, guilt stabbed briefly in his gut. Maybe he could give her a brief respite. Time to compose herself.

"All right. I'll give you one hour. When I come back, we'll eat dinner and talk. No more excuses."

She didn't answer, just stared at the comforter on the bed.

"Do you understand, Gemma?"

"Yes," she bit out and raised her heated gaze again. "Now, please go."

Unable to resist, he leaned forward and pulled the pillow away from her body, cupping one breast in his hand.

"I'll be back." He grazed one nipple with his thumb, and triumph seared through him when it tightened and she let out a soft gasp. "And deny it all you want, angel, but you'll be looking forward to it."

She needed to find a way out of here. To get the hell away from Hunter. Before she did something completely stupid. Like sleep with him again.

Gemma sat up on the bed, wrapping her arms around her knees as she stared at the closed door he'd just exited.

God, she hated herself right now. Despised her weakness. He'd barely had to touch her, and she was a puddle at his feet. How could she have made such a horrible choice to let him into her body again?

Going to bed with Hunter didn't feel horrible.

Even her subconscious betrayed her.

"Shut up," she whispered to herself, rocking back and forth on the mattress.

The door clicked, signaling the lock was being undone. Cold and hot swept through her. Oh, please, no. Was he coming back?

A cool breeze rushed in as the door swung inward. Her body sagged with relief once she saw her cousin enter the room.

"Megan!"

Was her cousin alone? Had she managed to escape the other two?

Brad stepped into the doorway and gave them both a quick look. His gaze lingered on Gemma, and his expression turned knowing.

Gemma flushed, drawing a blanket around her body. It wasn't being nude that embarrassed her—he'd already seen her naked on the drive over—it was his expression. Clearly he had no illusions about what had happened between her and Hunter.

Brad cleared his throat and looked back at her cousin, saying softly, "You have half an hour, Megan."

Megan nodded, tucking a strand of pale blond hair behind her ear. "Thank you, Brad. I appreciate it."

Brad? Gemma glanced sharply at her cousin. They were on a first name basis?

The door closed behind him as he left again.

"So-o-o," Megan said brightly. "I'm going to take a wild guess here and assume you and Hunter had some crazy wild sex a few minutes ago."

"*Megan.*"

"Good thing you're not married yet, girl. What a way to start a marriage, huh?"

Gemma's jaw flapped, her cheeks burning. "None of this is a joking matter."

Regret flashed in her cousin's blue eyes before she sighed and gave a short nod. "You're right. I'm sorry. I think I was just trying to lighten the mood a little."

Gemma was silent for a moment, guilt tearing her apart inside. She finally whispered, "I shouldn't have let him touch me. I shouldn't have liked it."

Megan crossed the room and sat down on the edge of the bed. "Don't be so hard on yourself, Gem. You love the guy. And he took advant—"

"I don't love him." The denial came out quicker than she would've liked. "I don't, Megan. Maybe at one point, but now . . . now I've got Jeffrey."

Megan didn't look convinced. "You know, speaking of Jeffrey, at dinner Brad was asking me some interesting questions about him."

"At dinner? You had dinner with Brad?"

Megan glanced away, her cheeks turning pink.

Gemma shook her head, marveling at the change in her cousin. This afternoon after they'd been taken, Megan had been petrified, pale, and barely able to form a word. Now she was back to her old self, bubbly and funny. As comfortable as if they were just spending the weekend at a spa in the mountains.

"Brad's not a bad guy," her cousin finally said. "He's actually pretty cool. We've been talking a lot. And he agreed to let me come see you for a while, even though Hunter told him not to."

Panic clutched in Gemma's belly, and she leaned forward to grip her cousin's hand. "Brad hasn't . . . have you two—"

"No!" Megan laughed and rolled her eyes. "Jeez, Gemma. He hasn't tried anything. Though I've gotta say, I'm almost disappointed. The man is *hot*."

Gemma's mouth tightened. "He's too old for you, Megan. Besides, have you forgotten that part where he kidnapped us?"

Megan's expression turned schooled; she suddenly looked older, wiser than her years. "They have their reasons, Gem. I'm not defending what they did, but it sounds like there's something going on. Something with Jeffrey."

The reminder of Jeffrey had Gemma leaning forward, brows

drawn together. "You said Brad was asking you questions about Jeffrey. What kind?"

"He was wondering how much I knew about his business."

"The shelter for runaways?"

"I guess so. I couldn't tell him much. There's not a lot I know about what he does."

"What else did Brad ask you?"

"Whether I'd ever noticed anything strange about Jeffrey." She paused. "And he asked if I ever got a bad vibe off him."

Okay, this was weird going on weirder. Gemma frowned and looked out the window into the dark night. "How bizarre. You of course told him no."

"Actually," Megan's voice grew more wary. "I told him yes."

Gemma's head whipped back, and she stared at her cousin incredulously. "What do you mean? Megan, what aren't you telling me?"

"Gem, I didn't want to say anything. But I've always got a really weird vibe from Jeffrey. In fact, I'll say it: the guy straight up freaks me out."

Gemma flinched as if she'd been slapped. "Are you serious? Why didn't you ever say anything—"

"Because I wanted you to be happy. I knew how important it was for you to move on with this guy." Megan cleared her throat and looked down at her hands, which she twisted in her lap. "But I'm going to be honest now—like I should have been in the first place. I'm almost glad Hunter took you today. I don't think you should marry Jeffrey."

Shock ripped the breath from Gemma's lungs. When she finally recovered, it was only to sputter, "I don't believe it. This morning you were all too eager to get me down the aisle. You came to warn me about Hunter."

"I was wrong."

Gemma stood up, pulling the sheet with her to cover her

body. She swallowed hard against the lump in her throat. Against the panic that everyone she trusted was turning against her.

"You were wrong," she repeated. "What, have they brainwashed you? You sound just like Hunter. There is nothing—"

"Gemma—"

"*Nothing* wrong with Jeffrey."

Megan stared at her, expression wary. "Okay. Well, I hope you're right then, Gemma. I hope Jeffrey really is the prized citizen of the community. And once the guys let us go, you can run back and marry him. Because of course that's what you want. Right? To spend the rest of your life with Jeffrey Delmore. Forget Hunter ever existed."

Nauseous now, Gemma rushed toward the door, but it opened before she got there. Brad stepped inside, his gaze taking in the scene. From Megan's pale face to Gemma, who couldn't control the tremble from the mix of fear and rage rushing through her body.

"Everything okay, ladies?"

"No." Gemma didn't even look at him as she responded.

Megan slid off the bed, her face crumbling with disappointment as she walked toward the door.

"I'm sorry, Gemma," she whispered and touched Gemma's arm lightly. "But it had to be said."

Her cousin left the room, but the door didn't close immediately. Gemma looked up and met Brad's hard gaze. "What?"

"You shouldn't take out your own uncertainties on your cousin. She just said what you needed to hear." Brad closed the door, pausing long enough to say, "Hunter will return shortly."

5

Hunter had just finished his shower when someone entered the small gym in the safe house. He glanced up to see Brad step into the hall. Hunter nodded his head in acknowledgment and passed him, heading to the locker.

"I haven't had a chance to speak with Gemma," he admitted before his friend had the chance to ask.

"I gathered."

Hunter pulled his stack of clothes from the locker. "What makes you say that?"

"I just came from her room."

Hunter went still, icy fury rushing through his blood. Brad had been in her room? Why? "And just what the hell were you doing in her room?"

Brad leaned back against one of the lockers, folding his arms across his chest. "Megan asked to see her cousin. So I let her."

"You had no authorization to do that."

"I don't really think I need any. It's not right keeping Gemma isolated up in the south tower. There's no reason she can't be with her cousin."

"I'll decide what's right for her," Hunter shot back, pulling on his clothes.

"Right. Like you decided it was okay to forgo questioning her for a good fuck instead?"

Hunter had his hands wrapped around Brad's T-shirt in seconds, slamming him back against the locker. "Don't presume to tell me how to do my job."

Brad twisted out from under him, forced an arm across Hunter's shoulders, and reversed their position. The cold metal from the locker bit into Hunter's back, and he clenched his jaw.

Brad brought his face in close. "I'm not telling you how to do your job. I'm reminding you that we don't have much time to nail Delmore, and you're busy screwing around. Literally." He released him and stepped away with a curse. "This wasn't supposed to be about getting your girl back, man. I know we joked about it being a nice bonus, but this is consuming you, and there're bigger things at stake."

Hunter stepped away, grinding his teeth together. "I'm on my way back up to talk to her now."

Brad was quiet for a moment. "I'm sorry, Hunter. I'm a bit high strung tonight. Headquarters just got word that another body was found."

Hunter stilled, his heart slamming in his chest. "Another one of Delmore's?"

"Yes. She went missing last week. She was found up on a ranch in Canada this morning. She was in jaguar form when she died. Shot three times."

"*Fuck.*" Hunter's throat grew raw with anger, helplessness, and guilt. He swallowed hard. They needed to shut down Delmore's operation. Now. They couldn't afford to wait—to let another girl die. "What did you get from Megan tonight? Anything?"

Brad's shoulders visibly relaxed, his tormented expression easing some.

"Nothing tangible. Though she admitted to me that Delmore has always scared her a bit. That the guy always gave her a bad vibe. And she said that she thought Delmore might have hit on her once."

"She couldn't tell?"

"I'm getting the impression that she doesn't have a lot of experience with men." Brad's lips twitched before he cleared his throat. "Apparently Delmore offered her a backrub when Gemma was in the shower one day. Kept telling her how pretty she was."

"Hmm." It wouldn't surprise him in the least if Delmore had tried to make a move on Gemma's younger cousin. Though it definitely made him a scumbag, it didn't give them anything to convict the guy on.

"Keep me posted on whether Megan remembers anything." Hunter slammed his locker closed again. "I'm heading back upstairs. I think I've been way too soft with Gemma."

Hunter dropped a plate of food next to Gemma, and it bounced on the mattress, the roll almost sliding off the plate.

"We're talking. Now."

She didn't glance up at his announcement or look at the food. Just kept her eyes closed as she lay on the bed, arms folded above her head.

"I'll start." He drew in a slow breath. It was time to tell her everything. "I haven't been completely honest with you, Gemma."

That got her to open her eyes—or at least one peeked open. She regarded him warily.

"I'd like to say I'm surprised," she said. "But not so much."

"Five years ago we had a connection that neither of us could have expected." He sat down on the edge of the bed but didn't touch her. "You gave yourself to me—"

"Can you not remind me of that please?"

"We marked each other."

Her head snapped back to him, both eyes wide open now.

"That means nothing. Marking is an old sentimentality that the elders believed in. Nobody in our generation actually takes it seriously anymore. It's the equivalent of a hickie."

Hunter's blood pounded and he swept his gaze over her— from the tawny hair that fell around her shoulders to her deep brown eyes that condemned him to pink compressed lips and then over each curve and dip of her body that he loved.

"How many times do I need to tell you not to lie to me, Gemma?" he asked softly. "It meant something to us. To me."

Her gaze flashed with regret and anger. "Well, guess what? Even if it did, you left me after that night. You lost any rights to me the day you walked out of my life."

His jaw clenched just before he ground out, "Because I was *dead*."

Gemma's mouth fell open, disbelief rushing through her. Was he completely delusional? He was dead? *Dead?*

She gave a slow shake of her head. "Well, once again you confirmed my theory that you're certifiable."

"Angel—"

"You were dead. Oh, right. Well, I have to give you originality for excuses, Hunter. Because that's certainly one I haven't heard before."

He slid forward on the bed, reaching out to encircle her wrist. She tugged, but he refused to let her back away from him.

"I'm not who you think I am."

She gave a bitter laugh, her stomach twisting. "Hunter, I figured that out a long time ago."

His mouth tightened, but he plunged on. "I'm not a martial arts instructor. I'm an agent for the Elite Shifter Agency and have been for the last eight years."

Gemma blinked and then blinked again. She couldn't have formed a word if she tried. Thick silence hung above them as his words looped in her head.

"The ESA?" she finally said in a flat tone. With a forced laugh, she shook her head. "You. An ESA agent. That's rich, Hunter."

He didn't even look offended, just watched her and then gave a slow nod. With his free hand, he reached into the pocket of his jeans and pulled out a badge, flipping it open. Before she could completely take in what she was looking at, he went on.

"When we first met, I was working on a case that dealt with a pretty high-profile drug dealer. When our target made an attempt on my life, the agency made the decision to let it appear that he'd succeeded in killing me." He flipped his badge closed and pocketed it again. "I spent the next four years without exchanging a word with my family or anyone I loved. I was reassigned to cases on the other side of the country, even then only under deep cover. It wasn't until the dealer and his team were finally prosecuted, convicted, and locked up that my agency felt it safe for me to resurface."

Gemma's pulse raced within his grasp, and she felt strangely light-headed.

Hunter's lips twisted into a smile, but there was no humor behind it. "To come back from the dead essentially."

She shook her head slowly. "You're really an ESA agent? You told me you were a martial arts—"

"I know what I told you, Gemma." He stood up with a sigh and released her, walking to the window to look out over the night. "The agency encourages us to keep a low profile. To be careful with whom we divulge our careers to."

"Right," she choked on emotion. "And I was just some woman you were screwing."

His fists clenched. "You were so much more than that. You can't possibly know how much you meant to me. I'm so sorry, angel. If I could have sent word, I would have. My own parents didn't know where I was. . . ."

"But they knew you were an ESA agent."

"Yes." He turned to look at her. "And I would have told you as well, not long after our night together. I wanted so many things for us after that night together."

Something warm sparked inside her. Maybe hope. Maybe not. She snuffed it out, knowing there was no room for such an emotion.

"When I was told I could resurface, I went to find you first." He paused. "You were already engaged."

Pain ripped through before the anger overpowered it. "Don't turn this on me. I had no clue what happened to you," her voice shook. "You have no idea what I went through—"

"I can guess, angel," he said gently. "And I'm so sorry. I would have left you be, let you get on with your life." His jaw hardened. "But once I realized who you were marrying, everything changed. I couldn't let you marry Jeffrey Delmore."

Gemma stood from the bed, her heart pounding in her chest now and tears of frustration prickling. Everything he said sounded crazy. Like something out of a bad thriller movie. Hunter was an ESA agent who'd had to feign his own death? The fact that he worked for the ESA alone was surreal enough.

And yet not once since the moment he'd shown her his badge had she doubted him. Her stomach flipped, and a hope she'd long ago smothered threatened to resurface. *No. Never again.*

"You lost any right to interfere in my life, Hunter. Fine, you've explained where you were the last five years—but let me be clear. There is no chance of us being together again. Ever."

Hunter crossed the room in seconds, pulling her flush against him. When she struggled, he slid his hand into her hair and tugged to hold her still.

"Don't be so quick to say that, angel." His gaze raked her face and then her body. "Not after this afternoon."

Her body stirred to life, moisture already gathered heavy in her pussy. *Stop.* She silently willed herself to be strong. "This afternoon was a mistake. It won't happen again."

"And I've told you that it will." He gave a soft laugh and moved his other hand down her back to cup her ass. "Many times."

"Never."

"Always." His mouth covered hers, gently, almost lovingly, before his tongue slipped inside to explore.

She pushed at his chest, arched away from him, but he gave her no leave. Instead, he reached down to hook one of her legs around his waist.

A second later, his thumb was on her clit, stroking away any leftover inhibitions. Slow and steady, his hand moved on her. The sounds of her slickness filled the air when he pushed a finger inside her core. Her hands ceased to push him away, instead moving over the hard contours of his shoulders as she moaned softly into his mouth.

Physical. It was only a physical reaction her body was having. He meant nothing to her anymore. Nothing.

Her heart tripped, calling bullshit on her inner pep talk.

Hunter's fingers moved faster on her, bringing her closer and closer to that intense release. His mouth sought the pulse beating wildly in her neck, sucking hard as he marked her in the same spot he had years ago.

Her body exploded, sending her mind into a zone of colors and free falling. She gripped his shoulders, holding on for dear life as she trembled through the aftermath.

Hunter lifted his head and brought his fingers—which had just brought her release—up to his mouth. He licked the tips and closed his eyes, desire and pleasure sweeping across his face.

"I rest my case."

Her pulse still thundering, Gemma blinked to clear the fog from her mind. *Rest my case?*

"You should eat your dinner. You've got to be hungry, and we still have some serious things to discuss."

Oh, God, he'd simply touched her just to prove that he could. That she would let him. And dammit, she had. She was such a complete fool.

My body, not my heart. She repeated the mantra in her head as she went to pick at the food on the plate. She would need the energy from the food, because tonight she would escape. She had to escape.

Already her heart was at risk, not to mention her future. Guilt twisted in her gut.

"What else do we have to talk about?" she asked quietly, cutting into the steak on the plate he'd given her.

"Jeffrey Delmore."

Her knife and fork scratched against the plate as her hands jerked in surprise.

"What about him?"

Hunter's gaze clouded, and he sighed deeply, folding his hands across his chest.

"What do you know about the man you were supposed to have married, angel?"

She ignored the "supposed to have married "comment and took another bite of meat. Once she swallowed, she cleared her throat. "He's a very generous man. Runs a nonprofit organization for runaways."

"Is that so?"

Gemma lifted her chin. "Yes. Where are you going with this, Hunter?"

"How does he help the runaways?"

"He helps send them home—if they wish. Or if they don't wish to return home . . . he finds another ideal situation for them. But he gets them off the street."

"I'm curious about this . . . other ideal situation."

She ate a bite of roll, eyeing him warily.

"Have you met any of these girls, angel?"

"I have."

"Do you follow up with them?"

"Why on earth would I? Hunter, I don't run the organization. Jeffrey does."

Hunter answered her question with another one of his. "How does Jeffrey Delmore make money, if it's nonprofit?"

Gemma drew a slow breath in. He was treating her like she was on the witness stand. This was ridiculous! "I really am under no obligation to answer your questions, Hunter."

"I could send Joaquin or Brad to question you if you'd like."

"Maybe that would be better."

His eyes narrowed. "Answer me, angel. They may not be so nice in their efforts."

"This is nice?" She snorted and shook her head. "Jeffrey comes from a very well-off family, if you must know. Money is rarely an issue for him."

"Have you ever noticed anything suspicious? Anything that caused you to think something wasn't right?"

She opened her mouth to say no and then hesitated as something flickered in the back of her mind. But just like that, the thought was gone again.

"No. I've never noticed anything." She set her knife back down. "Now it's my turn to do some questioning. What's your deal with Jeffrey?"

"Besides the fact he took my woman?" Hunter raised an eyebrow, his lips twitching. Then his expression sobered again. "The ESA has been investigating Jeffrey Delmore for several years now. We have reason to believe his organization to help runaways is a front for something entirely more sinister."

"Sinister?" she sputtered. "Like what?"

"Like trafficking women in the billion dollar industry of underground fuck hunts."

"Fuck hunts?" Gemma stared at him, not sure what a fuck hunt was and not sure she wanted to know. But she was certain Jeffrey had nothing to do with it.

"I'm not surprised that you've never heard of them. In fact, it relieves me. Some of the men at the agency were convinced you were in on it."

"In on what? Hunter, you're not making any sense to me. Tell me what a fuck hunt is and why you think Jeffrey has something to do with it."

Hunter's jaw flexed. "Shifter women have been disappearing for years now, turning up dead from being shot in their animal form. We got a lead a few years back from one woman, a werefalcon, who escaped. The story she told was that she had been driven to a farm and handed off to a man who savagely raped her. Then she was injected with a drug that forced her to shift into her were side, after which she was set free on the expansive property. Set free and hunted."

Gemma gripped the edge of the bedspread, her blood chilling as nausea threatened. Being raped in human form and then hunted and killed in shifter? Who would do such a thing? The idea was too horrific to even be believable.

"You can't be serious. Surely nobody would—"

"Listen." Hunter sat down on the bed and held her gaze. "The woman was a runaway, Gemma. She told us it was one of Delmore's employees who'd taken her to the ranch."

"*No.* You'd say anything to keep me from marrying him. You lie, Hunter!"

"Not about this, Gemma."

"Get out." She scurried off the bed and away from him. "Get out!"

He stood and gave a slight nod. "Don't believe me, angel? Fine, let's watch a little movie. Maybe you'll change your mind after watching the recorded statement of the woman who survived."

She ground her teeth together, watching him move to the door. It was a farce. It had to be. Was Hunter framing Jeffrey to get her back? The idea was ludicrous, but she couldn't discount it.

The door shut behind him and locked.

When he came back, she'd be prepared for him. She'd find a way to escape and get back to Jeffrey and discover for herself just what was going on.

A twinge of unease kicked in her gut, and she rubbed the back of her neck. A little voice in her head argued, *What if Hunter's right?* Jeffrey was a wonderful man. For God's sake, the city had given him an award for being an outstanding citizen last year.

There was no way he could be involved. This was just Hunter being ultrapossessive and doing anything he could to get what he wanted. He'd probably even suckered in a few of his friends at the ESA to help.

She paced the room and clenched her teeth. Well, this time, Hunter wouldn't get her.

6

Gripping the film that would hopefully persuade Gemma, Hunter made his way back to her room. Frustration ate at his belly—that she didn't believe him, that she'd be so quick to even dismiss the possibility.

Unlocking the door, he pushed it open and frowned. It was dark. Shit, what the hell was she trying to pull? He crouched on the defense, moving inside, looking for the light switch.

"*Ummph!*"

He staggered under the weight of whatever she smashed across his back. The pounding of her feet echoed as she shot past him and through the open door.

"Dammit!" He stumbled after her as broken glass fell from his clothes.

Up ahead he could hear Gemma thundering down the stairs, putting more distance between them as she made a run for the front of the building. And chances were she'd get there before him.

Shit! He'd been an idiot, treating her too soft, giving her too much damn freedom. Reaching the bottom of the stairwell, he turned just in time to see the front door swing open and Gemma sprint out it—shifting midleap. And then she was off—running to God knew where. Hell, she probably didn't even know where she was going.

Joaquin appeared in the hall, eyebrows raised. "Who just went out the front door?"

"Gemma."

"Well, that's not a good sign," Joaquin drawled and followed him onto the porch; they both glanced around. "You want me to help you search?"

Seeing a flicker in the moonlight to the north, Hunter shook his head.

"I've got this." His low response trembled with barely restrained anger.

Hunter leapt down the few stairs and headed out after her. His body stretched and popped in a smooth transformation to jaguar. The clothes he'd changed into earlier exploded from his body—which was the reason he preferred being naked. He'd only put on clothes tonight to make Gemma feel more comfortable. *Stupid.*

She'd pushed him too far this time. And when he found her, she'd know just how foolish it had been to run—to run from the house, but, even worse, to run from what they had together.

He growled and picked up speed. Tonight everything would change. Tonight he would take her full submission.

His paws slapped the earth as he let out a frustrated growl. His temper spiked as he jumped over a large rock along the riverside. Who was he kidding, though? He wasn't just angry with Gemma; he was angry at himself. He'd ignored all his training and instincts and let his guard down. Dammit, he *knew* better. But she did that to him, made him lose all sensibility.

He slipped in the rocky banks, trying to find purchase as he kept his speed.

One good piece of luck was that he'd picked up her scent.

She had indeed gone this way. His gaze flickered out over the water, and he pushed aside the brief stab of unease. He highly doubted she'd have tried to cross the river. Not at night.

Hunter slowed his run; the fur on his back lifted in a warning that something had changed.

The surface of the shoreline narrowed, merging into the hillside. He glanced at the ground, sniffing to keep her scent. That's when he noticed. The paw prints had changed to footprints. *She'd shifted back to human.*

He hesitated, debating whether to continue in jaguar form or shift back as well. With his dark fur he'd be more stealth in the moonlight, but he knew the terrain well and could acknowledge that manipulating it in human form might be easier at this point.

Knowing he had already lost too much time, he shifted back and a moment later ran with quick intent across the hill—following the trail of her footprints in the moonlight.

She'd turned away from the river. Interesting. Was she heading up toward the hills? But why? That would be the complete opposite direction of the road back to the city.

He froze as something blocked out the moonlight to his left. Hunter spun and dodged to the right, barely missing getting smashed in the head with a fist-sized rock.

"Are you insane?" He stepped toward her, but she danced backward.

"I won't go back, Hunter. I won't listen to your lies." Her shoulders quaked, her pale skin luminescent in the moonlight.

"Gemma." He put out his hand to calm her.

She lunged at him again, but he grabbed her wrist. Spinning her away from him, he wrapped his arm around her waist and squeezed her slight bones until she cried out and dropped the rock.

She struggled against him, groaning with frustration.

"You'd hit me over the head with that?" he rasped harshly,

his fury hardly abating. "Do you realize it could kill someone?"

Gemma stilled, her breathing uneven, before she let out a
choked sob and crumpled against him.

He tightened his arm around her, pulling her body harder
against his. His cock ground against her back, just above her
ass.

"Why, Gemma?" he asked again, his voice hoarse. Incredulity
still rolled through him. And yet his body reacted to being so
close to her softness, to her scent, and to the sound of her rapid
breathing.

Releasing her wrist, he moved his hand to cup her breast,
squeezing the soft flesh until she whimpered.

Against his rough palm, her nipple hardened.

His voice cracked. "Answer me, angel."

He needed to know. Needed to hear her admit that she'd been
willing to use such violence against him. If she said the words,
she wouldn't need the rock. The realization alone would kill
him.

Gemma's heart thudded so loud in her chest she was certain
he could hear it. Realization at what she'd almost done sunk in.
She'd tried to bash Hunter's head in with a rock. Her throat
tightened with emotion, and she choked out a gasp.

How had it gotten to this point? What was she doing? Facing the truth and her fear with violence? She hadn't wanted to
believe what Hunter had said about Jeffrey, but deep in her gut,
she knew he was telling the truth. And each mile she put between herself and the house had compounded her suspicion
that it wasn't a lie. Especially when she'd started to remember
things. . . .

"Gemma?"

"No," she whispered, her words barely audible. "I could
never hurt you, Hunter."

Hunter's relief was evident as he buried his face against her neck.

"Then tell me why," he demanded roughly and moved the arm that was around her stomach, sliding his palm downward to tease his fingers into the curls between her legs. "Why do you continue to fight me? To fight us? When your body makes no such pretenses."

Her head fell back against his chest, tossing from side to side. "Because I have to."

"But you don't, angel. Not anymore." He turned her around in his arms, his gaze fervently seeking hers. "Do you love him? Forget everything I told you about Jeffrey earlier and just answer me that. Are you in love with him?"

Did she love Jeffrey? Her heart skipped a beat. And then it was so damn clear. She didn't love him. God, not even a little bit. Probably never had. The implications of what that meant rocked her entire foundation. It was all she could do to answer Hunter with a tiny shake of her head to indicate no.

His breath released on a whoosh. "Stop fighting us, Gemma. *Please.*"

A tear spilled down her cheek as she blinked. She didn't want to fight anymore. Couldn't. Her heart rebelled against the idea of pushing away the man she just wanted to hold her. "No more fighting, Hunter."

He pressed his forehead against hers and whispered, "Thank God."

Her heart slammed against her rib cage. Once again her life had just changed course. And this time, she knew it was heading in the right direction.

When Hunter lifted his head, the mood had shifted, crackling with awareness and tension. The possessiveness and determination in his gaze took her breath away.

"You shouldn't have run tonight, Gemma."

"I know." She swallowed hard. "It was just too much."

He touched her cheek, and his expression softened just a bit. "You are my mate, angel. You belong to *me*. You will deny it no more?"

She swallowed hard, her knees going weak. "I will deny it no more."

Then the significance of what she'd just done hit her. She'd verbally agreed to be his mate. And she knew what was about to come; every part of her body responded at the idea. Her breasts swelled, the tips tightening. Cream flooded her pussy, and she squeezed her thighs together to ease the ache.

His gaze darkened, moving over her. "Tonight your body and mind will know and accept me completely." He ran a finger across her bottom lip then slipped it inside to find wet warmth. "You will show your loyalty."

"Yes," she whispered.

Hunter curled a hand over her shoulder and gently pressed down, urging her to her knees before him.

The dirt on the ground bit into her knees, but she barely noticed the slight discomfort; her attention was already focused on Hunter's cock, thick and erect, the tip almost red in the moonlight.

She knew this was about dominance, that Hunter wanted her to prove her devotion by being submissive tonight. It was common after shifters mated. After how hard she'd fought him today, she could understand his need for her total surrender. The idea of giving into his every demand and want aroused her more than she could ever have realized.

"Take me in your mouth, angel."

His soft command left no room to argue, not that she had any inclination to.

She wrapped her fingers around his flesh. He felt like hot silk wrapped over the hardest of steel. When her finger caught the tip, she found a drop of fluid.

"Taste it."

Gemma leaned forward, her hair falling around her face, and let her tongue flick out to capture the precum. Salty and warm. All male. All Hunter.

His breath caught, and she licked the tip again, watching his thighs tighten in response.

Hunter took her hair in his hand and held her in a grip that kept her close. He pressed her head forward, until his cock slid past her lips.

Gemma's eyelids fluttered shut, and she relaxed her jaw, bringing him fully into her mouth. He plunged deep, until the head of his cock hit the back of her throat, then he eased back a bit.

She sucked on his flesh, licking over the length of him. When he relaxed his grip on her hair, she took the freedom to move on him again, bringing him deep and then sliding her lips back off so she could suck on the plump head.

"Gemma," he rasped, his hips bucking in response.

Awareness zinged through her. She knew he was in control, but when his cock was in her mouth, there definitely seemed to be a shift in who held the power.

She slid back down the length of him again, reaching a hand up to caress his sac.

"Yes." He groaned and pulled her mouth from him, pushing her lower, until the softness of his balls brushed her lips.

She opened, obeying his silent command as she sucked and licked over his flesh. Wrapping her hand around his cock, she slid her fingers up and down, still paying extra attention to his sac with her mouth.

"Shit." He gasped and pulled her head up again, plunging his cock back deep into her mouth.

He held her still, not giving her much room to move as he began to fuck her mouth. Faster. Deeper. Harder.

Gemma relaxed her mouth around him, knowing he was close to his release. She continued a soft massage of his sac while he plundered her mouth. He tightened in her hand and his thighs clenched.

"Gemma." He choked out her name and then came in her mouth.

She drank from him everything he gave, enjoying the feel and taste of his salty release on her tongue, loving the intimacy and trust required for her to have let a man come in her mouth for the first time.

His hand slipped from her hair and he cupped her face, his thrusts nowhere near as strong as they had been. When he was finally spent, he slid out past her lips a moment later, rubbing the head of his cock against her cheek as he groaned.

Gemma licked her lips and swallowed the last drop of him before lifting her head to look at him.

His gaze was smoky, his chest rising with each ragged breath he drew in.

In an instant, he was on his knees next to her on the ground. This time when his hand cupped her shoulder it was to propel her backward onto the dirt.

Confusion swept through her, and she tried to sit up. Surely he needed her to bring him to arousal again before he joined them.

"Hunter—"

"First I need to taste you."

With her back against the earth and grass, she trembled at his ardent admission.

His large rough hands wrapped around her legs, pushing them wide and forcing her knees up toward her chest.

Her heart pounded as he lay down between her thighs. A second later his mouth was on her. His tongue found her hypersensitive clit; he licked at it and rubbed, showing no mercy before he slid lower to plunge his tongue into the depths of her pussy.

A guttural moan ripped through her, and her hips ground

against his face. He ate at her without pause, so aggressive and fervent in his purpose she could barely keep a thought in her head.

Lifting her head, she watched him. Watched his dark head move between her legs as his mouth made love to her.

She dug her fingers into the earth beneath her, letting the dirt and rocks sift through her hands while she rode Hunter's tongue, letting the sensation of his mouth bring her higher and higher.

"Fuck, you taste good," he muttered and caught her clit between his teeth, tugging lightly.

"Hunter." She gasped, her ass clenching at the exquisite stab of pleasure and pain.

He released the tiny nub, soothing it again with his tongue before drawing it into his mouth to suckle. Releasing her legs, he slid his hands under her bottom, lifting her.

His mouth found a closer fit against her pussy, and the intensity of pleasure skyrocketed. She twisted her head back and forth, digging her hands deeper into the earth

"Oooh. Yes." Her hips jerked, her body arching against and then away from him. "Oh. Oh, Hunter!"

"Mmm." Hunter buried his tongue deep into her slick channel once more, and she exploded.

Her legs fell to the ground on either side of his head, and she lifted her ass into the air, riding his face as the spasms of pleasure assailed her.

Thinking wasn't even an option, so many sensations and emotions rushed through her. She struggled to breathe as her heart slammed hard against her rib cage. And Hunter's tongue, wet and rough, continued to move over and around her pussy.

She reached down to stroke his hair, her pulse slowing as she fell back against the dirt. Watching the moon, she heaved an unsteady sigh. It was almost terrifying how quickly she had fallen back in love with him. But then, had she ever fallen out?

Hunter kissed the inside of each thigh before returning to press his mouth gently against her clit.

She felt him grab her ass again, lift her lower body off the ground, and then without any warning, he'd plunged his cock into her swollen channel.

Gemma gasped, her body arching at the sudden invasion. He was erect so soon? She blinked in surprise as he moved to lie on top of her, his arms braced on each side of her head, his biceps bulging.

She met Hunter's fiery gaze as he sank deeper, stretching her and invading each inch of her body.

"You're mine, angel," he said vehemently. "Never forget it." He looked down to where they were joined. "Never forget who owns this pussy."

Heat flooded her body, staining her cheeks and breasts. His possessive claim on her sent another rush of heavy arousal between her legs. Softened her heart a bit. Because behind his words, she heard the desperation, the fear that he might lose her again.

"I'm yours," she whispered and wrapped her arms around his neck, pulling his mouth down to hers. "All yours, Hunter."

7

Hunter plunged his tongue between her lips, the blood rushing through his veins. The fear he might be too rough with her disintegrated. She understood his right to dominate tonight. That he was traditional in so many aspects of their culture. And he even suspected the little vixen was enjoying being submissive.

God, she was an amazing woman.

Her flesh hugged him, wet and hot, dragging his cock deeper into her body until he was nestled at her womb and she squirmed beneath him.

He lifted his head again to look down at his cock buried inside her. Pulling out a bit, he was captivated by the shimmer of her slick juices on his dick. He pressed back into her, harder this time, unable to hold back a strangled groan.

Leaning down, he caught her mouth once more. Her tongue met his halfway, tangling in a frantic dance while his plunges turned savage.

His thoughts grew jumbled and he slowed again, pulling

fully from her body. No. He couldn't finish this way. He needed to have her complete submission. In every way.

Her eyelids fluttered open, confusion in her gaze.

"Turn over, angel. On your hands and knees."

She inhaled sharply and her breasts rose, hard nipples scraping his chest. Understanding flickered in her eyes and then a mix of excitement and maybe panic. But wordlessly she obeyed, moving to the position he'd requested.

Her smooth back glowed in the moonlight, the curves of her ass an invitation he had no plans of declining. The cleft of her sex just below her derriere was already slick with the lubricant he'd need.

He moved forward on his knees, pressing two fingers against her pussy and then inside. Gathering the cream there, he brought it back to the tight rosebud of her ass and pressed inside with one finger.

Her body went rigid, and he heard her small whimper.

Pausing, he asked, "Have you ever done this with anyone, angel?"

"No. Besides you, there's been only Jeffrey, but we never . . . not there . . ." She trailed off, her voice soft.

At the mention of Delmore, Hunter's jaw hardened. He hated the bastard. Hated even more to think he'd touched Gemma. *Never again.*

He leaned down to brush a kiss against the small of her back, adding a second finger into her tight little asshole.

"I'll go slow, Gemma," he promised.

Working the two fingers inside her, he stretched her and prepared her for his cock. Reaching his other hand in front of her, he found her clit and began a slow pressure rub.

When she began to relax again, made those sexy little moans, he added a third finger, forming a triangle out of the three to penetrate with.

He pulled his three fingers free and gripped his cock, quickly placing it at the rosebud entrance between her cheeks, pushing in just enough to keep the momentum.

Gathering more moisture with his finger, he continued the steady massage of her clit and pushed in past the first tight ring in her ass.

Gemma moaned and her thighs trembled slightly.

"Am I hurting you?" he asked, stilling in his progression inside her.

"No," she shook her head and rotated her hips. "It feels . . . not bad. Different."

"Different good?" He pulled his finger from her clit and licked it, loving the brief taste of her juices again. With the pad of his finger dampened, he brought it back to the swollen nub between her legs.

"Oooh, Hunter. Yes, good." She let out a ragged breath. "But I'll let you know if that changes when you're all the way in."

He gave a soft laugh, helping ease some of the tension in his body. He was strung like a damn violin, resisting the urge to just plunge into her and take his own pleasure. His balls hurt; his cock was hard enough to pound nails.

Slowly now, he eased farther into her until he hit the second tight ring in her ass. He rubbed her clit steadily as he pushed past it. Her body stiffened.

"Relax, angel. Just relax." He clenched his teeth, slowing even more in his advance.

He eased past the second ring and all the way into her. She let out a sharp gasp, her thighs trembling.

"Gemma, fuck you feel so good."

Hunter almost came on the spot. Her body squeezed around his dick so tight, so hot. He used his free hand to rub her ass cheek, giving her a second to adjust to him.

She drew in a big breath and then exhaled loudly.

It was all the go-ahead he needed. He began a slow penetration, making sure she wasn't too uncomfortable. But the longer he rubbed her clit and slid his cock in and out of her ass, the more her pussy got wet. He felt her slickness on his finger, heard her arousal in the panting breaths. And then she began to move, pushing back to meet his thrusts.

"*Hunter.*" The channel of her ass tightened around him as she came, more cream coating his finger.

"Gemma. Sweet Gemma," he moved faster in her, rubbing at her clit blindly. His sac tightened. "Not . . . going . . . to last much . . . *fuck.*"

The climax slammed him. His vision blurred as cum exploded from his cock, again and again, until he couldn't breathe and his grip on her hips was the only thing keeping him from falling over.

His blood slowed again and clarity returned. Gemma had slid forward, half-lying, but her ass was still in the air.

He pulled his cock from her, wiping the sticky remains of his spend off with a nearby leaf.

"Gemma?" He came to his feet, surprised to find his legs still a bit unsteady. He glanced down at her, hoping she wasn't hurt. Or more so, that she wasn't ashamed at what had happened between them like she had been last time.

He crouched down and touched her shoulder, asking gently, "How are you?"

She rolled over and came to her knees, a tiny smile on her full lips. "I'm okay."

Her response was soft, almost uncertain. He touched her cheek, concern flaring. "Are you sure, Gemma? Did I push you too—"

"Not at all, Hunter. I promise," she assured him before her lashes lowered. "It was . . . not at all what I thought it would be."

"Did you maybe even . . . like it?"

She made a noise that was a cross between a sigh and a laugh. "I think maybe . . . I did."

Hunter tucked a strand of hair behind her ear and smiled. "Good." Because he had serious plans to take her ass again in the future.

She stifled a yawn and pushed her way into standing position. "I'm also a little tired."

A wave of tenderness swept through him. She looked every bit as exhausted as she sounded. He'd put her through hell today. Damn. Had it only been this morning that he'd seen her again, come back into her life after five years?

He stepped forward and pulled her against his body. Her head nestled against his shoulder, and her arms moved around his waist.

Hunter brushed a kiss across her forehead and closed his eyes. His heart twisted, expanding with love for her. Never again would he lose her. Never.

"Let's head back to the house, angel. We'll get some sleep."

Hunter slipped from the bed and went to the window, looking out at the moon that had sunk lower in the sky. Sunrise would be upon them in a few hours. And then not long after that, the sting on Delmore would be set into action.

His blood pumped quicker with excitement. They would nail the guy this time. He was certain of it.

Hunter thrust a hand through his hair and glanced back at the bed. Beneath the tangled blankets, Gemma slept, her body curled up on her side and her hands beneath one cheek. Tawny hair spilled over the white pillowcase, pink lips parted in an endless sigh. One round breast peeked out from beneath the sheet, the pink tip hard from the cool night air.

His cock jerked at the image, but he snuffed out the urge to roll her onto her back and take her again.

She'd barely made it through the long shower they'd taken together. More than once, he'd had to kiss her back into alertness. The moment her head hit the pillow, she'd been out. It was obvious the day had been both a physical and emotional drain for her.

Damn. Though she'd passed out, he couldn't sleep for shit. He pulled a pair of jeans on and headed downstairs to grab a snack.

The kitchen wasn't empty though. His eyebrows rose when he spotted Joaquin and Brad sitting around the small round table in the kitchen.

"What the hell? You guys got a poker party going in the middle of the night or something?"

Brad scowled and took another swig on a bottle of beer he was nursing. He muttered something under his breath about sleeping with a hard-on, but Hunter didn't catch it all. Probably a good thing.

Joaquin leaned back in his chair and sighed. "I can't stop thinking about tomorrow and the sting."

"Yeah?" Hunter glanced down the hall. "I forgot all about the rookie arriving tonight. Sorry. Got a little distracted with Gemma trying to run."

"She cool now?" Brad asked.

"She's cool. We . . . worked things out."

Brad guffawed. "Worked things out. Is that what they're calling it nowadays?"

Hunter shot him a warning glance even as his lips twitched. "So did the rookie get in okay?"

"Her name is Kimiko. And yes, she got here a few hours ago. She's sleeping now. Gearing up for tomorrow." Joaquin shook his head and rubbed the stubble on his jaw, his expression tight. "I don't know. I think she's too green. This is a helluva assignment to be her first."

Hunter paused. "She graduated from the academy with flying colors."

"She's young."

"Twenty-two," Hunter argued, turning around a chair and

sitting backward on it. "She just looks young—which is why we need to use her."

Kimiko Roberts was new to their team. With her shifter blood a mix of Japanese and Caucasian, she easily passed for an older teenager. She was the perfect agent to go undercover into Delmore's supposed sanctuary for runaways.

"She's the best fit for this," Brad agreed and set his beer down. "Tomorrow we send her in there. Hopefully Delmore takes the bait and tries to send her out."

Joaquin grunted but didn't look convinced. "If I see anything that indicates she's not ready, I'm pulling her."

Hunter clenched his jaw, wanting to argue but knowing he couldn't. Joaquin ran this operation.

Brad set the empty beer bottle down on the table and stood. "I'm going to try and grab a couple hours' sleep."

Joaquin sat the chair back down on all four legs and nodded. "Yeah, I should, too."

Once the two men had left and Hunter was again alone, he headed to the fridge to get the snack he'd initially come downstairs for. He'd fed Gemma tonight but hadn't had time to eat. Not after she'd run.

He hurried through the leftover steak then headed back upstairs. He was already itching to spend those last few hours before dawn with Gemma back in his arms.

The hint of sunlight trickling through the window woke her. Gemma blinked and adjusted her eyes to the room. What time was it? She'd slept hard, which was unusual for her. Maybe it was because she'd been so exhausted. She yawned and stretched beneath the sheets; her leg brushed against Hunter's hairy leg and she flushed. *Or maybe it was because Hunter had been with her.*

She rolled onto her side and propped herself up on an elbow, gazing down at him. His face was relaxed in sleep, those sexy lips full and curved into a slight smile. Maybe something in his dream was amusing.

Not wanting to disturb him, she slipped silently from the bed. She'd woken to find him gone at some point in the night, and he hadn't returned too long ago to fall asleep.

Pulling on the dress he'd given her yesterday, she left the room to go downstairs. The house was dark, and she searched for a light switch, but a noise from where she guessed the kitchen would be gave her pause.

She bit her lip and crept the last few steps to the landing then peeked around the corner into the lit up room. It was the kitchen, and her cousin and Brad were standing near the stove arguing.

She slipped back before they could hear her. She could go back upstairs, but they'd probably creak again and maybe this time announce her presence.

"I told you, Megan, it's not you," Brad's voice sounded strained, a little harsh.

"How can it *not* be me? Yesterday I thought we were really getting along. And then last night you kind of just wigged out. Didn't talk to me. Didn't want to see me."

"Megan—"

"I just want to know what I did to make you pass me off to Joaquin to deal with."

"You didn't do anything, okay?" he rasped. "It's what *I* wanted to do."

"What? What did you want to do?"

Brad gave a defeated laugh. "God, how you push me, girl. I wanted to do this."

There were footsteps, and then her cousin gasped. A second later she made a soft moan.

Gemma frowned. What the hell? She peeked her head around

the corner and her eyes widened. Brad had Megan in his arms and seemed to be doing a thorough exploration of her mouth with his.

Jerking her head back again, Gemma bit her lip and shook her head. Not a good idea. So not a good idea.

"Shit," Brad said raggedly, obviously having come up for air. "I'm sorry, Megan. That wasn't a good idea."

Gemma nodded. Hmm. Well at least he agreed with her on that.

"I don't think it was a bad idea." Her cousin's voice had turned breathy, wondrous. "At all, actually. Brad? Where are you going?"

"Out for a run. Go back to bed, Megan."

"Brad . . ."

"What just happened; didn't happen. Got it?"

"Uh, not really."

Brad didn't answer, and a few moments later, the front door opened and shut.

Gemma winced. Damn. She didn't like the idea of Brad putting the moves on her cousin; she was barely eighteen and leaving for college next month. She didn't need to get into a complex relationship with an ESA agent. But he could have at least let her down a little gentler.

After counting to ten, Gemma took a deep breath and trudged loudly into the kitchen to announce her presence.

"Wow, you're up early," she said brightly, noting Megan's pink cheeks and swollen mouth.

"Yeah . . . I couldn't sleep. Heard Brad out here and just got up." Megan lowered her gaze. "He's out running."

"Probably a good thing," Gemma said quietly.

Megan's head snapped up, and Gemma held her gaze. Realization flared in her cousin's eyes, showing that she knew Gemma knew what had happened. She sighed and looked away, her expression more than a little disappointed.

"I suppose." Megan crossed the room and poured herself a glass of water. "You're up pretty early yourself. Everything okay with lover boy this morning? Have you realized that resistance is futile and you need to stop the fighting and work on the lovin'?"

Gemma gave a soft laugh. "Something along those lines." She paused. "And you were right about Jeffrey."

"Yeah?"

"Yeah. There's something up with him, Meg. Hunter told me about it earlier. And . . . there were signs, when I think about it. I just can't believe I couldn't put them together."

"They were out of context. Besides, Jeffrey is a charming bastard—as much as I hate to say it. Brad kind of filled me in on the situation. It's pretty horrific, Gem."

Down the hall, a door slammed shut, followed by the sound of someone being sick. A moment later, the toilet flushed.

"Yikes," Megan lifted an eyebrow. "Somebody's dinner didn't agree with them."

Another door opened, and Joaquin strode out wearing nothing but pajama bottoms. His expression pinched.

When the bathroom door opened, a girl stepped out, pale, her entire body rigid.

Joaquin approached her, shaking his head. "I'm pulling you from the operation, Agent Roberts."

8

Agent Roberts? Gemma's gaze darted back to the girl—woman rather, though she looked so young. The agent flinched and paled even further before her almond-shaped eyes narrowed.

"Why would you do that? I'm fine. I'm ready for this—"

"You haven't slept. I heard you pacing your room. And that's the second time you've thrown up since dinner last night."

Her chin lifted. "So I drank some bad milk."

"Bullshit."

"Look, a lot of agents go through this. A mild case of nerves is common."

He shook his head. "You got little, if any, sleep last night. And it doesn't appear to be a *mild* case of nerves, Roberts."

"What's going on here?" Hunter appeared in the hallway directly between the kitchen and bedrooms, fully dressed, and glanced both ways.

"I'm pulling her from the operation." Joaquin walked past her, his jaw tight.

The agent hurried after him, desperation in her gaze. "You can't do this to me. I'm ready."

Joaquin spun around, snapping harshly, "You're *not* ready, Kimiko."

Hunter folded his arms across his chest. "Someone want to tell me what's going on?"

"She's been puking all night. Hasn't been to sleep."

"I'm not going to choke. I promise." Kimiko's face finally gained some color back, but the red stain on her cheeks didn't help her case much.

Gemma's stomach twisted, and she felt a stab of sympathy for the younger woman.

"Shit." Hunter sighed and turned, shoving a hand through his hair. "She'll probably be fine, Joaquin."

"It's my operation. I don't think she can be convincing undercover right now, so I'm pulling her."

Hunter paused. "Can we get another agent up here to replace her?"

"Don't replace me," Kimiko pleaded, though her shoulders remained stiff, her expression stoic. "I can do this. I'm ready."

Joaquin and Hunter exchanged a long glance, and then Hunter shook his head.

"I'm sorry, Agent Roberts. I don't make the final call. If he says you're not ready, you're out."

She let out a ragged breath and then her lips pursed. Casting a hard look at Joaquin, she turned and walked back to her room. The door closed a second later.

Gemma glanced at Megan, who looked just as puzzled by the encounter. That poor female agent—though she'd tried to keep a professional appearance—had obviously been devastated. What was her part supposed to be in the sting anyway?

"Fuck." Joaquin crossed the room and opened the fridge.

"It'll take us days to get a replacement up here and briefed on the operation. Roberts has been studying this case for weeks."

"At least."

"Maybe I could help." Gemma cleared her throat. "What was she supposed to do?"

Hunter gave a harsh laugh. "Be the bait. Pose as a runaway to get into Delmore's ring."

The color drained from her face, and Gemma let the air out of her lungs on a hiss.

"Do you realize how dangerous that is?" she asked when she could finally speak.

"Danger is all part of the job for an ESA agent," Joaquin murmured and glanced down the hall toward the closed door. "But we don't send someone into a situation they're not ready for."

Gemma bit the inside of her cheek, casting furtive glances around the room at everyone. So they'd just send up another agent to fill in as bait? Ask another girl to risk her life by getting thrust into the world of fuck hunting?

Her stomach clenched and she swallowed hard. No. She couldn't let them do it. There was another way. And even though it sent a small stab of terror through her, she knew it was the answer.

"I have another suggestion," she said quietly, and all eyes turned toward her. "Send me instead."

There was a moment's silence before both men laughed.

"Just one problem with that, sweetheart," Joaquin said, with a sardonic smile. "Since you were supposed to be Delmore's wife, you can't exactly pose as a runaway."

"No . . ." she began slowly. "But since I was *supposed to be Delmore's wife,* I do have access and knowledge to where he keeps information regarding his . . . business."

Hunter straightened from the counter, his brows drawn together. "You told me you didn't know anything."

"I didn't . . . or I thought I didn't. It all started to come back to me last night. There were men who would come by for parties . . . discussing recent hunting successes. When I asked what they hunted, they would never respond, just laugh." And stare at her like she was a piece of prime rib. She drew in a deep breath and pushed a wave of hair back over her head. "And when Jeffrey and I first got engaged last year, we threw a party. The invitation list was saved on his computer, and I needed it. So when he wasn't home, I went to print it out."

She licked her lips, visualizing the document in her head. "I opened the list, but . . . it took me a few minutes to realize I was looking at the wrong thing. The only names were of men . . . and there were dates on it, followed by dollar figures." She swallowed hard, guilt stabbing in her gut. "I closed it out and brushed it off, figuring it was nothing. Then I forgot all about it. Until last night."

Joaquin approached her. "Do you think you could get access to his computer again if we sent you back?"

"No," Hunter said vehemently.

Gemma nodded. "Probably. I'd find a way. He trusts me. I'd just slip in when he wasn't in the room and transfer some files to a jump drive."

"We're not sending her back to that bastard," Hunter snarled, straightening to his full height, shoulders quaking. "He'll probably be suspicious as all hell the minute she walks in the door."

"Maybe not . . . hang on for a second." Joaquin disappeared down the hall, reappearing moments later with a folder in his hand. He dropped it on the table and smacked his palm on top of the thin file. "These are the transcripts of all the phone calls going in and out of Delmore's estate in the last twenty-four hours. Several of the calls are from Jeffrey Delmore himself."

Gemma's pulse jumped, and her gaze dropped to the file.

"Did he give you anything that could be used against him? Evidence?"

Hunter's harsh laugh exploded in the room. "He's not that stupid. He knows there's always a possibility of us bugging him."

"Does he know he's bugged?" Gemma asked.

"No. Not that we're aware of."

Joaquin scratched the back of his head. "Signs indicate he doesn't. He's even said a few times his compound is too air tight for anyone to get a bug in."

"But you did."

"We did," Joaquin agreed. "Anyway, the last few calls—same old stuff as usual, except one call with his father. They talked about you."

"About me?" Gemma backed away from the table, not sure she even wanted to know.

"He doesn't seem suspicious. He seems distraught. Worried something happened to you. He's had people looking for you since yesterday morning."

The idea took root inside her head. "So this could work. . . . I could call him, explain I had cold feet, and ask him if he'll take me back."

Hunter snarled and paced the room. "It won't work."

"It might," Joaquin argued.

"Hunter, you don't have a choice. I'm the best option you have." Gemma touched his shoulder, feeling how rigid his muscles had become. His eyes now glinted with panic.

Joaquin cleared his throat. "She's right, Hunter. She can go in and be under the radar. If we sense something changes, we can pull her."

Hunter shook his head. "I don't like the idea of putting her safety at risk."

"Jeffrey adores her," Megan spoke up. "Obviously those

transcripts prove it. I don't like this any more than you do, Hunter. But if anyone can pull this off, Gemma can."

The front door opened, and they all looked up to see Brad returning from his run. His gaze immediately sought out Megan, who cleared her throat and excused herself, walking quickly from the room.

Brad's jaw tightened, but he didn't say anything. Instead he just glanced at the other men.

"Pull what off?"

"Agent Roberts isn't ready. We pulled her and we're sending in Gemma," Joaquin said then proceeded to explain their reasoning.

"I like it. Let's do it," Brad immediately agreed.

"*Fuck.*" Hunter pushed away from Gemma and slammed a fist into a wall. "This is a bad idea."

"I'm in charge of this operation," Joaquin said resolutely. "I'm sorry, Hunter. But if Gemma agrees to do this, I think we'd be stupid not to." He turned and looked at her. "Gemma?"

Her pulse jumped and she swallowed hard. Her gaze darted to Hunter. His eyes were locked on her, and it was hard to miss the blatant plea for her to say no.

She thought of the shifter women who'd been killed, who'd died such horrible deaths. How long had it been going on? Would it continue to go on? Her stomach rolled with revulsion. It made her sick to think that she'd been engaged to the man behind their deaths—that she'd slept with him.

Licking her lips, she gave a slight nod. "I'll do it."

Fear and pain flickered across Hunter's face before he turned and left the room.

"Great. Thank you, Gemma." Joaquin touched her arm. "Go talk to him. You've got two hours before we leave."

* * *

Hunter paced the bedroom, wanting to throw or hit something. Most of all, he just wanted to show up at Jeffrey's estate and kill the bastard on the spot. Screw a trial.

Sweat beaded on the back of his neck, and his head pounded with the beginning of a headache. He groaned and slapped his palm against the wall. What was she thinking? To volunteer to go back to Delmore's and get the evidence. It was too damn risky.

What if something happened? What if—

"Hunter." His name was a soft caress on her voice.

He turned, his heart in his throat.

Gemma stood in the doorway, her body leaning to one side of the frame, her hip thrust out against the cotton dress she wore, her breasts hugged by the fabric. She looked feminine. Entirely too delicate. An easy target if Delmore were to turn on her. His gut clenched.

His gaze moved up her body again, and he met her eyes, finding her expression imploring.

"Please, Gemma." He shook his head. "Don't do this."

"Hunter." She said his name on a sigh, closed the door, and then crossed the room to him. "I have to."

"We can find someone else. There's—"

"I have two hours." She touched a finger to his lips before sliding her hands to his shoulders. "Two hours before I leave. You can spend it arguing with me, and I'll warn you that I won't change my mind, or we can do other things. . . ."

He knew by the determination on her face that she meant what she said. There would be no changing her mind. He hesitated for only a moment and then slid his arms around her waist, pulling her hard against the contours of his body.

She buried her head against his shoulder, her arms wrapping around his back. "Thank you," she whispered. "I want you. Need you before I do this."

"You're crazy," he muttered and lifted the dress from her

body, tossing it across the room. "And so brave. I don't know what you're thinking."

He cupped her breasts, thumbing her nipples into tight points.

"Right now? I'm thinking about you," she admitted with a gasp.

"Good." He unbuttoned his jeans and adjusted them enough to free his cock. He sprung free, erect and aching. "Because you've got me."

Without any preliminaries, he grabbed her ass and lifted her, impaling her down onto his dick.

"Hunter!" Gemma choked out his name, gripping his shoulders.

Despite her obvious surprise, her pussy was already soaked and ready for him. The soft walls gripped his cock, massaging him as he sank deeper inside her body.

He backed her up against the wall, pinning her against it to hold her still for his thrusts and to give him better leverage.

"Gemma," he whispered her name, his fingers biting into her ass cheeks as he pounded harder into her. "What if something happens to you?"

"*No.* Please, Hunter, don't think like that." She angled her head, her mouth finding his.

His lips crushed against hers before he slid his tongue deep to plunder her mouth. He slammed his cock harder up into her, faster. Almost blind with need and fear.

Gemma cried out, and he knew by the way her nails broke the skin on his back he was using her rougher than she was used to. But she didn't protest, just gave him her mouth again and hugged him tighter with her inner muscles.

He pounded into her pussy, making her body slide up farther against the wall. Gripping her ass, he pulled her back down onto his cock until his vision blurred and his sac tightened.

"*Hunter!*" She ripped her mouth from his, clenching her eyes shut, her whole body shaking in her climax.

"*Yes.*" He buried himself to the hilt and exploded, letting everything, including a bit of his soul, empty inside her.

Gemma pressed her hands against his shoulders and lifted her head, a small smile of regret on her face. "I think I really needed that."

"You and me both, angel."

She kissed the side of his neck. "Mmm. We should shower. I can't go to Jeffrey's smelling like sex."

At the mention of her mission, he stiffened. He didn't want her to go at all. Unfortunately he had no choice in the matter. Lowering her to the floor, he bit his tongue and led her to the shower.

Hunter remained quiet the entire drive to the drop-off point. The team had agreed to release Gemma several miles from Delmore's estate, in case he was monitoring the grounds.

"How are you feeling about all this, Gemma?" Joaquin asked, glancing back from the driver's seat.

"Good. I feel real good about it." She gave a confident nod and glanced over at Hunter.

Hunter tightened his grip on her hand, his mouth curling downward. His stomach clenched, and he forced a steady breath. He still hated that she was putting herself in this situation, but he had ceased trying to dissuade her. Knew it was pointless.

The vehicle slowed, pulling to the side of the road at the edge of the forest.

"This is it." Joaquin turned in his seat. "If you have any hesitation, tell me now."

"None at all." She unfastened her seat belt and opened the door, climbing out.

Hunter followed her before she could close the door again. She turned, surprise registering on her face.

"Be careful." He cupped the back of her head and closed his mouth over hers. Brushing her lips once, then twice. "I'll be nearby."

"I thought you were going back to the safe house?"

He shook his head. "If shit hits the fan, I'll be nearby. I'll be your first response."

She gave a soft sigh and then kissed his cheek. "Nothing will go wrong, Hunter."

"I know. But just in case." He gave her hand a reassuring squeeze.

"Good. Jeffrey thinks I'm running back from the coast. So he'll expect me to arrive just shifted." Gemma gave a rueful smile and pulled her dress from her body and tossed it back into the SUV. "He's going to be waiting for me. And before you say it again—yes, I'll be careful."

With a wink at Hunter and a wave to Joaquin, she sprinted off into the forest, the sleek curves of her body already shifting into jaguar form.

Hunter's throat tightened with fear, and tension radiated from every muscle in his body. He didn't like this. Dammit, he didn't like this. She'd made the call earlier this morning to Delmore, and it had gone surprisingly well. Her fiancé had held only a small amount of suspicion, but overall he had seemed relieved to have her returning.

"Hang in there, Hunter." Joaquin jerked his head at him in a reassuring nod. "She'll be fine. I need to head back."

Hunter gave a terse nod and shut the door to the SUV, slapping the door good-bye as Joaquin pulled a U-turn and headed back to the safe house.

Turning, he focused on the forest Gemma had just taken off into, hoping everything would be okay but unable to shake the dark premonition in his blood.

*   *   *

"Can I offer you a drink, darling?"

Gemma fastened the last button on her dress, relieved to once again have her flesh hidden from Jeffrey's gaze.

He'd been waiting in the front hall, a dress in hand for her to put on. She'd barely managed to sneak the tiny monitoring device Joaquin had given her out from under her tongue and stick if between her breasts before slipping the dress on.

Turning, she offered him a rueful smile. "I could certainly use one. I'll have a dirty martini."

His gaze, already lingering on her body, flared with heat. "Of course. Stedman, please bring us a dirty martini and glass of white wine."

The butler, who'd been lingering in the hall, nodded and disappeared.

Jeffrey's eyes narrowed, and he took a few steps toward her. "A dirty martini for a dirty girl." His hands slid out to cup her hips, pulling her firmly against his body. He was shorter than Hunter—skinnier. Pale, with light blue eyes and almost white blond hair.

His cock, thin, long and already erect, brushed her hip. Revulsion swept through her, though she tried her best not to react. Instead, she let her fingers trail over the collar on his crisp white shirt.

"I know I've already apologized." She licked her lips and looked at him through her lashes. "But I'm so sorry about yesterday, honey. I panicked."

"Did you now?" he asked in a lazy tone. Cupping her chin, he forced her head up so she had to look at him.

Giving a delicate shrug, she let her lower lip protrude into a seductive pout. "Yes. The idea of marriage just seemed so overwhelming. So . . . committed."

"And is that not the point, Gemma?" He gave a soft laugh.

"To commit yourself to me . . . and only me, for the rest of your life?"

"Yes. And yesterday—"

He cupped her breast, his hand squeezing her flesh almost to the point of pain. Swallowing back her disgust, she wrapped her arms around his neck and pressed her body tighter to his.

"Yesterday?" he prodded, the expression in his eyes unreadable.

"As I just said . . . I panicked. I bolted from my cabin and shifted, running all the way to the coast. I spent the day at my favorite lighthouse. Thinking."

"And your decision?"

She gave a husky laugh. "I was being a spoiled fool. I . . . love you, Jeffrey."

She'd been proud of her acting abilities until she'd choked on the word love. Damn. That had been hard to force out. This man, whom she'd once thought she cared for—had shared a bed with—now made her want to hurl up her breakfast.

"Hmm." His fingers moved inward on her breast until they caught her nipple and pinched. "You ruined your dress, darling. And if I recall, it was very expensive."

She winced in pain but forced another light smile. "I'll purchase a new one."

"And all the money that went into a ceremony that never occurred."

"Please, Jeffrey, I already feel awful." She forced herself to brush her mouth across his then whisper, "I'll make it up to you. Any way you want."

"Any way, darling?" His expression relaxed, and a shimmer of lust filled his eyes. His hand moved down her body before grabbing her crudely between her legs.

She jerked away before she could censure herself. Before she could rouse his suspicions, she gave a husky laugh and stepped close to him again, pressing a kiss against the side of his neck. "I'm in dire need of a shower, honey. You wouldn't want me now. My skin and hair are salty from the sea water. Tonight, though. *Anything* you wish."

"Hmm. You are right. I prefer you clean. Although . . . there's no reason you couldn't pleasure me."

His zipper went down and Gemma about fainted.

"Your drinks, sir."

The butler's sudden reappearance had Jeffrey pulling his fly back up.

"Tonight it is," he murmured with a grimace and turned to greet the butler. A moment later, he handed Gemma her drink.

Gemma wrapped her fingers around the thin stem on the glass and took a quick swallow, needing the liquid courage.

"Come, let's make ourselves comfortable in my study." Jeffrey caught her hand and escorted her down the hall into the other room, then shut the door, locking it firmly. He gestured to the leather couch for her to take a seat.

She sat down, crossing her legs and glancing over at the laptop on his desk. Now she just needed a chance to get on there and grab the information.

Jeffrey went to his desk, pulling something out and fiddling with it. But with his back to her, she couldn't see what.

"I'm glad you came back, darling. You have no idea the distress I was under when you simply disappeared."

"I . . . can't imagine."

He crossed the room and sat down beside her, catching her chin in a ruthless grip. "Tell me, Gemma. How *was* the coast?"

She swallowed hard. "Breezy."

"Hmm." He leaned his face toward her and grabbed a handful of hair, nuzzling it. Then he turned his head, and she felt his tongue graze across her cheek.

A shudder ran through her body, and she closed her eyes.

"You don't taste like sea air, darling," he said softly. "In fact your skin tastes clean . . . your hair smells like shampoo. But not your normal shampoo . . ."

Cold sweat broke out on the back of Gemma's neck, and she felt the blood drain from her face. She'd showered with Hunter. God, she'd walked right into that one.

"Oh, that's right. I . . . showered at the beach."

"Gemma, my darling." His grip tightened on her chin, and he gave a soft laugh. "Just how fucking stupid do you think I am?"

She stopped breathing. "What do you mean?"

"I have cameras in every cabin, including the one you used to prepare for the wedding." He rubbed his thumb across her mouth. "I saw those vile ESA agents take you."

Gemma's head spun as panic slammed into her full force. She hadn't foreseen this. She knew he monitored various parts of his property, but each cabin that guests stayed in? Oh, God.

"I trust no one," he went on as if reading her thoughts. "I watch everything."

"Then you knew they took me?" she whispered. "And did nothing?"

"Why did you lie to me, Gemma? Tell me you went to the coast?" He answered her question with a question. "If you had truly been an innocent victim, then when you returned to my estate, surely you would have told me the horrors you endured."

Shit! Twice now she'd walked right into his verbal traps.

"But I don't think you endured horrors, darling. You let that man fuck you, didn't you?"

She licked her lips, her heart pounding against her rib cage. "You knew your phone was bugged, didn't you?"

"Of course I did."

"You weren't at all worried about me."

"Answer me, darling. You enjoyed having that filthy ESA agent's hands all over you."

Her chest rose and fell as she held his cold gaze. It didn't matter what she said. In Jeffrey's mind, she was already tried and convicted. By now the ESA was probably making plans to come in and rescue her. And they'd never have—would be lucky to ever get—solid proof on Jeffrey's organization.

Taking a deep breath, she made an impulse decision and hoped it wouldn't cost her her life.

"Yes," she replied quietly. "He did have his hands all over me. And to say I enjoyed it would be an understatement. He is my mate, and I love him with all my heart."

The sound of Delmore slapping Gemma came through loud and clear. At her startled gasp, rage exploded inside Hunter, blurring his vision and sending his pulse into overdrive.

"Fuck this, I'm going in," Hunter rasped and charged through the forest on foot.

Unlike Gemma, he hadn't thought to use one of the oral communication devices that could be placed in his mouth. He'd settled for the head unit, which wouldn't hold up if he shifted. And he needed to be able to hear what was going on.

"Careful, Hunter," Brad came through on the radio. "We're sending in backup."

Hunter barely heard him, his body too tense as he listened for further conversation on Gemma's end.

What was she thinking, goading him like this? God, you'd think she wanted Delmore to kill her.

"He told me all about this fuck hunt ring you run, Jeffrey." Gemma's voice was harsh. "What kind of man are you?"

"It provides me with an absurd amount of money. Besides, what is the world with a few less freakish shifter girls?"

"*Freakish?*"

"Yes, Gemma. Your kind is an abomination. You're not normal."

"I'm more normal than a sick fuck like you could ever be."

Another slap resounded. And Hunter's stomach rolled. *Stop, Gemma. Stop goading him.* At least until he could get there and kill the bastard.

"I suppose you came here today to find evidence. Perhaps find something on my computer?" He laughed. "What, you think I didn't notice you'd been looking at my files? I've been watching you, darling. For months now. That's why I'm not really surprised to be having this conversation.

"I spared you, Gemma. I could have made a nice coin on your sweet ass. But I kept you for myself. And this is how you repay me?" His voice grew louder, and Hunter new Delmore must have gotten closer to her.

"Get off me, you bastard." The sound of her struggling was clear. "I would have turned you in sooner, had I known. You make me sick."

"I don't participate in the pleasures, I just arrange them." Delmore paused, and when he spoke again, his tone was silky. "Until today. I think I shall partake in my very first fuck hunt. Of course, my darling, I'm going to need your participation. I'm sure you understand."

Hunter stumbled, his blood turning to ice. No. Oh, God, no!

"No!" Gemma's scream came shrill after a moment's silence. "Stop, get off me!"

The sound of fabric ripping could be clearly heard.

"Shit!" Hunter picked up the pace, plunging through the trees. "Joaquin, Brad, you guys almost there? You hearing this?"

"We're hearing," Joaquin confirmed. "Our location is about ten minutes out. How far are you?"

"Just a few minutes."

"Get there, Hunter. Get there in time, because we may not."

"Jeffrey, please don't do this," Gemma begged, the sounds of a struggle in the background.

"A little late for . . . what the *fuck* is this?" Delmore roared.

"You're bugged? But I watched you when you came in naked. It wasn't there."

"Should've checked my mouth, asshole."

"God*damn* it. You fucking bitch. I'll show you what you can do with your mouth."

Gemma screamed before everything went silent.

Hunter's knees almost buckled, fear paralyzing him. And then he snapped. Delmore had just sealed his own death warrant. With a ferocious war cry, he pulled the communication device from his head and ran. Shifting into jaguar form, he let his primal side take control. He ran. Ran to try and save Gemma, and ran to satisfy the bloodlust that now consumed him.

Gemma hit the floor hard, landing on her hands and knees. She gasped in a breath in an attempt to fill her lungs again. Her dress hung from her body in shreds, ripped down the middle.

The punch Jeffrey had landed on her diaphragm—just after grabbing the bug from her chest and smashing it—had left her dazed and winded.

"Get up." He gripped her elbow, jerking her to her feet. The next moment, she felt a sharp sting in her arm.

She pulled away, but a moment too late. He'd already injected her with a hypodermic needle. *Oh, God. What had he done?*

She backed away from him, her stomach rolling with terror. "What . . . what did you inject in me?"

"It appears we don't have time to fuck, darling. But no worries, I've done that before." Delmore's face contorted into a sneer as he crossed the room again. "We'll just have to skip to the hunt part."

Hunt? Her mind froze on the word. Oh, no. She could barely form a thought. What had been in that needle? A spasm rocked her body, and realization dawned with horror. She was shifting without trying. Even now fur spread across her hands and her nails turned to claws. He'd forced her to shift.

Her gaze jerked up, and she watched Jeffrey unlock a cabinet in the corner of his office; behind the glass was a rifle clearly on display. He was going to shoot her.

Run! Her instincts kicked in, and she ran for the door, unlocking it and throwing it open before she sprinted outside.

Jeffrey's ominous laugh followed her. "That's right, run, Gemma. But you won't get far."

Heart pounding in her throat, she stumbled down the front steps of his house. With her body only half-shifted, her movements were awkward and sluggish as she attempted to put some distance between him.

She charged into the forest, willing her body to finish the transition. But even if it did, thinking was still difficult. Her head seemed to be filled with cotton, everything seemed delayed, like she'd had a few drinks. This was how the women had died? Drugged and barely functioning? Running for their lives?

Hunter. Please, where are you?

The first shot rang out, and she roared with a mix of terror and rage. He'd missed. But she could hear him . . . and he was close.

A whimper escaped her, and she plunged on, her body almost fully changed into jaguar form now. But it probably didn't matter . . . she was as good as dead.

Hunter froze at the sound of a rifle being fired. Son of a bitch. The bastard was already hunting her.

He ran faster, harder, using all his senses to find them. He picked up Gemma's scent first then Delmore's.

A second shot rang out, and he heard Gemma's terrified growl in response. *Thank God.* He hadn't hit her yet.

Spotting a flash of orange off in the distance, his blood warmed. Delmore was a fool for not making an effort to blend in with his environment. And it would cost him his life. Just as long as he could get to her in time.

The second shot pinged off a tree next to Gemma, and she screamed inside, trying to increase her pace. It wasn't easy. Her body was pretty much refusing to obey her mind's orders. Whatever he'd shot in her was a powerful substance.

She dove between two trees, seeing the road up ahead. Relief spread quickly, and she lunged forward.

"Here kitty, kitty."

Her chest tightened; she couldn't breathe. And just like that, the relief was extinguished and defeat rode her soul hard. Delmore was right behind her; she could hear his unhurried footsteps.

Hunter had been right, she was a fool for going in here alone today. But at least the ESA had Jeffrey's confession on tape. Tears pricked at the back of her eyes. She hated leaving this earth when she'd only just found Hunter again. It wasn't fair.

"Turn around."

He was literally right behind her.

"Turn around," he ordered again, amusement in his tone. "I want to see the pretty pussy I'm about to kill."

She drew in a slow breath. He could kill her, but not before she made an attempt on his life.

Gemma turned, and the long barrel of the rifle filled her gaze. With a growl, she leapt at him.

The rifle fired at the same moment he fell to the side. There was an enraged roar as dark fur mixed with the orange of Jeffrey's jacket.

She moved to the side, heart pounding as she watched Hunter struggle with Jeffrey. Jeffrey raised the rifle between them, brushing the underside of Hunter's body.

No! Her world tilted, and she waited for the shot, but it never came.

The rifle fell to the ground and Jeffrey's body went limp, blood seeping into the dirt beside him.

Hunter unwrapped his jaws from the dead man's neck and stepped back, shifting back to human form, wiping the blood from his mouth.

"Gemma," he knelt down beside her, brows drawn together. "Angel, are you okay?"

Her head spun, relief weakening her. Or maybe it was the drug. She whimpered, wanting to shift, but not able to force her body to. Crawling toward him, more dizziness assailed her. Her legs wobbled, and then blackness rushed up to claim her.

9

Gemma stirred, realizing right away she was back in human form. Her legs moved against soft silk, and she blinked her eyes open.

A cream-colored ceiling was above her. Shifting her gaze, she took in the unfamiliar room. Inhaling the scent deeply, she twisted her head on the pillow. Relief washed through her. This was Hunter's room.

"You're awake."

Pushing herself up in bed, the sheet fell away from her body, exposing one breast before she could grab it again.

"Please, my love, don't cover yourself on my account." Hunter laughed softly and crossed the room to sit beside her. He pulled the sheet from her grasp, easing it back down so he could again look at her. "I'm sorry he hurt you."

Hunter cupped a breast, tracing a finger over the scratch mark across her chest from when Jeffrey had ripped her dress from her body.

The tenderness in his soft words flooded her eyes with tears.

"He didn't get to . . . he would have forced me, but then he found the bug."

"I know."

She swallowed hard, emotion forming a thick lump in her throat. "I shouldn't have . . . I didn't—"

"Shh, angel." He brushed a kiss across her lips and her eyes closed. "It's over now. Delmore is dead, and the ESA is putting together a case against all those involved in the ring as we speak."

"You saved my life," she whispered and moved her body so her breast fit tighter in his hand. The need to have him touch her consumed her, burning white hot in her center. "Remind me I'm alive, Hunter. . . ."

Desire flickered in his gaze, and he pushed her back gently on the mattress, dragging the sheet all the way off her body.

Straddling her body, he leaned down to close his mouth over one of her breasts, suckling the nipple deep.

She buried her fingers into his hair, her body twisting on the bed beneath him.

"Beautiful," he murmured, transferring his attention to her other breast. "So beautiful. I don't deserve you, angel."

"You do." She gasped when he bit down lightly on her nipple. "And you have me."

He lifted his head, and possessiveness flared in his gaze. "Yes. I do. And thank God you're alive."

His hand slid over her belly to cup the mound of her sex. Sparks shot through her body, and she bit her lip.

"So hot. Warm." He slid down the bed to lie between her legs, his warm breath feathering on her inner thighs.

Gemma gripped the bedspread and let her head fall back against the pillow. Closing her eyes, she waited for the first stroke of his tongue.

It didn't come. Instead the rough pad of his finger found her clit and began moving in slow circles.

Her chest rose with a slow breath, and her ass clenched against his knowing touch. Only he could make her body respond like this, turn her brain to mush.

"I love watching you get creamy for me," he murmured, and she felt him probe the entrance of her pussy with two fingers.

She squeezed her eyes closed tighter, her breathing more erratic. Inside. Oh, God, she wanted those fingers inside her.

He teased her for a moment, running his digits up and down her slit and spreading her moisture while continuing the agonizing assault on her clit.

A frustrated gasp escaped her, though she tried to hold it back. Her hips lifted against his hand.

"Easy, angel. I'll take care of you, but first I want to enjoy you."

He probed her entrance again and then slid the two fingers slowly inside her.

She released a shuddering breath. He pressed deeper, sliding over the walls of her vagina while his thumb continued its maddening rotations.

The sounds of her wetness filled the room when he began to steadily thrust his fingers in and out of her.

"You feel so good." He kissed her thigh again. "And your pussy tastes even better."

His tongue found her clit, teasing the swollen flesh and causing her hips to buck in response.

"Mmm. Yeah, just like that, angel." He flicked her clit again, faster this time.

The ache between her legs increased, and she could feel herself grow wetter against his fingers.

He closed his mouth over her clit and suckled her, moving his fingers deeper and harder inside her now.

"Yes. Oh, God." Gemma reached blindly for his hair, clutching at the strands while rocking her body against his mouth. "Oh . . . oh . . . *please*."

His tongue flicked over her again. Faster and harder. Her stomach clenched, and she gasped, her ass lifting off the bed.

He followed the bucking of her body, his mouth and fingers never leaving her.

Behind her closed lids, the light spiraled upward with her growing pleasure.

"*Oh!*" She tugged at his hair as her world exploded, clenching her thighs around his head while her body trembled.

His fingers slowed to a tender exploration, his mouth suckling her gently through the orgasm.

Sweaty and weak, she sank boneless into the mattress, gasping, her eyes still closed.

Hunter moved to lie between her thighs, nudging her legs open wider.

She opened her eyes again and found him watching her with steady intensity.

"You told Delmore you loved me," he said quietly. "Did you mean it?"

Her throat tightened with emotion, and her pulse slowed before quickening again. She licked her lips and shook her head. "Never doubt it, Hunter. You've not only claimed my body, but my heart. My soul."

His mouth tightened, pain and regret in his gaze. "From day one, I knew you were my mate. If I could change the past five years—"

"But we can't. We're together now, and that's all that matters." Her heart ached for the years he'd been gone and the fact that he couldn't seem to forgive himself.

He gripped her hips, his cock probing her entrance. "Be more than my mate, Gemma. Be my wife."

Tears flooded her eyes, and she managed to choke out a watery, "Yes."

His eyes closed. "I came home from being dead a year ago. But having you in my life is the only way I truly feel alive." He pressed his forehead to hers and plunged deep into her body. "I love you, Gemma."

"I know," she sighed. Gripping his shoulders, she lifted to meet his thrusts, whispering, "I'm yours, Hunter. Always."

"Always," he repeated and laid claim to her mouth.

Turn the page for a preview of
DEVOUR ME,
by Lydia Parks!

On sale now!

1
_____

"You look *delicious* in moonlight. More wine?"

Rachel gazed up into the dark eyes of her unusual host and smiled. "Sure."

At something like six-four and amazingly handsome, Max's high cheekbones, firm jaw, and thick, dark, shoulder-length hair gave him an exotic air. She'd never seen anyone quite so attractive.

She'd certainly never spent the evening with anyone so attractive.

He filled her glass with cabernet.

She turned to watch the full moon shatter on the gulf's surface, trying her best to appear mysterious, and enjoyed the tropical breeze as she sipped. Warm, salty air sighed across her skin.

The wine was good. Probably expensive, like everything else—the hotel room on the beach, the food, his clothes. Max was wealthy, good-looking, and sexy as hell.

Yes, this was a date no one back at camp or at school would believe.

"You, my dear, have wonderful lines."

He spoke from right behind her, and a shiver tripped up Rachel's spine.

"Lines?"

"Yes." The tips of his fingers slid across her shoulder and up the side of her neck. "Quite classic, like Aphrodite."

His touch did strange things to her skin, leaving behind tingles that sizzled deeper into her body. She closed her eyes to enjoy the erotic sensations.

"Tell me, dear Rachel, what are you doing so far from home?"

She swallowed hard. "I was, uh, working a dig. For school."

"A *dig*?" His fingers blazed trails down the outsides of her arms.

"Yeah. Archaeology. You know, Maya ruins and all."

"Ah, I see." He spoke directly into her ear in a quiet voice full of lust and danger. "Looking for secrets perhaps?"

Rachel grabbed the railing with her free hand to stabilize her spinning world. "Yeah, secrets." She hadn't had enough alcohol to be drunk, but she felt intoxicated nonetheless. "Legends."

"Hmm, legends." His palms grazed her hips, and then slid up to the tender sides of her breasts. "I know several legends from this place. Which is it you seek?"

Even through her cotton blouse, his touch felt incredibly intimate, as if she were standing before him naked, unable to move. When his lips brushed the top of her shoulder, her breasts swelled with desire and her nipples puckered.

She tried to focus. Although she'd accepted Max's invitation to his room knowing she'd likely end up in his bed, she didn't want to appear too eager. Stanley, her ex, had told her that men enjoyed a challenge, just before he left her for her prudish former roommate.

Focus.

Work. What was it he'd asked about work?

"Legend," he whispered, as if answering her silent question.

"In Mutankah, near Chichen Itza, a priest created a talisman that was supposed to be magical or something. Probably ... worth a lot."

His fingers traced a line around the top of her jeans, grazing bare flesh, and his mouth moved to a tender spot at the side of her neck. He kissed and gently sucked, and her knees began to tremble. His hands moved around her waist and he eased her back against him as he unsnapped her pants.

She drew in a breath of surprise at the size of the erection pressing into her lower back.

"Ah, yes, the Mutankah talisman," he said. "And have you found it?"

"No." She rested her head against his solid chest, marveling at the scent of cloves and strange herbs. Wild aftershave, unlike anything she'd encountered before. Ancient and enticing. "We, uh, don't even know ... if it exists. No proof."

"But you will continue to search?"

"Not me. I'm going ... home. Others will."

He caressed her breasts with an expert touch, teasing the sensitive nipples through the cotton, and desire tightened her crotch. She wondered how long it would be before he removed her clothing. Would he take her gently, as he now seduced her, or would he throw her onto his bed and fuck her brains out? Just the thought brought juices that soaked her panties.

"Max," she whispered, "you're good."

"Hmm," he said, his chest vibrating against her. "And you are quite lovely."

One hand slid down her belly and into the front of her pants.

A strange fog invaded her thoughts, making it hard to decide what to do, as if he had total control over her. She couldn't move away from him, and wasn't even sure if she wanted to.

She wondered if anyone stood on the beach, watching them, and surprised herself when she realized she didn't care. Let them watch. At the moment, she just wanted to come in this man's arms. As his cool fingers slid between the folds of her wet pussy and across her swelling clit, she nearly did.

She pushed back against him, and then rocked her hips forward, and his fingers hinted at entering her. Muscles tightened and she groaned at the promise of ecstasy.

"Oh, yes," he said. "Delicious." He kissed the side of her neck.

She moved her head to one side to give him access to more, as she pushed back and forward again, drawing his fingers inside.

He sucked on her neck, and her pussy tightened.

He slid out and back in, deeper, and again.

Her back arched at the impending release, and her world narrowed to just his touch.

"Yes," she breathed, "yes."

He slid deeper still as her climax started with hard, urgent pulses. She cried out and her entire body convulsed from the inside out. His arm tightened around her waist, holding her close.

A scream froze in her throat when he pierced the flesh of her neck, and the wineglass tumbled from her hand.